THE VATICAN RIP

The Lovejoy series

AN ORIGINAL

LOVEJOY

MURDER MYSTERY

THE VATICAN RIP

JONATHAN GASH

Constable & Robinson Ltd.
55–56 Russell Square
London WC1B 4HP
www.constablerobinson.com

First published in the UK by Collins (The Crime Club), 1981

This edition published by C&R Crime,
an imprint of Constable & Robinson Ltd., 2013

A copy of the British Library Cataloguing in
Publication Data is available from the British Library

ISBN: 978-1-47210-289-8 (paperback)
ISBN: 978-1-47210-290-4 (ebook)

Typeset by TW Typesetting, Plymouth, Devon

Printed and bound by
CPI Group (UK) Ltd, Croydon, CR0 4YY

1 3 5 7 9 10 8 6 4 2

In Rome, effort is unknown, energy is
without purpose . . .
– Stendhal

Dedicated to the Second Biennial Festival of Bolton, Greater Manchester (formerly Lancashire) – August 1981 – in gratitude for the rich appreciation of community feeling instilled in the author by his unique home town.

Chapter 1

The trouble with life is, you start off worse and go down-hill. I'd bought the rip in winter, two days before my Italian lessons with the delectable Maria were to begin – though I didn't know that then.

I'm an antique dealer. The antiques game is always at a lowish ebb in January, probably because everybody's spent up after Christmas and is knackered by the weather anyway, so I was on the scrounge and feeling very sorry for myself. It hadn't been too easy of late, what with inflation and all that. And the scanty tourists who knock about East Anglia in deep midwinter tend to be holy, on their way to carol services in our ancient little chapels. They aren't so keen on our priceless (or indeed worthless) antiques.

On this particular day the roads out of my village were bad. There had been one of those heavy snowfalls the previous night after a solid weekend of sustained gales. Typically, the buses never even started out from the nearby town, and as far as civilization was concerned our village might have been on Mars. A couple of lads from Hall Farm managed to shift the worst snowdrifts using tractors and got the south road partially cleared by noon. I was lucky – so I thought – and got a lift in from Ann Scott, the cheerful and pretty lace-mad wife of an insurance assessor. She tried telling me that the famous nineteenth-century torchon lace was superior to Honiton if properly made. We argued all the way. She was wrong, of course. 'Torchon' means dishcloth, but she wouldn't be told. She has a valuable collection of lace samplers I'd been trying to buy from her on tick for years. We'd had several intimate afternoon negotiations. I'd lost every one on a pinfall.

'You can show me the error of my ways, Lovejoy,' she said, straight-faced and careful as she dropped me off in front of the town hall. 'Before five, this afternoon.'

'Any chance of you selling?'

She smiled, not looking. The traffic swished slowly past through the mush. 'Come and find out.'

'When is Henry back?' I'm always worried about new risks because there are so many old ones knocking about.

'Six. Come early.'

'Right. Thanks.'

She checked the traffic in her driving mirror and pulled out with a cool disregard for the road code. I winced at the squealing tyres and the honks of protest and observed her serene passage off down the High Street. That's women for you. All the breaks and none of the breakages.

The auction was well under way when I finally made it out of the cold and into the fug.

Seddon's Auction Rooms is basically a long derelict shed with alleged antiques crammed into every available bit of space. I saw that today's auctioneer was Millon, a florid-faced, waistcoated know-all who believes the world owes him a living. My spirits rose. He was a newcomer and therefore by definition dimmer even than the regular auctioneers, which is to say beyond belief. Fewer dealers than ever had turned up today on account of the snow. I offered up a prayer of thanks, because fewer bidders means cheaper prices, even among this load of crooks. Still, the one thing you can say about crooks is they're honest, not like the good old law-abiding public. And speaking of crooks, the auctioneer was gavelling again.

'Lot Forty-One. A small genuine antique silver bookmark. Who'll give me fifty to start?'

A hand touched my elbow. Even before looking round I knew from the pong it was Tinker. Bleary as ever, a crumpled alcoholic old reject in a stained army greatcoat, greasy of mitten and threadbare of gear. A stub of a person, but my one and only employee. He's my barker, a sniffer-out of antiques. The greatest.

'Hiya, Lovejoy. Your crowd from the arcade have gone for a bite.'

I knew better than to argue. Tinker locates dealers and antiques by some kind of mental beam. Somebody morosely bid a fiver for Lot Forty-One and the bidding was off, to the auctioneer's relief. He didn't deserve such good fortune. Instead he should have been gaoled, because he had deliberately called a false description, an offence punishable by law. The 'genuine antique silver bookmark' was no such thing. Genuine and silver, yes. Antique and a bookmark, no. It was late Victorian and thus not 'antique' by honest definition (and here I exclude the Customs Office which, being unable to count above double figures, has reluctantly pretended for years that antiques begin at a hundred years of age). And it was a *page* marker. These delectable little objects are very collectable, being usually silver or even gold. Most have a split blade to slide over a page's edge leaving

3

the decorated handle protruding. About two-and-a-half inches and all sorts of shapes – scissors, carving knives, pipes, swords, leaves and the like. Lovely. My mouth watered. If I hadn't been broke . . .

'Jane Felsham with them?'

'Aye.'

I cheered up even more. She would be back for the paintings which I saw began about Lot Ninety in today's heap of gunge.

'Jason?'

'Him too.' My spirits fell again. Lately Jason had been seeing Jane more than he deserved. Only I deserved to see Jane Felsham that much, but seeing I was broke and Jason wealthy . . .

Tinker cleared his throat, warming up for one of his famous rasping coughs. I drew a deep breath to last me through the droplet haze. Tinker's cough started as a deep rumble full of such powerful reverberations that several of the crowd glanced idly towards the windows, wondering what kind of monster vehicle could possibly be making that racket on East Hill. It then intensified, growling and lifting in tone and bubbling as the phlegm in Tinker's stringlike windpipe churned. The volume intensified and swelled sending shudders through the brickwork. Finally out it came, a great explosion in a slamming din of sound, a noise so cacophonous it rapped your eardrums. Tinker's wiry little frame jerked double and bobbed with the effort. It's a pity they don't give Olympic coughers' medals. The Russians wouldn't stand a chance. Tinker would walk it.

I opened my eyes in relief as the appalling noise dwindled, Tinker rejoined the human race, wiping his nose on the back of his filthy mitten, his rheumy old eyes streaming from the relief of having coughed and survived. The entire auction room was stunned into an appalled silence.

Tinker was contentedly rolling himself a fresh cigarette when he noticed the ominous stillness.

'Pardon,' he croaked.

A few of the dealers chuckled and nudged each other. And even Helen from the arcade, the loveliest dealer in East Anglia, smiled at Tinker. The trouble was that Millon chose to be offended, which led to his downfall. Antiques are dear, but there's nothing so costly as pride.

'Who made that awful noise?' he parped. He knew very well who.

The place stilled. Tinker stopped rolling his fag.

'That corf? Me.' Tinker was indignant. 'I said me pardon.'

Millon lost his rag. 'Get *out*! I will not have this auction interrupted by any old doss-house lounger!'

Poor old Tinker was stricken. He glanced apprehensively at me, knowing I needed him for a Kwangtung temple-door carving I had my eye on among the high numbers. A couple of the local dealers, suddenly nervous, shot glances at me. I saw Alfred Duggins, an elderly bowler-hatted collector of hammered coins, roll his eyes in alarm. He'd known me since I was a callow youth and guessed what was coming.

Mortified, Tinker shuffled sideways towards the door. 'Sorry, Lovejoy. I'll see me quack, get something for me chest. Honest.' He thought I was mad at him for one lousy cough.

I said nothing. I was looking at the floor, planks in a row and worn to the nails by generations of people coming in this crummy auction just because they wanted an antique, a piece of the loving past to cherish them against the shoddy crapology of our modern world. In this generation those ordinary people just happen to be Tinker and me. And you.

'Do-you-*hear*-me?' bleated this nerk on the rostrum.

'I'm going, mate,' Tinker muttered.

'Tinker.' I gave him a quid. My voice sounded funny. 'Wait in the pub. I'll only be ten minutes.'

'Ta. But the auction won't be over till—'

He peered at my face and then quickly went, his old boots clumping until the door pinged shut behind him. By now old Alfred was at the door, nervously measuring distances for a quick getaway. Trust him to suss me out before the rest.

Millon announced, pompously tugging his waistcoat neater, 'Now we can get *on*! Lot Forty-One. The bid's with you, sir.' He pointed to a tall neat gabardine-suited bloke, who had bid last in a foreign accent. 'It was fifty pounds. Who'll give fifty-five?'

I found Helen's hand on my arm. '*Please* no, Lovejoy,' her voice begged. But it was miles off and I shrugged her away.

Millon was chanting, 'Fifty-five anywhere?' when I coughed. The place stilled again. It was nothing like a Tinker special, but I did the best I could.

'Who'll give me fifty-five for this—?'

I coughed again, a non-cough phoney enough to gall anyone. Millon glared in my direction. 'Sir. Please control your noise or I shall have to ask you to leave also.'

So I was a sir and Tinker was a doss-house lounger. I coughed again, looking deliberately at Millon. He reddened and for the first time noticed that the other bidders had silently begun to recede, leaving a clear space around me. I heard Alfred mutter, 'Oh Gawd!' The door pinged once as he slid out. Wise old bird.

Millon's voice wavered but he gamely went on, 'In

view of the interruptions we will leave Lot Forty-One in abeyance and go on to Lot Forty-Two, which is Chippendale—'

'No.' That was me, trying for a normal voice but it came out like a whipcrack.

He stared. I smiled back. In that moment one of the strangers next to the big bloke started to say something but he was pulled up by a kindly friend, which saved him a lot of trouble, whoever he was. I heard another voice murmur, 'Watch it, mate. That's Lovejoy.'

Millon's gaze wobbled. For confidence, he stared belligerently to where his three miffs were standing. Miffs are auctioneers' callers who hump stuff about and make sure potential bidders get the barest glimpse of the lots next on offer. They were looking anywhere else. You have to smile. Sometimes they behave like real people.

'What do you mean, *no?*' Millon snapped, which only goes to show how dumb auctioneers can be.

'I mean your "Chippendale" bureau is a fake.'

There was a babble of alarmed chatter, quickly fading. Millon practically went berserk.

'This is outrageous! I'm putting you out this instant! And I'm having you sued for—'

That old familiar white heat glow came in my head. I gave up trying to be patient and found myself walking forwards, the mob parting like a bow wave. Everybody gave me their attention, especially when I told them to.

'All of you listen,' I said. 'Lift his Chippendale bureau up. It's the wrong weight for its size. Look at the right-hand drawer – you'll find a pattern of old filled-in screw holes. It's oak all right, but nicked from a World War One vintage bedroom cupboard. And the ageing stain's phoney. Invert the drawers and you'll see the paler shrinkage lines round the edges.' I looked up at Millon,

7

now looking considerably less assured. I added, 'It's not Chippendale, chum. It's a bodged mock-up.'

An angry murmur rose from the crowd. Millon paled. I felt so happy.

Blithely I sailed on, 'Like that old sextant.' It had been proudly displayed in the window all week. 'Did you tell them it isn't really seventeenth-century, Millon?' I explained how even with a small hand-lens you can spot modern high-rev lathe work.

Millon was going green. The ugly groundswell of muttering intensified. He bleated, 'These allegations are quite unfounded—'

'And that old Dutch microscope, Millon,' I announced with jubilation. 'You catalogued it as a mint original. The lenses are whittled-down spectacle lenses from a three-penny stall. Any optician will tell you how it's done.'

Somebody shouted, 'Well, Millon? What about it, eh?' Another dealer yelled, 'I bought that ivory, Millon—'

'Taiwan,' I put in before the dazed auctioneer could draw breath. 'They simulate the grain.' With a wax coating pitted by a kitchen cheese-shredder and a dilute solution of phosphoric acid you can give almost any plastic a detailed texture of ivory. Unscrupulous forgers of antiques can mass-produce them if you make a template, though I've found (er, I mean I've *heard*) the moulds don't really last very long.

'Please, gentlemen.' The nerk tried to gavel but it only irritated everyone still more.

'What about this miniature?' That was the big Continental bloke. He was looking not at Millon but directly at me, which I thought odd. Nor did he seem worried at having risked his money on a load of tat. The man next to him, obviously one of his many serfs, was holding up a small filthy medallion-sized disc covered by a dirty piece of glass. Even across the angry crowd in that dingy hall I felt that luscious shudder deep inside my chest. My breathing went funny, and I shook to the chime of heavenly bells.

For me all strife momentarily ceased, and I was in Paradise. I was in the presence of a genuine sixteenth-century miniature, possibly even done by the great Hilliard himself. I groaned audibly and felt tears start in my eyes.

The big geezer laughed, a strange noise like a cat's cough. I didn't need to explain my jealousy because it must have showed on my face. He had made himself an absolute fortune and suddenly I hated him more than fried liver, the bastard.

I turned away and raised my voice over the babble. 'Pay attention, troops. That bobbin tree catalogued as late Hanoverian is actually brand new, and imported pinewood at that.' I could have gone into details of how fruitwood and laburnum can be simulated in these delectable household necessities of Regency days, but you can't educate antique dealers so it's no use bothering.

'Please. You're ruining—'

'That Civil War cavalry pistol's a fake,' I continued, pointing. 'A cut-down Eastern jezail with a Turkish barrel. Note the—'

I would have gone on because I was just getting into my stride, but with a howl the dam broke. A beefy gorilla in from the Smoke shouldered me out of the way. The furious dealers grabbed for Millon, the poor goon shrieking for help but of course his three miffs had vanished and he disappeared in a mound of flying limbs. I spent the next few seconds eeling my way from the pandemonium, smiling blissfully. The place was in uproar as I pinged out into the cold.

Happier now, I plodded the few snowy yards to the Ship. I could still hear the racket from the auction rooms as I pushed open the tavern door. Tinker was hunched over a pint at the bar. He started at the sight of me. 'Look, Lovejoy. I could get old Lemuel to help instead.'

'Shut it.' I gave him the bent eye and he subsided into silence but still managed to drain his pint. His gnarled countenance led me to understand a refill was a matter of survival, so I paid up. It was in that split second while Tinker's pint glass remained miraculously full that I felt the most horrid sense of foreboding. I started to slurp at my own glass in an attempt to shake it off just as a hand tapped my shoulder.

'*Lovejoy.*'

Chris Anders was normally a taciturn geezer but now his face was puce with fury. He is domestic pre-Victorian furniture – that treacherous shifting sand of the antiques world – and late Victorian jewellery, and good at both. I quite like him but at the moment I wasn't exactly in the mood to have my shoulder tapped. I sighed and put my glass down. It was one of those days.

'You bastard! You shambled the whole bloody auction!'

'Me?' I said innocently.

'*You!* I wanted one of the lots and you stopped me, you—'

I tried to calm him. 'Sorry, old pal. Anyway that Chinese funereal terracotta bird shouldn't be glazed, Chris.' I was only trying to be reasonable, because he's famous for coating with polyurethanes any antique that stands still long enough, the maniac. The object Chris was after shrieked authenticity. It was one of the terracotta figures from Fu Hao's tomb, excavated at Anyang in China during the mid-1970s. Anyway, I have a soft spot for that tempestuous empress Fu Hao who lived such a stormy life. Wife of the Emperor Wu Ding, 1300 BC or thereabouts, and not above leading his armies into battle if the need arose. A real woman.

'I have a right—' Chris was storming.

'You're thick as a brick, Chris,' I said, honestly trying to be kind.

His eyes glazed and he grabbed me by the throat – or would have done if his rib hadn't cracked on the stool I slammed up under his ribcage. The broken glass suddenly in my hand opened a slit down his sleeve and forearm through which blood squirted.

'You should only *dust* terracotta figures,' I told him as he reeled back aghast and squealing. I heard Sal the barmaid shriek. 'And use a sable paintbrush. Okay?'

The pub was silent, except for the quiet jingle of the door behind old Alfred. The poor bloke was like a refugee today. Chris clutched at his arm as the blood refused to stop and moaned, 'What's Lovejoy done to me? Get an ambulance.'

'Oh Gawd,' Tinker muttered. 'Scarper, Lovejoy.'

The scattered drinkers were simply looking. That is, all except one. And he was smiling, clapping his hands together gently in applause. Pigskin gloves, London-made. Clap-clap-clap, standing by the door. His two goons were there but simply watching.

I slid past Chris and out of the side door. Tinker's hunched form was just shuffling round the side of the pub on to the snowy slope of East Hill. I wisely took the other direction, slushing past the small timber yard and the Saxon church into the little square where the Three Cups pub stood. I took my time, stopping in the bookshop to price an Irish leather binding, but their prices read nowadays like light years.

Alfred Duggins wasn't in the Cups when finally I

reached there. He'd probably given up. But the big stranger was waiting for me just inside the taproom.

'Look, mate,' I said to him. If you're narked about the auction, say so and let's get on with it.'

'Drink?' His voice was man-sized, cool and full of confidence.

'What's the catch?'

'Catch?' He gave a lopsided grin. 'No catch. I just thought you deserved one, that's all.'

Without thinking, I said, 'Well, ta,' and we pushed in to the fug.

Arcellano was instantly at home in the Three Cups, exactly as he'd been at home in Seddon's crummy auction rooms, and just as he had seemed in the spit-and-sawdust Ship. While he ordered at the bar I glanced at him. This bloke was a hard nut and no mistake.

Jason and the delectable Jane were just settling down in one snug corner, which failed to cheer me. I glimpsed Big Frank over among a huddle of barkers, all of whom glowered my way. Nobody waved. I guessed my popularity was lower than ever because of spoiling the auction.

'Here, sir.' The stranger passed me my pint. I crossed to the fireplace to dry my shoes. I noticed we were out of earshot of the others. A careful geezer too.

'My name's Lovejoy, Mr Arcellano,' I told him. Oddly, my name caused no screech of merriment. It always had before.

He said slowly, 'You know my name?'

'You bought at Seddon's, remember.' That was the name he had given Millon. Too late now to wonder if he'd made the name up. 'You a collector?'

He shrugged my question off and cautiously he tasted

the beer before drinking properly. 'You're pretty definite about antiques, Lovejoy. Other dealers aren't.'

'Most dealers are like Chris, can't tell an antique from
a plastic duck.'

'You're famous hereabouts.' He smiled as he spoke but
with no warmth. I began to see why his tame goons did
as they were told. 'Lots of people gave me your name.'

I didn't like the sound of that and said, all innocence,
'Me? Oh, you know how people are.'

'Yes, I know.' He said it with utter conviction. 'And
people say if there's an antique to be got, Lovejoy's the
man to get it.'

'Do they indeed?'

'Sure do. In fact,' he added, 'they seem to talk pretty
guarded when I asked about you.'

I didn't like the sound of that, either. In fact, I wasn't
at all sure I liked the man, but he seemed like a customer with money and I was sick of living on fried
tomatoes and what I could scrounge from bored housewives when I was forced to go on the knocker. Things
had been really terrible lately. So I smiled affably. 'Take
no notice.'

'Oh, but I have, Lovejoy. You're hired.'

'I am?'

He smiled at the irritation in my voice. 'For lots and
lots of money.'

The dull world exploded in a blaze of gold fireworks.
The muted mutter of the taproom soared into heavenly
cadences. The entire universe was once again a magnificent carousel of dazzling lights and brilliant music. I
was suddenly aware of how pleasant a bloke he actually
was. I cleared my throat and squeaked, 'Have another,
Mr Arcellano?'

I reeled back to the bar and gave Jean a weak grin.

She's the barmaid, sometimes cooperative. 'Trust me, love. Stick it on the slate. I've a deal on. Pay you back tonight.'

She drew the pints and slid them over, holding my stare. 'I'll hold you to that, Lovejoy. I finish at eleven.'

'You're wonderful, Jean. I'll come, love.'

She smiled mischievously. 'I might hold you to *that*, too, Lovejoy.'

The big man was lighting a cigarette when I rejoined him. I'd never seen so much gold in my life. There were rings, the lighter, watch, tiepin and collar clips, teeth. He didn't offer me a smoke. So I was already one more minion. I'm no smoker, anyway, but the message was there.

'Hired for what?'

'To get me an antique.'

He probably meant for me to bid for him in an auction. 'You want it valued?'

'I already know what it's worth. And where it is. I just need it collecting. You see, I own it.'

My brow cleared. A simple vannie's removal job. Well, in my state I wasn't proud. 'That's easy.' For some reason I'd been getting anxious.

'It isn't, Lovejoy.' That horrid smile was worrying me. The more I saw of it the less I liked it. 'But I saw the way you broke the auctioneer's arm—'

That got me mad, because people have no right to go suspecting things people don't want suspected. 'I did no such thing!'

'You did,' he said flatly. 'I've used the same trick myself. Pretend to help somebody in a brawl and put their elbow backwards over the edge of a desk. It never fails.' His face was expressionless now. I noticed his eyes were always on the go, flicking glances here and there as we talked. My brow cleared and I thought, oh Christ. What have I got into?

He continued, 'And that dealer in the pub. Big and tough. But you sorted him out. Never seen anybody move so fast in my life. You're the man I've been looking for.'

'To do a vannie's job?' He looked puzzled till I explained. Vannies are the humpers of our trade, mere shifters. A right mob of brainless old boozers they are too.

He heard me out and shook his head. 'Nothing that simple. You see, Lovejoy, somebody else has got my antique. And I want you to get it back.' His voice chilled me, and I'm not easily chilled.

He'd said 'get'. Not buy, not bid, not collect. Get. As in rob?

'Why can't you, erm, get it, Mr Arcellano?'

'Because it's risky. I might get caught.'

I thought, bloody hell. It's a rip. The bastard actually wants *me* to do a rip. Not him, note, because it's frigging risky. I rose, full of bitterness. It had all been too good to be true. Back to the cold snow and a quick rape over Ann's lace in the village. Maybe there was a slender chance of fitting in a quick hot nosh, though other times I'd called round I'd had to nick what I could from her fridge while she went to the loo.

'Sod off, mate.'

'Sit down, Lovejoy.' His face lifted. His smile was there again. I'd never seen such an unhappy smile. 'You just risked gaol for that old man—'

'Tinker's my barker,' I said. My chest felt tight. I was in some sort of scrap and losing fast. I'm responsible for him.'

'And Margaret?'

How the hell did he know about Margaret Dainty? She and I have been close friends a long time. She's not young, yet despite her limp she has that elusive style some older women carry like blossom. I glanced around. Arcellano's two serfs were now sitting at a table by the door.

I subsided slowly. 'What is this?'

He blew a perfect smoke ring. 'Do the job and no harm comes to any of your friends – or you. You'll not cry when you hear the fee.'

I swallowed. 'To nick an antique?'

He looked pained. 'Not *steal*, Lovejoy. I did say I already own it. Think of it as returning it to me, its rightful owner.'

'Who has it?' I said.

'The Pope,' he said.

'The *who?*' I said.

'You heard.'

'Fucking hell,' I said. 'You're asking *me* to . . . ?'

'Another drink?' he said. He was still smiling.

Chapter 2

I've always found that youth's no deterrent to age. The ultimate proof was the Pinnacle Peak Language Academy, a big, modern but old-looking house on the outskirts of town. Arcellano had instructed me to report there, making all heads turn by snapping his fingers that snowy January day in the pub and passing me the card one of his goons whisked over. The card read *Specialists in Modern European Languages*.

'You're going to school, Lovejoy,' he'd said. 'To learn Italian.'

'I'm hell as like.' I'd hated school.

'You register tomorrow.'

This was beginning to look too organized for my liking. 'Can't I just buy a phrase-book?'

'Not for this job.' He rose then, a gentle picture of threatening behaviour but still smiling. 'Your wages will be delivered every Friday.'

'Oh.' I cheered up. These language schools are all the same — a convenience for foreign students to get a visa and for our own students to go on the scive. Simply register, attend the first couple of lessons to show willing, then it's off to the boozer with a part-time job on the side for extras. I thought what a nice simple bloke this bloke

17

was. And a charming nature. 'Right,' I said, keeping the card and carefully not yelping with delight as Arcellano and his grovellers made to depart. Money for jam at last. He paused.

'One thing, Lovejoy. About your wage.'

'Oh, that.' I tried to sound only casually interested, but was pleased he'd remembered the details, like how much.

'It depends on how you do.'

'Eh?'

His blank smile was beginning to get me down. 'Good progress, you get good money. Little progress, little money.'

I thought, what bloody cheek. 'Then you can stuff your schooling.'

'And no attendance,' he said quietly, 'no Lovejoy. *Arrivederci.*'

I watched the unpleasant bastard go. Thoughts of Margaret, Tinker, Jane and the rest rose within me and stayed. Antiques is a rough game. Antiques plus Arcellano was unthinkable. I thought for an hour before leaving the pub.

There was no doubt left in me. Some failures were just not worth having. Back to school for Lovejoy.

I have to tell you this next bit because it's where I met Maria. And she became more of the rip than ever I wanted, and in a way I hate to remember even yet.

The next morning was bright with that dazzling winter brilliance you get living near the cold North Sea. To the east the sea-marshes glistened, trees standing in spectacular white silhouette against the blue. Even the thought of schooling didn't put me down. I'd wangled my unlearned way through childhood. A day or two more would be peanuts. And maybe they included dinner.

I got a lift into town on a horse-drawn wagon, since there had again been snow during the night and all the modern mechanical wonder-gadgets were frozen under drifts. At such times East Anglia's one useful vehicle is Jacko's cart. He is a smelly, cheerful old devil, much addicted to light opera, who runs a ramshackle removal van in summer and Terence in winter. Terence is his gigantic shire horse, ancient as a church and about twice as big, and he pulls this wooden farmyard cart which Jacko, a born comedian, rigs up with nailed planks he calls passenger seats.

'Is it true you're going to school, Lovejoy?' Jacko called as I climbed up. He was falling about at the notion.

'Shut it, Jacko.' I hate the way word gets round our village.

But he choked with laughter all the way down to the brook and across the water-splash where the town road begins. I had to grin weakly and put up with him because he lets me on for nothing. It was a lot kinder than it sounds – I still owe him for six journeys from last winter when the black ice had blocked us in for three days.

Jacko put us all down at the Albert tavern, from where we could walk up the slushy hill into town. I ploshed my way out to the Pinnacle Peak Language Academy, my chirpiness dwindling with every wet step.

The lowering sky to the south-west was leaden, promising yet more snow. The wind was rising, the air dank and chill. I was hungry as hell, perishing cold and imprisoned in a trap of utter misery by that lunatic Arcellano. My antiques trade would vanish. My life was a wreck.

So I went to school – and met Maria.
From then on things went downhill.

The so-called Academy was heaving. I'd never seen so many shapes and sizes and ages. Somehow a motley mob of people had battled their way to this emporium of learning and were noisily finding acquaintances among the press. There were kids, geriatrics, housewives, workmen, and elegant ladies obviously bolting from boredom. The Pinnacle Peak's idea of welcome was a handshake in the form of grievous bodily harm from a bluff language instructor called Hardy ('everybody calls me Jingo'), a sermon full of veiled threats from a geriatric grammarian headmistress, Miss McKim, and a gentle reproof from old Fotheringay. He was heartbroken because I'd never done classics at Balliol. I sympathized, because so was I.

Jingo Hardy enrolled me in a dusty side room. I nearly fainted at the fees printed on the form. One week's worth would have kept me six months.

He boomed a laugh. 'Don't worry, Lovejoy. Yours have been paid. Ten weeks of special instruction.'

He told me to wait in the hall so I sat on one of the radiator pipes and watched Jingo Hardy, in the thick of things, inform a small disorderly bunch that they were intellectuals about to tackle Russian literature. With poisonous cheerfulness he bullied them off into a side room, leaving only a moderately-sized horde milling blindly to and fro.

What with the warmth and the comfort I must have nodded off or something because the next thing I knew I was being criticized and prodded with a shoe, which proved I was awake again. The hallway was empty. This woman's voice was saying sharply, 'And what do you think *you* are doing?'

'Waiting.'

I blinked up at her. She was one of the loveliest women I had ever seen. Dark, slender, bright and stylish with a warm tweed-and-cardigan look. Pearl stud earrings. I fell for her. She toed me again. The crowd had vanished. A faint hum arose from the rooms all about, school now in session.

'You're a tramp, aren't you?'

'Not yet.' I said. The irony was lost on her.

'Please leave, or I shall call the police.'

I said, 'Lady. Prod me again with your toe and I'll break it. *Off.*'

She withdrew a yard. 'Why have you no socks on?'

'Drying.' I got them off the radiator and felt. Still damp, but I started to put them on. All I could do now was tell Arcellano I'd tried and they'd threatened to have me run in.

'And shoes?'

'Give me a sec.' I'd sloped them on the pipe, heels down, in an attempt to dry the cardboard which covered the holes.

She was watching. 'Do you have far to go?'

You can't help staring at some people. There ought to be Oscars or something for hypocrisy. Today's message from this luscious bird: piss off or I'll call the police, and have a pleasant journey strolling through the blizzard. People amaze me.

'Yes.'

'Oh. Well. Where's your overcoat?'

'Still at my tailor's.'

She flushed then and developed the injured look of a woman wanting some man to take up this particularly cumbersome crucifix. I didn't help by spinning out my dressing process. She stood her ground, though.

'One thing, love.' I stood and stamped my cardboard inners flat. 'Swap that painting to the other wall.'

'I beg your pardon?'

I stepped across and lifted the watercolour down. '*Never* over a radiator. *Never* in a centrally heated hallway if you can help it. *Never* facing what sun we get. And *never* where people smoke.'

The little watercolour sketch was a Thomas Robins, the sort of thing he did before doing the proper Dutch fishing-boat scene. He liked storms in harbours. I'm not all that old, but I can remember the time four years ago when his best paintings could be got for an average monthly wage.

'Take your hands off our property—'

She came at me so I cuffed her and yelled, 'You could have made me drop it, you silly bitch! Look.' I dragged her near to the modern photorepro of 'The Stag at Bay' which I'd just taken down. '*That*,' I explained into her stunned eyes, 'will stand anything. *This* original watercolour is vulnerable.' I spelled the word to give her cortex time to adjust to the learning process. 'So we put your repro picture anywhere, see? It'll not warp, change or fade in the sun. On the other hand, love, original paintings by Thomas Sewell Robins need care.' I spelled that too, mounted the watercolour, then walked to the door.

'You hit me.' She was still preoccupied with being annoyed.

'I'll come back next week, love, to check you've not swapped the pictures back. And I'll accept no crappy excuses about your painting being school property.' I wagged a finger to emphasize the threat. 'A genuine antique is everybody's, no matter who owns it. Remember, now.'

She suddenly said, 'You're Lovejoy.'

'True,' I said, opening the door to the kinder world of winter. 'And goodbye.'

She suddenly became a supplicant. The abrupt transformation was really weird. 'Please. Don't go.' She even tried a winning smile. I'd never see a quicker – or more desperate – conversion. 'I'm – I'm your special instruction counsellor assignment.'

'You're my what?' Nowadays everything sounds like the UN.

She gave in and used language. 'Teacher. Please come back in.'

I hesitated between the blizzard and the deep blue sea. Normally I'd have stormed out in a temper, though I'm usually very mild. The reason I didn't was the sheer desperation in her eyes. Somehow I'd annoyed her at first, but now there she was full of frantic appeasement. I could have sworn she was afraid. Maybe she needed the money or lived in terror of mighty Miss McKim.

'Can I dry my shoes on your radiator?'

'If you wish.'

'And socks?' I added shrewdly.

'Of course.' She moved past me and pushed the door to

'And I'm not in trouble for, erm, telling you about the pictures?'

'You mean hitting me,' she said evenly. 'No.'

It seemed there was no way out. Time for a truce. 'All right.'

'Thank you,' she said, and meant it, which was odder still. She extended a hand. 'I'm Maria Peck.'

We went all Regency. 'Pleased to make your acquaintance. Lovejoy.'

She didn't look local, not with those lustrous Italianate features and that complexion, but Peck is unshakably East Anglian and I commented on it while we shook.

'So I'm told,' she said, and added sweetly, 'Nothing like as unusual as Lovejoy, is it?'

Smarting, I thought, okay. Truce, not submission.

'This way, please.'

I followed her lissom form. Whatever lissom means, it's the right word.

Most women have an inherent grace, don't they, with awareness sort of built in. Well, the ultimate was Maria. I swear I was demented for her by the time we reached the classroom, though her attitude seemed to be one of instant aloofness once she'd got me to stay.

But why the terror when I was making my sullen exit? Last time I'd been at school they were glad to get rid of me. Fool that I was, I shelved the little mystery and forgot it.

Late Friday of that week it happened. I was in my cottage frying some pieces of apple. It's supposed to be a countryman's delicacy, but was proving a failure. For a start you need oil for the pan, and I'd got none. Then you need a good stove, and the bastards had cut my electricity off in the midweek. The methylated spirit lamp, which I use for wax modelling, was going full blast – an erg an hour – and the sliced apples were barely warm.

The knock on the door surprised me. My cottage is fairly remote, on the outskirts of a small village. The lane leading to it is narrow and long and goes hardly anywhere else. The daylight had faded an hour since. I cheered up as I went into the little hallway. My first week's wages were due for having attended that punk language school. Apart from having the opportunity to gape at the delectable Maria it had been a real drag, so I deserved every penny.

It was Arcellano and his two nerks all right, but not

with my wages. The three of them were crammed into
the tiny vestibule, blocking out the vague haze of snow
light.

'Mr Arcellano!' I yelped with false delight, thinking
of money, and hot pasties and beer at the White Hart.
Hunger makes crawlers of us all. 'Good of you to call!
Come in!' Nobody moved.

'Where's the lights?'

'Erm, well, I've had the electricity cut off,' I said
smoothly. 'Temporary repairs, you understand. This
wretched weather brought down a cable—'

'What's the stink?'

'Stink?' I swallowed my irritation. The bastard was
speaking of my staple diet. 'Ah. Delicious country recipe.
Fried apple. Actually takes hours to make. I haven't done
the flaky pastry yet, or I'd offer you supper—'

A flashlight blinded me. With the beam flickering
into every corner the two goons bore me backwards
and slammed me down in a chair. Heavy hands pressed
on my shoulders when I tried to rise. It's horrible to
discover you are suddenly out of breath for no known
cause. In that instant all I could think of was that quick
glimpse of terror on Maria's face when I had started to
cut out from the school.

'Is this how you live, Lovejoy?'

'Only temporarily,' I answered, narked. 'I'm having an
extension built—'

'Hold him.'

A flashlight was beamed at my face so I could see
nothing. With my eyes screwed up against the beam
I sat and listened while somebody, probably Arcellano
himself, shook out drawers and emptied cupboards and
slammed doors and tore things in the darkness beyond
the light. I knew better than to hope for neighbours or

the police to arrive. The former wisely leave me alone, and the latter are only more trouble and I'd enough to be going on with.

Quite ten minutes later I heard Arcellano return. He sounded slightly winded from all his exertions. I felt the same and I'd done nothing but sit.

A lighter flared, showing his face full of unpleasant shadows. The light snapped off and a cigarette glowed.

'Why do you live here like a pig, Lovejoy?' He sounded surprised but honestly interested.

I tried to shrug but his berks were still pressing me down. 'I'm a bit short. I've done a few good deals, though—'

'You've not, Lovejoy.' Even when smoke came into my eyes making me cough and blink I knew the sod was smiling. 'You are penniless.'

'Only temporarily,' I shot back. 'If I hadn't wasted the week on your frigging school I'd have—'

'How *was* school?'

That gentle query pulled me up. 'Oh. Horrible as ever.' I tried a chuckle. It sounded like a trapped wasp.

'Make much progress, Lovejoy?'

I swallowed. This didn't make sense. He sounded too gentle for somebody who had come in like Attila the Hun and wrecked the place.

'Quite a lot,' I lied cheerfully. My mouth was dry.

A paper rustled. 'Your report says different.' A silence. 'That's bad news, Lovejoy. Not for me. For you. Light.'

I found I couldn't swallow any more. The beam moved to show his gloved hands and the crested school paper.

'Inattentive,' he quoted. 'Six reprimands daily for reading journals on antiques during lessons.'

Had it been that many? 'Rubbish.'

'Homework: nil per cent.'

I'd done none. 'I've been a bit pushed lately—'

He read on relentlessly, 'Altogether a hopeless start.'

I protested weakly, 'Most of the others are young, still in school. They're naturals—'

'That's not true. There are only four children in your class. The rest are adults. One is fifty and did better than you, Lovejoy.'

I seethed in silent fury. The bastard had checked up What kind of employer checks up? Where's trust gone?

'The others distract me.'

'But your afternoon teaching is individual. I should know. I paid for it. And your teacher says: "Total lack of motivation." Well, Lovejoy?'

That sounded Maria all over. She and I had wasted every afternoon in a soundproofed room, if you can believe it. I took three goes to start my voice up. 'I suppose this means no wage this week, eh, Mr Arcellano?'

He rose and I got the light back in my eyes. 'True, Lovejoy. But I have to go away for ten whole weeks. I can't leave you here without motivation, can I?' There was some shuffling nearby. One of the goons was getting ready for something. Arcellano's voice hardened. 'Our deal's on, Lovejoy. It's on because I said so. Play dim if you like, but you suffer the consequences. Understand?'

'Well, yes,' I was saying when somebody clouted me. 'Hold him.'

Gloved hands gripped my head while Arcellano extinguished his cigarette on the point of my chin. I whimpered but they held me fast. I was going to bring up some very convincing excuse when they started on me. Even now I can't for the life of me remember what it was, but I know it would have been a cracker. I'm good at excuses.

* * *

There's a knack in cooking. I've not got it, but I once had a bird who was really great. Sally used to make these fantastic meals, never the same twice and so many different flavours you never knew what you were eating half the time under all that taste, which is quite an achievement because eating's a right drag. We parted when she developed suspicions – almost quite unjustified – about a rich widow who used to call sometimes when Sally was out at work. I've found that women always want to believe the worst, when it's so much simpler to believe what's easiest.

I had stopped being sick about eight o'clock or thereabouts. By a fluke no bones were broken and the bleeding had stopped on its own while I was flat out. In the light of my spirit lamp I could see my face puffy and battered, with a prodigious blister the size of an igloo bulging from my stubble where the bastard had burned me with his fag. No cuts, but dried blood down my neck from one ear, one eye black and bulging, and my right shoulder sprained. The cottage was a hell of a mess.

For some reason I was tired, even after such a long enforced slumber, so I dozed on my divan for a while. Then my hunger returned and I started warming the pan again. The cold slices of apple stared reproachfully up at me in the gloom. What with the state I was in, she must have been knocking donkey's years before I heard and let her in. My favourite teacher.

I need not say much about the rest of that evening, or of that night. Maria shot a handful of terse questions at me, to which I gave terse unfriendly answers, seeing she was to blame for the battering Arcellano's serfs gave me. She looked closely at me with the aid of the spirit lamp's watery blue flame. Then she did a quick reconnaissance while I glowered sullenly at my pan through my one good eye. Eventually she said she'd be back and went. I heard her tyres skittering and crunching on the snow.

Ever the optimist, I was trying to raise a brew-up when I realized she was back. She must have nicked my key somehow, or maybe I'd given it her. I forget which. She lit a candle and stuck it on a plate. Then another. The lovely golden light bathed the cottage's shambled interior. It looked in a worse state than me. I wondered where she'd managed to buy candles at this hour.

She took the saucer of apple off me and scraped it into the bin in my kitchen alcove. That was the start. She must have made them work — an all-time first — at the Treble Tile because she'd fetched some hot nosh as well. Chips, fish, sausages, a pot of soupy stuff, and bags of cheese, bread, a cake and milk and tea and, among the rest, apples by mistake. I didn't grumble. I'd run out of Ann's grub two days before. Playing at being an angel of mercy was obviously doing Maria a power of good because she was silent for the first time ever. Until then I thought I'd never met such a talkative bird in my life.

I ate her nosh slowly and slurpily while she tidied, always a bad sign in a woman. The more racket they make the more you're for it. Not saying a word, I whittled my way across two platefuls while her slamming and rattling went remorselessly on, a sort of creeping barrage. She was watching me by that sort of feminine feel which requires tight lips and no actual stare. I could tell because the instant I finished she swept the dishes aside and sat washing my face in a cupful of lukewarm water. The sensible lass had used eight whole candles brewing tea.

We reached midnight in total silence, sitting primly side by side on my folding divan, knees together and politely clearing throats and watching candles glow. I always feel at a disadvantage when women tidy me up. Maybe that's why they do it. The battle started.

'Lovejoy,' she said carefully. 'What happened here is none of my business.'

How true. 'A disagreement with a customer.'

'Be that as it may.' She spoke the words exactly like she taught in pronunciation class, with gaps a mile long. 'But I'm not so stupid that I fail to see the connection between your bad first week's report, and this beating you have suffered.'

I told her rubbish. She fumbled in her handbag and brought out the crumpled report. Arcellano must have left it.

'Then how did this get here?'

'It was posted to me by mistake.'

'Miss McKim *never* makes mistakes.' She read through it quickly, folding it after seeing her own handwriting. 'These reports are sent only to the sponsors.' She rose and paced, obviously going to put the boot in. 'Tell me the truth, Lovejoy. You've got to do well or suffer. Isn't that right?'

'Yes.'

'Very well.' She turned to face me. Two candles shone from behind her, casting a subtle corona round her from the shadows. I'd never seen such beauty in a woman in all my life, not since Helen, or maybe Lydia or maybe Sally the nosh queen.

Entranced, I mumbled weakly, 'Very well what?'

'We must knuckle down.' She spoke so full of sadness that for an instant I misunderstood and thought she'd spotted a way out for me. Then it dawned she meant working, and my bitterness returned. I was trapped between Arcellano, that non-smiling smiler, and this gloomy optimist. 'You sold your Italian grammar text—'

'I did no such thing!'

'I saw you,' she said calmly. 'In the junk shop on the Hythe. So I bought it back.' And she brought it out of her handbag, the treacherous bitch. 'It's no good glaring, Lovejoy. Your signature's on the flyleaf.'

'You have no right following me—'

She smiled over my protest. 'And on the rare occasions you *do* pay attention in open class, Lovejoy, it's to Joan Culpepper.'

I asked innocently. 'Is she one of our group?'

'She's the lady next to whom you sit, Lovejoy. You started the week in the opposite corner.'

'Oh, *her*!' I'd obviously hardly noticed her, but Maria was not dissuaded, as usual suspicious without a single cause. 'The one with the Justinian period Roman quartz intaglio ring, modern setting in garnets on gold with raised platinum shoulder mounts?'

'Yes, *her*.' She tapped my knee with a finger, not knowing Arcellano's lunatic serfs had kicked it to a balloon size. I nearly screamed. 'From now on, Lovejoy, your Friday reports will be superb.'

'They will?' I brightened. Not only was this luscious woman delectable, but she'd obviously fallen head over heels for me. With Arcellano away for weeks and my bonus money rolling in . . . It was my trillionth mistake of the week. I asked, 'How'll we fiddle Miss McKim's reports?'

'You mean *cheat*?'

I saw her face. 'Well, er, no. Not exactly—'

She went cold as charity. 'There's only one way, Lovejoy, and that's to *earn* a good report.' She collected her coat and gloves. 'Don't worry, I'll see you'll get the right sort of help.'

'Erm . . .'

She walked towards the small hallway, rabbiting on. I had the idea she was smiling deep down. 'From now on, Lovejoy, you eat regularly. None of this heroic starving for the sake of old pots and ramshackle furniture—' I gasped, outraged at this heresy. It only goes to show how boneheaded women actually are. 'And from tomorrow your electricity bill will be paid. Light *and* warmth.' She smiled, adding sweetly, 'And distractions will be minimized. I shall see to that first thing tomorrow.'

She meant Mrs Culpepper. My head was spinning with all this. Or maybe it was the unusual sensation of not being hungry.

'Er, look,' I mumbled, 'can't we discuss this?'

'Yes. In Italian.'

'Eh?'

'You heard, Lovejoy.' Now her smile was open and visible, a beautiful warm silent laughter. 'From now on, ask for anything in English and the answer's no. But ask in Italian and the answer's . . .'

'. . . And the answer's yes?'

For one instant her smile intensified to a dazzling radiance. 'The answer's . . . quite possibly.' She stepped into the darkness, leaving me in the candlelight. I heard the cottage door go.

'Good night, Lovejoy,' she called from the winter midnight.

'Good night.' I was trying to say thanks as well but the latch went and she had gone.

You can't teach women anything about timing an exit. I've always noticed that.

Chapter 3

From then on it was hell – but a peculiar kind of hell, with torment interspersed with a haunting promise of ecstasy. For a time. Under the white-hot attentions of Maria, I quite forgot about Arcellano.

Unaccountably, the attractive Joan Culpepper attended no further classes, apart from one hour's collective conjugation, so to speak, I got the full teaching blast. 'Incentive teaching,' she often reminded me with hardly a trace of her secret hilarity.

By Tuesday of the following week I was showing withdrawal symptoms which caused a bit of upset. Maria had kept me at it twelve and fifteen hours at a stretch. Apart from that glimpse of Mrs Culpepper's 'tassie', as we call such incised semi-precious carvings, the only antique I'd seen was a Newhall painted cream jug with a 'clip' handle – these are always pre-1790 and still a bargain. It had somehow crept from its place of honour in the little dining room and was found on our table. I honestly had nothing to do with it, but a poisonous epsilon-minus cretin called Hyacinth reckoned I'd moved it nearer and blew the gaff on me. A tight-lipped Maria came across and restored it to its place on the sideboard. I was heartbroken. Newhall porcelain's enough to melt the hardest heart – Maria's excepted.

I was really peeved. 'Why d'you believe Hyacinth and not me?' Hyacinth's only twelve but she always came top in Italian at the end-of-day test.

Maria let the tea-lady pass with a loaded tray before accusing, 'It's antiques, isn't it, Lovejoy?'

'I'm fine.'

'You're not.' She was eyeing me as if for the first time, in serious puzzlement. 'You're a wreck and going down-hill like a pining child.' That was a real laugh. At my age.

'It's just I'm used to one way of doing things—'

'Wait here,' she said suddenly. 'Learn the past perfect of *essere*. I'll not be a minute.'

I shrugged. She hared off, obviously in the grip of some vital decision, while I wheedled a ton of cake from one of the tea-women and sat noshing it while admiring the clip-handled jug. You can still get these little polychrome beauties for a song – almost. And when you think they are *always* older than two whole centuries, made with love and elegance by potters with all the gifts of God in their gnarled fingers, and less than a day's average wage . . . I had tears in my eyes when finally Maria returned and jerked me back to reality.

She was dressed to go out. 'Get your coat, Lovejoy.'

'I've got none.'

'Sorry. I meant get ready.'

'I'm always ready. Where are we going?'

'Round the art galleries, antique shops and ruins of this fair town. Folk Museum. Minories.'

My eyes misted and I reached for her, ignoring the delighted gaze of the canteen women. 'Darling,' I said. She was seeing things my way at last.

'Yes, darling,' she murmured, misty too. 'There's only one thing, Lovejoy.'

'Eh?' I drew back full of apprehension.

'Everything in Italian, please. You know the rules.'

Breathlessly but angrily I raced upstairs for my dictionary and the grammar, thinking of that sly bitch falling about laughing down in the porch. As I hurried I raged at myself, I'll kill her one of these days, just see if I don't.

I wish I hadn't thought that terrible thought now, but you can't look into the future, can you? And honest to God none of this was my fault. None of it.

That day was sheer torture. There was I, frantically trying to tell Maria about the engravings on the Jacobite drinking glasses in the town museum, and of the really serious need for ultraviolet light to distinguish between the fluorescence that demonstrates a glass's origin, and there she was nodding encouragement as I ballsed up my declensions time and again. At the finish we both knew it was hopeless. I was the only known language learner with zero vocabulary, which is some handicap. I lost half a ton in sweat that afternoon.

Maria dropped me off in the village at the end of a harrowing day. I had an idea she lived somewhere down on the estuary but didn't dare ask. During the somewhat uncontrolled journey out of town the snow was still about with the roads pretty grim she hit on the idea of one particular item per day.

'It'll work, Lovejoy,' she asserted confidently. 'Pick a card.'

'Illuminated manuscripts,' I said. I've a real love for those.

She glanced at me, oddly amused. 'Fine. See you after midmorning break. We might as well go together in the car.'

That night I worked in a maniacal fever, slogging like

a mad thing to scrape together enough language to tell the stupid woman about the purity and complexity of style in the mediaeval illuminator's work. Our town museum can only afford this one mediaeval Psalter, but there was so much to say. I was desperate to convert Maria's moronic mind from materialism to a proper appreciation of love in human skills. The trouble is, nothing shuts you up like having no words.

By dawn I was knackered, but capable of bleating a few short sentences about the most beautiful things on earth.

Five weeks later I had worn out my first pocket dictionary and I kept going in grammar only by the neat trick of nicking Hyacinth's text. I'm good at swapping flyleaves without trace so I could prove the book I'd pinched out of her satchel was mine. Anyhow, by then I was streets ahead of the rest. They were even leaving me out of the end-of-day tests. I out-smirked Hyacinth by miles, which served her right.

It was that day too that Maria came to me for the first time. We were speaking in her language all the time now. Admittedly, I had to pause every minute or so for a feverish fumble through the book, but basically it was all progress. I'd discovered the most curious thing: learn one word and use it, and before long it somehow grows into two. Also, by then I wasn't hungry any more and had started filling out. Maria bought me a second-hand overcoat and my wages were already sparkling with bonus gelt. Likewise Tinker had prospered, the parasitic old devil. Maria and I had taken to using our pub hour for revision, and Tinker would bob up in the Cups to cadge enough for five pasties and get paralytic drunk. I didn't mind – though Maria presumably found him hard going – because when he's sloshed his mental radar works best and he starts to find antiques.

Just before everything closed one day Tinker found a small piece of *pietra dura* in Jeff Archer's shop in the antiques arcade. We shot over, me blathering halting explanations to Maria. Jeff's a pleasant bloke who lives with a young blind woman in Arlesford. He has the most phenomenal luck. I don't actually believe in luck, but there's a lot of it about.

'Wotcher, Lovejoy.' Jeff shoved a small gold box on the counter. Tinker took the quid I slipped him and faded like grinning mist, duty done. 'Genuine Florentine, seventeenth century.'

'*Pietra dura*.' The lovely pictorial stone was beautifully laid on the box lid. 'But Derbyshire, early nineteenth.'

'Sure?'

In raptures, I began to explain how the Duke of Devonshire's fluospar mines actually made a continuous profit but the resultant craftsmanship never quite matched Italian work. You can't help being enthusiastic.

I came to feeling my smile dying on my face. Maria was looking at me. Shoppers were dwindling all around, pausing only for a glance on their way through the arcade to the bus station. Nothing seemed wrong, but there again was that wrong feel. As if she was comparing me with . . . with . . . ?

I guessed, 'Wrong declension?'

'No, Lovejoy.' She was holding my arm. 'But I just can't see it.' She sounded helpless. 'You have such potential. You could be doing so much—'

I dragged her to one side. I've had all this before and you can't let it get a hold of you. All this reasonable criticism can be very corrosive if it isn't soldered shut. Fast. Jeff hastily busied himself in a corner.

'You ever heard of love, Maria?'

'Love?'

'Yes. That stuff two people occasionally make.' I saw her almost imperceptible nod. 'Antiques *are* it. Love's not a feeling, or a mystic dream. And sometimes,' I finished brutally, 'antiques are the only true pieces of love some people can ever find. So don't knock them. Okay?'

'But—'

'Shut it,' I said savagely. I drew back then, looking at the ground because I could feel people staring, thinking we'd had a row. An elderly couple were going tut-tut.

Maria thought. 'I hope you're wrong, Lovejoy.'

'Women always do.'

She was glancing round Jeff's antiques with new eyes. 'Which antique do you like best, Lovejoy?'

'The next, love.'

She looked back at me then, and asked sadly, 'And is there no stopping?'

I had the strange notion she was asking me something about herself. I hadn't a notion what. Not then.

'You mean relax?' I snorted. 'Sooner or later we relax for ever. What's the point of starting early?' My answer did not please her.

She said abruptly, 'I think that's enough for today, Lovejoy.' Jeff was relieved it hadn't come to blows and took my promissory note for a deposit on the lovely box. He was glad to see the back of us.

Maria walked with me through the churchyard to her car. She seemed morose, withdrawn for some reason, though I could have sworn I'd got the grammar more or less right. Her skin looked drawn and tired, her eyelids developing a faint crinkled texture as if she had begun to age. Normally she'd have been gunning verbs or rattling off sentences for me to construe, but she drove in silence right to my cottage garden. I got out in a bit of a huff because guilt makes you feel bad, especially if it's someone else's. I've always been able to get rid of my own pretty quick.

'Look,' I said miserably. 'If it's another bad report—'

She averted her head and started to reverse. Just put the kettle on, Lovejoy,' she ordered wearily. 'While I bring my things.'

I said, 'Eh?' but she simply drove off up the lane leaving me standing there feeling a pillock and wondering if I'd heard right.

Then I went in with the dusk falling round the cottage like a huge coverlet, and frantically began tidying up before she came.

That was how Maria and I really began And I really loved her. I honestly mean that. We lasted until they gave me my final examination. I've already said how I screwed (I mean obtained) the result from Maria.

Six next evening Arcellano came, dead on time.

Chapter 4

After the previous day's examination Miss McKim had given a little tea party. All eighty of us stood about with little fingers hooking air, and trying to look as though we were in a rave-up. Miss McKim made a tearful little speech. We gave her a bunch of flowers and a book token. Hyacinth shook me by giving me a ruler which she had decorated in oils. In return I gave her a hair slide of brilliants in a bow-shaped setting, only 1870-ish but quite bonny. In the final farewells she whispered to me that she quite understood about Mrs Peck and me because after all it was Only Natural These Days, though I should be On My Guard Against Duplicity. I wish now I'd listened to her warning. She kissed my ear, her specs practically gouging my right eye out. Everybody shook hands with everybody while Jingo Hardy boomed a last speech full of jokes in bits of everybody's languages so we all understood two per cent. Old Fotheringay creaked out a farewell poem in Latin modelled on Catullus, while we applauded at the wrong place. We'd all clubbed for theatre tickets to give all our teachers. Then it was break up and goodbye.

Next day with Maria gone by eleven the cottage felt bare. It only looked the same. For a while I hung about and walked the garden, gave the robin his cheese and all that. There was no trace of her anywhere. She might simply never have been there at all, never crooked her fingers in midair when we made love, never called exhortations against my neck, never uttered hoarse cries for the light to be switched on . . . Finally I couldn't stand it and walked through the drizzle to the pub.

Tinker brought the suitcase to the Queen's Head about one o'clock. It was there that I was called to the phone in the saloon bar and heard Arcellano's voice telling me he would be at the cottage by six. From the background noise I guessed he was at some airport or other.

My money used to come in an envelope simply marked 'Lovejoy'. I still had my final envelope, and shared the gelt with Tinker. I told him I'd be away a few days.

'With that bird with the big bristols, Lovejoy?' He nearly fell into his pint at this witticism, his only joke.

'Very droll, Tinker,' I said. 'Remember. While I'm away buy nothing. Just look out for musical boxes, William IV jewellery and anything that even smells of Nabeshima porcelain.'

'Christ.'

'And try for commemorative plaques, especially any with town names. There's word of some being unloaded in Coggeshall soon. And dancing automata. You'll find two already at Southwold, but don't touch them because they're crap. Somebody's subbed them.'

'Bastards.' Tinker spoke with feeling. 'Subbing' means to replace a few parts of an antique with modern bits. Do it often enough and you have all the spare bits for a genuine original. It is done most often – for this read always – in the field of watches and clocks, automata, early scientific instruments, and early printed books where it's done by dissecting pages. Dealers call this illegal process 'twinning', though that's illogical because you finish up with 'antiques' of different ages.

I drew breath to tell Tinker to keep an eye out for a rumoured Brescian miquelet-flint pistol but that made me think of modern weapons which made me think of revolvers which made me think of Arcellano so I shut up.

Tinker got the vibes. 'Want me to come wiv yer, Lovejoy?'

'No,' I said. 'I'm in enough trouble.'

He would have, though, if I said yes. What he didn't know was that he and the rest – and maybe Maria too by now – were hostages.

'It's in the Vatican,' Arcellano told me, tilting back on the chair legs. He looked bigger than ever. His two animals were outside in his car. I'd insisted on that and to my astonishment he had agreed. It didn't make me feel any more secure.

'Whereabouts?'

'No idea. Finding out's your job. Listen, Lovejoy—'

'No,' I told him wearily. '*You* listen, Mr Arcellano. You want me to pull a rip. You'll blam my friends if I don't. Okay, I'll do it. But what if I rip the wrong antique?'

'You got a photo.'

'It's useless. There might be ten, a dozen tables like this.'

The photograph had been taken by an instant camera, by someone riding a camel to judge from the blur. The lighting was abysmal, the angle atrocious. I'm no photographer but I could still have done better with a cardboard shoebox and a pin. The table had the look of a rent table, standing against a wall by a window. It could have been anywhere on earth.

'What do I do when I nick it?'

He did his smile thing. 'You'll have a contact. Marcello. And you will obey the orders to the letter.' He was smoking a cigarette and gazed reflectively at the glowing tip with his humourless smile. 'And you will never use names. Not mine, not yours. I'll hold you to that, Lovejoy.'

He narked me. Threats are all very well, but it was me taking the risks. This vagueness just would not do. 'Do I get *any* help?'

He raised his eyebrows in mock surprise. 'Not much. Remember you were carefully selected for the task because of your undoubted talents.'

Well, I'd tried. 'Which leaves the small matter of payment. I've no money to fly there.'

'So it does.' He rose and stubbed out his cigarette right on the surface of my wobbly table, the pig. Still, it wasn't on me this time. He took back the photo, careful man that he was. 'The travel agent in town has your tickets and flight bookings. You go tomorrow night.' He dropped a bundle of notes on the table. 'That will give you luxury for five days, or survival for twenty. Choose.'

'What if—?'

'No more questions, Lovejoy.' He moved to the hall. Mechanically he raised a hand to stop me switching the light on. A very cautious man, every gesture the subject of detailed planning. 'You have a job to do. Do it.'

'And this Marcello pays me?'

'You get ten times the going commercial value of the antique in question, plus expenses. And a basic weekly rate averaged on your past four weeks.'

I worked that out. As far as I was concerned it was a relative fortune. Once I'd pulled the rip I'd be able to eat until Christmas and still have enough left to give a turkey the fright of its life.

I stood at the door of the cottage and watched his big Merc leave. One of his nerks, a gross unpleasing man with the pockmarked face of a lunar landscape and bad teeth, wound down his window and bawled, 'Good luck – you'll need it!' I said nothing back because I could hear somebody laughing. The laughter continued until the closing windows sliced it off. Idly I wondered what the joke was. It couldn't have been Arcellano laughing because clearly he'd never learned how.

I went inside to pack.

Chapter 5

On the whole I never like travelling much. It always seems to me a waste of all those places in between. No, for me a little distance goes a long, long way.

Absence is great therapy, but during the journey to Heathrow Maria kept coming to mind. Her rather weary acceptance of me as a lover, those occasional remote silences like that time in the arcade with the Derbyshire *pietra dura*. And most of all those vivid flashes of apprehension − practically wild terror − so soon suppressed yet memorable as a gleam of gold in a lake. Twice I'd asked her outright if she knew Arcellano, describing him, and she said no. I believed her. Even though I can't fathom women I think I know them pretty well. At least, I think I think.

The previous night I'd tried contacting her, but realized I didn't even know her address. She once told me she lodged somewhere down the estuary, but that was as far as I got. The phone people were unable to help. The school was closed.

By a fluke Joan Culpepper was in when I'd phoned, and was able to get away to meet me that evening. We went back to the cottage for a farewell chat, which helped me to forget my worries. A little sublimation does you a power of good. The silly bitch laughingly refused to sell me her tassie ring, though – 'to keep you interested, Lovejoy'. She asked with a great show of sweet innocence what I had done with Maria ('. . . somewhere in the garden, I hope, Lovejoy . . .') but I put a stop to that. One war's enough.

The flight to Rome wasn't so bad, two hours ten minutes stuck in a reclining seat and fed to bursting by those girls who always look sterile. I may have missed Maria yesterday but would definitely see her once I got back. That notion pleased me so much I became quite eager to land and get on with the rip. It was bound to be dead simple. 'Easy as stealing from a church' is a saying in the antiques trade. As the plane banked in from the Mediterranean stack over Ostia I was even smiling. Maria would give me a hero's welcome. I knew that.

Then the Customs bit, and Rome.

Marcello was the least likely crook I'd ever seen, and, knowing as many dealers as I do, I must have notched up four figures by now. He was fairly tall, dark-haired, fairly well dressed and youngish. He took me aback somewhat because I suppose I must have been expecting to meet a mini-Arcellano. So when a voice said, 'Lovejoy?' as I hung around the exit concourse among mobs disgorging from the Customs, I was surprised to turn to see this pleasant bloke smiling a real-ish smile. 'Welcome to Roma. I'm Marcello.'

We shook hands, him quite keen to get on with the chat and me thinking Arcellano was playing a very mixed game. 'I've borrowed a friend's car to take you into the city.'

'That's very kind.'

'Good journey?'

'There's no such thing.'

He gave me an appraising glance and asked, 'Didn't you want to come?'

'Yes.' My own answer seemed to satisfy him but it shook me rigid. Surely I couldn't have meant that? All the way into the city I wondered, but stared politely at the novel scene.

Marcello's car turned out to be a microscopic gadget which had room only on its roof for my suitcase. I'd somehow had the idea everybody in Rome had enormous Ferraris.

It was dark outside. I'd never seen so many cars driven at such speed and with such noise. Marcello entered into the spirit of things, occasionally raising his hands heavenwards and parping the hooter angrily on any excuse. Later he told me quite calmly he enjoyed driving. He could have fooled me.

An hour later we were finishing a bottle of wine in a trattoria somewhere in the centre of Rome. I'd no precise idea where we were. The place was quiet, only two or three tables occupied and music covering everybody's conversation.

I couldn't get over how good the grub was. I told Marcello this. He was delighted and insisted that this particular trattoria was really below average and that he'd only chosen it on account of its central position and quietness.

Until then we had sparred around the main subject. We'd talked of all sorts. I'd mentioned the weather. Marcello had mentioned a shopkeepers' strike of the previous week. I said how pleasant Rome seemed. He praised my Italian, which was a bit effusive. I was relieved it worked with him as well as Maria. And

47

Arcellano. There was very little wine left when I decided to open up.

'Did you book me into a hotel?'

Marcello was surprised. 'I'd instructions not to. I can tell you the names of some you could try.'

'Thanks.' I paused, weighing him up. 'Look, Marcello. How much help are you supposed to be giving me?'

'Whatever you ask, with two exceptions.' He ticked his fingers. 'Money.'

'Great,' I said bitterly. 'And women, I suppose?'

He grinned. 'I'm a married man with two young children. I can't give a bad example.' He shook his head. 'No. Number two is the Vatican.'

'Jesus.'

'We're to be casual acquaintances, Lovejoy. I gave you a lift, a typical stranger at the airport confused on his first visit to the Big R. I showed you a good cheap trattoria. You,' he explained with a flash of wry humour, 'are to express your gratitude by paying for the meal.'

'*Grazie*,' I said.

'*Prego*,' he answered politely.

So everybody was to be protected, except good old Lovejoy. Marcello was to be shielded from the arriving thief – me – and Arcellano was nowhere to be seen. He was therefore immune. Only Lovejoy was to remain exposed like a spare tool, having come to Rome for no obvious legitimate reason. I felt a twinge – well, actually a wholesome cramp – of unease.

'Can I not contact you?'

He hesitated, obviously feeling sympathy. 'If necessary. Learn my home phone number. If you're desperate, you can leave a message. My wife is usually there. Just say you'll be at the trattoria. I'll know you'll mean here.'

'That casual?'

'Why not?' He seemed genuinely surprised but I'll bet I was more surprised than him by a mile. I'd never heard anything like this in my life. Normally crooks never divulge anything about their families. I tried to look as if I understood what the hell was going on.

'No reason. Just a bit more open than I'm used to.'

Piously he put his hand over his heart. 'Us honest Italians.'

We both laughed and I paid the bill.

At the third go I found a room in a fair-sized hotel about an hour later. Marcello had gone home, leaving me walking between the hotels and muttering his phone number to keep it in my thick skull.

My clothes I left in my suitcase. In my innocence I didn't expect to be staying very long. I lay on the bed and thought of the rip.

Arcellano's story was somewhat porous. Of course, he'd no need to give me any story at all. Most crooks don't – and I'd no doubt Arcellano was a hood of the first order. His family had owned this enormous suite of antique furniture, made by the great Chippendale himself as an entire household set, alcoves built for every single wall piece and suchlike. I'd been fascinated, half wanting to believe his account of an aristocratic family, a heritage in a mansion . . . I'd asked him where.

'Mind your own business,' he'd said straight back, which was fair enough.

Came the war and all hell broke loose, belongings scattered, families in ruins. Afterwards, Arcellano's family set about recovering the various pieces. All eighty pieces were found, except one. I quite understood his eagerness. Remember that most so-called 'Chippendale' pieces are conjectural, and in any case were made only by his workmen. A vast historic genuine documented set was worth a king's ransom. A vast but incomplete set was immeasureably diminished in value.

'My cousin,' he explained, 'visited the Vatican Museum last year. Recognized the missing table, the very one at which his uncle – my father – had been made a papal count.'

'Didn't you write and ask for it back?'

He let his wintry smile loose. 'You mean, simply walk in and say I want your priceless antique, please, Your Holiness?'

'Well,' I said lamely, 'you could explain.'

'Would you give it up?'

Indignantly I burst out, 'Would I hell!' before I realized. Of course, nobody would. 'Are you certain it's the missing piece?'

'Positive.' He held up his gloved fist. 'Like I know my own hand.' That too was fair enough. The rent table made the difference between a mindboggling fortune and a more ordinary fortune.

I lay in my hotel room listening to Rome closing for the night. All the usual sounds: voices in the hotel corridors, cars going, somebody speaking to a friend on the pavement outside, an elevator whirring, a woman calling to a neighbour.

My trouble was I was beginning to feel lost and threatened, maybe even set up. This Marcello, for instance. Nice as pie. Trusting, even. I wondered if he had only given me an accomplice's phone number instead. It was all wrong, so bloody unlike any carry-on I'd ever known.

Okay, I admit it. Over the years I've done the odd rip, though honestly every time was a deserving case and none had done anybody any harm. I mean, nobody had starved or gone broke, nothing like that. Looking up at the ceiling of my room, I cheerfully absolved myself of any blame. You see, I'm not big on motive. To me there's simply no sense in sussing out why people do things. There's altogether too much talk about psychology and suchlike crap. It's all rubbish. What matters is what a person actually *does*, not what he thinks or dreams. Consequently I was happy to accept more or less everything Arcellano had told me, except it was pathetically obvious that Lovejoy Antiques, Inc – all one of me – were the entire rip. I was the whole sodding army of villains, including the man driving the getaway Jaguar and piloting the Boeing out to a Bermuda haven. Still, nothing could be easier than knocking a single piece off, and from a church at that. I'd done much, much harder things. And here all around was beautiful Rome, a place I had only read of in awe.

Ignorant nerk that I am, I went to sleep full of optimism.

Chapter 6

Rome is beautiful. Seen in the cool daylight of early spring it was exhilarating. Oh, the traffic and the noise were same as everywhere these days, but the place has a definite quality. From my hotel window you could see only the apartments opposite and a bit of the main road to the right with a shop or two, but new is interesting.

Breakfast proved two things: Maria's language also worked in the mornings, and breakfast was unlimited coffee and rolls and jam, not the ponderous eggs-and-bacon slammer I'd never been able to afford. All my life I'd been making horrible coffee. Here in Rome there were real flavours in the cup you'd never dream of. Coffee will catch on.

Only a few people were down for breakfast early as me. We all watched each other with that surreptitious scrutiny of new acquaintances reluctant to become committed. I finally plucked up the courage to ask a woman and her daughter, poring over a tourist map of the city, where they'd bought it. They lent it me for a quick glance. The street and our hotel were marked with an inked cross.

'Very near the Vatican,' I remarked with delight.

'This is why we stay here. Ten minutes' walk.'

'Are people allowed in?' Subtle old Lovejoy starting reconnaissance.

They laughed. 'Of course! It's usually quite crowded.'

'Is it best to go early?'

'You get to see the Sistine Chapel before it fills up with visitors.'

That sounded promising. Caroline, the daughter, was a solemn lass, Elsie the mother a good deal chirpier and eager to chat. I deflected their kind offer to show me round on my first day, saying perhaps another time when I'd found my feet. Two women could be useful camouflage.

The conversation cheered me. I was ecstatic at the thought of all those crowds because crowds are concealment. When a rip is on your mind it is space which is the enemy.

I knew nothing of the Vatican beyond the travel agents' window pictures of St Peter's great church, and vaguely supposed the Vatican and the church must be one and the same thing. Elsie prattled that of course the Vatican, being nominally an internationally recognized city state, had its own everything. Post office, stamps, currency and—

'Police?' I joked.

That threw Elsie. Her face wrinkled in doubt. 'They have the Swiss Guards,' Caroline offered. 'They wear a special uniform.'

I scraped up a dim memory of the fancifully-garbed elderly blokes somewhat resembling the yeoman warders, the so-called 'Beefeaters', of the Tower of London. Well, I've been in the Tower often enough without paying, so a couple of geriatrics in fancy dress would hardly cause me to break step. They were probably failed cardinals.

I smiled. 'How quaint.'

Caroline touched my arm as we left the dining room. 'You'll *love* Rome,' she informed me earnestly. 'Everything about it is positively *rapturous*.'

'I believe you, love.'

'*Do* ask us,' Elsie trilled, 'if we can be of any assistance. We'll keep looking for you.'

'And I'll do the same,' I promised with poisonous heartiness, thinking, you see if I don't.

We parted and I hit the road.

The city was a-bustle. Cars were everywhere, including on the pavement in the slant-parked way I quickly came to expect. People pleased with their eagerness to talk. I had a great few minutes with a tiny elderly woman standing by a street kiosk, to the amusement of the kiosk man. She was drably dressed, hunch-backed and wistful behind her specs. She somehow provoked me into bargaining for the tourist map I wanted, and argued I had made a terrible choice. We went at it hammer and tongs, both of us laughing and threatening each other. She offered to show me round for a few lire but I couldn't afford a passenger. We parted friends.

It was all happening by then. Schoolchildren, housewives, and cars, cars, cars. Green buses, the gliding trams and the shops. I knew the essentials from Maria. For weeks now we had been over things like currency, the newly-opened Metro's Linea A, the coins you must have ready, that kind of thing, so I was not too taken aback.

Not knowing what was coming, I really enjoyed myself for an hour. I tried out the buses for a couple of stops. I had a go on the trams, and even went one stop on the cleanest Metro in the world and was appropriately confused to find nobody at the other end wanting to check my ticket. Badly shaken by this assumption of honesty, I walked into the Piazza del Risorgimento bus terminus for the best cup of coffee since breakfast. I remembered Maria's warning in the nick of time: stand and it's cheaper; sitting costs extra. I thought, let's live, sat and got the map out.

Wherever I had gone so far I had come up against the most enormous brickwork wall. Its foot sloped outwards from a point several feet above the pavement. It could not have been less than a good eighty feet high. Presumably the rear end of St Peter's church was in some churchyard behind it.

I drank my coffee feeling decidedly less full of myself. If *that* was the wall of the Vatican, there was no way of climbing it, for sure. Still, a church is a church is a church. There was bound to be a proper way in. And out. Nicking an antique from a church would be child's play. Always is.

Despite the early time of year, numerous tourists had begun to troop about when finally I left the café. I thought, follow the wall and you will come to the entrance. Nothing could be simpler. Full of resolution, I crossed by the tourist shops crammed with mementoes and religious statuary. A group of Germans, superbly organized, were already photographing a small gateway up ahead. I headed for them and mingled. I disliked what I saw.

The gateway was one car wide. It had everything except size. Its traffic lights worked. It had business-like gates folded back, but worst of all it had a group of vigilant blokes. They wore the navy-blue attire of tidy artists, slanted berets, cloaks with arm-holes, black stockings. That didn't paralyse me so much as their air of diligence. No car was allowed to enter but these chaps scrutinized each car's occupants and the passes. Worse still, an imposing-looking car earned itself the sailor's elbow.

'Excuse me, signor,' I asked a man nearby. 'What is this place?'

He did not understand and anyway saw his guide raise her folded multicoloured umbrella – the signal of the Roman guide – and was off with the rest. A hand tugged my elbow.

'You never heard of the Vatican, son?'

My drab old lady who had ribbed me so mercilessly at the kiosk, her hat still with its ludicrous black cherries.

'*That's* the Vatican?' I said weakly. 'What's the wall for?'

'To keep bad people out.' She chuckled at my face. 'We Romans have this joke – it's to keep the good people in.'

'What are those men doing?'

'In the gateway? They're the Swiss Guard.'

I looked again, this time harder. Young, tough, vigilant and very fleet of foot should it come to a sprint. My heart sank. That bastard Arcellano.

'How many of them are there?'

A slyness had crept into her voice. She tilted her head up at me, birdlike, her spectacles glinting. 'Enough. You want to go in? There's a museum, but the entrance—'

Irritably I shook her off and walked dejectedly along the wall pavement. People were drifting like a football crowd. Ahead were the pillars of the Colonnade rimming St Peter's square. A toffee-maker and a trinket-seller were doing a roaring business, blocking one of the arches leading into the square with tourists mobbing the stalls. The square itself was crammed. A pop group was singing somewhere on the Colonnade steps. There was a caravan shop selling Vatican City stamps, obviously an improvised post office. Ahead, between the fountains, rose the great basilica of St Peter's. It was a real ball, everybody agog and full of good cheer, but I drifted into the throng feeling a right yeti.

Until then I had really felt quite confident. Idiot that I was, I had assumed the Vatican to be a church – okay, a big one, but still a church, with perhaps one or two elderly vergers pottering among the churchyard flowers. Now I was sure Arcellano had bitten off more than I could chew. It was like a frigging castle. Those calm diligent guards . . .

The mob of us moved like a slow tide, across the great circle and up the steps. The sheer scale of everything was awesome, doors a mile high and the basilica unbelievable in size and splendour. The last thing I expected was to find the place used, but there it was with people praying and milling and a Mass being said. I joined the crowd round Michelangelo's exquisite *Pietà*, now behind protective glass, then wandered down to the main altar. The little birdlike lady happened to be standing near the great Bernini cupola, so I ducked in to see the Papal treasures, a mind-blowing session of rococo exotics. An hour later I reeled out exhausted in a state of unrequited greed. For somebody else to own all that wealth was criminal. And no sign of anything resembling Arcellano's piece of furniture.

That familiar little figure was now flitting among some Japanese tourists. She seemed everywhere, I thought irritably. Anyway I was getting peckish. No good could possibly come of hunger when I had to suss out the Vatican, so I left St Peter's in search of a nosh bar.

That bloody great wall was beginning to get me down. For one thing, it seemed formidably intact. For another, it emitted those chiming vibes which an antiques-sensitive soul like mine hears louder than any foghorn. This wall, I thought uneasily, is not only massive and intact. It is *old*. A couple of corners and a few hundred yards and the wall turned left up the Viale Vaticano.

Halfway along there was a grand doorway complete with police-like guards and ice-cream-sellers and tourists trailing in and out of a few coaches. A notice announced that this was the Vatican Museum. I sussed it out for a few minutes, dithering and generally getting in everybody's way until one of the guards started to notice. I found a pizzeria, a neat clean little place near the market. You choose a hunk of different pizzas cooked on trays, have your particular slice weighed and pay up. It's everything grub should be – fast, satisfying and cheap – but I was coming to recognize that, like all things Italian, this famous type of nosh has style, even a kind of grace. So there I stood, oozing tomato sauce and miserable as sin.

What little I'd seen told me the worst. The Vatican was no peaceful East Anglian church, as I had fondly imagined. I had so far done it all properly. Exactly according to the old antiques thieves' adage: *suss the outside, and the inside will take care of itself.* Only, the outside of this particular rip was a real downer.

Irritably I noticed I was being observed. My old woman was peering in at the window. Her face was sad, her gaze fixed wistfully on the hot food through the glass, a right Orphan of the Storm. This pest was getting on my nerves. I fidgeted and ate determinedly, but her stare bored into my shoulders. I finally surrendered and gave her a jerk of my head. She came in like Jesse Owens.

I asked grudgingly, 'Which?'

'*Con funghi,*' she said, really quivering with delight.

Wise in the ways of the world, the pretty serving lass gave her a chunk big enough to feed a regiment. Blissfully the old lady tore into it, while I paid up and left. I was narked to find the irksome old biddy trotting beside me, gnawing her pizza plank.

'*Grazie*,' she burbled. 'The Vatican now?'

I started to cut across the Andrea Doria among the market stalls. 'Mind your own business.' We risked life and limb reaching the other side unscathed. That vast dark brown wall was in clear view down the side streets.

'The Vatican makes you so sad.'

'What's that supposed to mean?'

She cackled a laugh. The market was already showing signs of winding up for the day. Stallholders were beginning to box up their unsold stuff for loading. It was all so pleasant and good-humoured I almost forgot how bitter I felt. I took no notice and tried to shake her off by walking quicker. The old biddy simply trotted faster.

I'll say this for her, she was a spry old bird. She seemed to know a lot of the market people and sprayed greetings right and left as we hurried through to the flight of steps where the street ended. I sat for breath. She sat beside me, still chewing gummily on the shredded remains of her pizza slab.

'Going in this time?'

I eyed her. 'Maybe.'

'You didn't before. You walked round the walls to study the entrances. Never seen a stranger do that before. Except once.' She smiled at me. I had to smile back. The old dear was nothing more than a fly little chiseller, a wheeler scavenging on the fringes of the tourist crowds. Harmless. She went on, 'Three years ago.' Her eyes were merry as a fairground. 'They caught him before he'd got a mile.'

My throat dried. 'Caught him? You mean—?'

'Si, signor. A robber. A bad man.'

'What's that got to do with me?'

She nudged me. 'What's your game, signor? Tourist clipping? A con? A hideout?'

'Just looking,' I told her offhandedly, but worrying like mad. Was I that obvious?

'So young and foolish,' she said mischievously.

I rose in earnest then. I wasn't going to take that from anyone, the stupid old bag. Anyway she was too shrewd for my liking. 'No.' I wagged a finger at her as she made ready to bustle after me. 'No more. You go your way. I go mine. Goodbye, old lady.'

'Anna.' She was enjoying herself.

'Goodbye, Anna.'

'*Arrivederci.*'

She was looking after me, smiling and shaking her head. The pizza was gone.

Chapter 7

Sickened, I stood looking at it.

The Chippendale rent table, for such it was, stood almost halfway down an immensely long gallery upstairs in the Vatican Museum. I checked its appearance against my memory of Arcellano's photo. It was the one all right. That didn't worry me, but its position worried me sick.

On its flat top stood a glass case containing a present from President Nixon to one of the Popes, a horrible ornithological Thing of white birds and ghastly synthetic grass. I reflected that President Nixon had a lot to answer for. Still, with any luck the Thing might get damaged when I did the rip, which would clearly be a major contribution to the world of art.

Hundreds of visitors were ambling about the Museum by now, a good sign. There were plenty of uniformed guards, which was really grotty, one at each angle and in every secluded room. This particular gallery was about twice as wide as the average living room. It couldn't have been situated worse. No exit near by, no doors. The white library near one end of the gallery was a good hundred feet off. Okay, wall-cupboards stood against part of the opposite wall, and the protrusion of a rectangular wall-pillar created an open recess here and there, but that was all the cover there was. And the bloody windows gave me heartburn the instant I clapped eyes on them. Wherever you stood in this long corridor-gallery you felt like a tomato in a greenhouse. I'd never seen windows so wide and tall before, great rectangular things, beautiful but full of the chances of being seen exactly at the wrong time. To one side the windows over-looked a raised terrace, landscaped gardens, lawns and walks. To the other, one could see a small macadam road with a line of parked cars. Each car displayed an offi-cial-looking sticker on its windscreen. More open grassy swards, and that was it. Not a place to hide.

The gardens ran off to include a lovely villa and a spectacular little grotto complete with miniature water-fall, but too far away to be any use. The entire place was a miracle of design. Lovely, but ruinous to any rip, at least in the safe old Lovejoy style.

As I hung about pretending to be overawed by the Nixon gift – as indeed I was – parties of visitors came along the gallery. I'd never seen people move so fast in all my life. Everybody simply stomped hurriedly past all the delectable antiques, for all the world as if on a route march. Most gave only a sweeping glance at the cased displays, further along, of early Christian burial artefacts and miniature votive statuary. Of course, this speed was very cheering. Except they would certainly notice, if that lovely antique table were missing and that Thing was left sitting there on the floor. You could hardly miss an aquarium full of white birds, especially if you fell over the damned thing. Simply nicking the rent table was definitely out.

A mixed party of Italians and Germans raced through. I could feel the floor vibrate and felt sad. Sad because the vibrations were small in amplitude, which meant a very substantial solid flooring. You feel these by rocking back on your heels as somebody walks past. And the lovely ceiling was an arched miracle of painting. Note that: the most difficult kind to penetrate from above. So no way in from above, through the windows, the walls, or through the floor. Gawd.

Miserably I tagged on to a group of Americans and plodded downstairs leaving Arcellano's beautiful table standing there.

The rip was impossible. Arcellano had had it. Now I had to tell him.

I phoned the number Marcello had given me. A young woman's voice came on, to the background of an infant's loud abuse. Pausing breathlessly to admonish the infant, which only made another sprog burst into discordant song, she told me Marcello was still on duty, and could she give him a message.

'On duty,' I said pleasantly, but not liking the phrase. 'Please tell him Lovejoy rang.'

'Right. I'll phone him at the station. Where can he reach you if he can't get away?'

That was a bit difficult. 'May I ring you again, in, say, an hour?'

'Yes. That will be fine.'

I kept listening after we said our goodbyes. I didn't like that word 'station', either. Her receiver went down without any special clicks full of ominous implications to an antique dealer like me. No special significance in the woman's voice, either, obviously just a young house-wife doing multihanded domestic battle with her two riotous offspring. Which in its way was as ominous as anything I had yet encountered since arriving in Rome.

I had bad news for Marcello. This rip needed Murph the Surf, not me. I cheered up and went out for a gander at the streets. It was high time other people started getting bad news, as well as me. Share and share alike, I always say.

You've never seen such neat shops as there are in Rome. I knew from Maria's relentless teaching that the shops shut for the afternoon and open again about four-thirty. They were just opening for their second rush.

I went down the Andrea Doria, a wide and pleasant street. You have to be an olympic pole vaulter to get across safely but I made it. Two cups of *caffé-latte* with a cake *columbe* the size of a tram and I felt full of myself. Within one hour I'd be free of the rip, the whole bloody thing. I'd simply tell Marcello the Vatican was a fortress, protected by vigilant guards who were obviously wise in the ways of the horrible old world. Then, duty done, I would spend a few happy nights in this lovely city's museums and art galleries until my money ran out, then off home. What was impossible was impossible. No two ways about it. I wandered on in a welter of relief. Even Arcellano would have to accept the obvious.

It was coming up to Easter. I'd never seen so many Easter things in my life. Shop interiors were hung all about with chocolate Easter eggs done in scintillating coloured papers, each egg decorated in a spray effect for all the world like a grenadier's badge. And windows with a zillion chocolate shapes, chocolate baskets full of tiny eggs and little creatures doing their thing. You couldn't help but be fascinated. I saw one that I don't know to this day how it stayed upright, a giant floating dove cake in creams and puff pastry. Marvellous.

Marvellous, that is, until I saw old Anna struggling in the grip of the proprietor, her hand pointing imploringly at me and screaming blue murder.

'Nephew! Nephew! Enrico! He'll tell you the truth!'

I looked round. The old bat meant me.

Shoppers gathered instantly, volubly joining in and having a whale of a time explaining opinions.

'Are you her nephew?' the proprietor demanded.

'Yes! Yes!' Anna screamed, yelling it was all a misunderstanding which her nephew would account for. 'Enrico! Tell them!' *Enrico*, for Christ's sake?

'It's your auntie!' people informed me. I was pushed at Anna. Faces were everywhere. A million voices were raised in tangled explanation as I looked about desperately for escape. And Anna was screeching and pleading, with the weary proprietor accusing Anna of stealing the things in her basket.

'Poor old woman!' people cried.

'Let my nephew explain!' Anna was bawling. She reached over and clutched at me. I could have strangled her.

'Hush! Let the nephew explain!' everybody babbled.

There was no way out. A horde of faces turned expectantly. I drew breath, trapped. The trouble was, everybody looked so bloody nice and interested. If they hadn't I'd have scarpered in a flash — and I'd have got away, too. Nobody scarpers like Lovejoy Antiques, Inc.

'Yes?' the proprietor demanded.

Italy abhors a silence, so I started. 'I'm so sorry,' I said to the proprietor, casting a loving glance on Anna. There was no doubt in my mind the sinful old devil had half the shop in her basket and, seeing me contentedly sipping coffee, had hit on the notion of using me for cover. 'Yes. I'm her nephew. Hello, Auntie,' I smiled.

'*There* you are!' everybody exclaimed triumphantly. 'He is her nephew!' They told Anna I *was* her nephew, after all.

'I've been looking for you, Auntie,' I announced loudly, quickly beginning to get the hang of Rome talk. This was one thing Maria hadn't taught me: use gestures and keep going. If everybody else talks louder, use a few more decibels yourself. The system of alternates used where I came from – saying your bit in turn – is regarded hereabouts as surrender.

'You *have*?' Anna said, amazed despite herself.

'For two whole days,' I lied, embracing her. 'And here you are!'

'Yes! She is here!' the shoppers chorused.

'My poor auntie,' I bawled into the din, eyes misty, 'has been expecting me for Easter and wanted to give me a present, but she is poor—'

'Ah, how *loving*!'

'– but,' I thundered, '*proud*!'

'Ah! How human!'

I had some of them in tears. The proprietor was glancing exasperatedly about. A strolling policeman across the street was looking across. One more problem I could do without.

If there's any misunderstanding, I'll pay!' My yell gained instant approval, even scattered applause on the crowd fringes.

'She stole—' the proprietor tried loudly.

'How much?' I bawled louder over the hubbub. 'I'll pay, this very second!'

The place was a riot of chatter. A couple of tearful old ladies and a well-dressed elderly man pressed forwards offering bank notes.

'Here! Take this, signor! For the old *povera*!'

No!' I carolled. 'This lady is my responsibility! My honour demands—'

'Such honesty!'

The proprietor named a sum beyond my resources. Thankful for the racket, I flourished my handful of notes and, howling explanations that my dear old auntie was in any case slightly loony, grandly miscounted out a complicated sequence of notes. Old Anna looked murderous. The pandemonium reached deafening proportions as I wrung the proprietor's hand. Several of the shoppers embraced me tearfully.

I left the shop a hero, with my dear old auntie clinging to my arm. We walked, smiling and reunited, round the corner to a small alley and paused, carefully looking right and left to check we were unobserved. Then she clobbered me on the side of my head, hissing abuse.

'Cretino!' she spat. 'Stopping them from giving us money—'

All for equality, I clocked her back hard enough to glaze her eyes. She leaned against the wall, moaning.

'You beast!' She was obviously at death's door from my criminal assault.

'Yeah, yeah,' I said calmly.

Her basket was crammed with chocolate delicacies under the cover cloth. No wonder the proprietor was narked. Old Anna had practically nicked his entire shop, the evil old witch. I found her purse and riffled inside. Two hundred grotty lire.

I flung the basket down. The old sod was falling about laughing at the expression on my face. I chucked the chocolate figures back, keeping a merry Easter rabbit out of spite.

'Here,' she said, sobering up long enough. 'Got any further on your Vatican job?'

'What Vatican job?'

'I understand,' she said slyly. 'But I could help you.'

'How?' I asked levelly, hating the old crab.

'You're new to Rome. Your Italian's good but raw. Learned too fast, see? Come and live with me.'

The old lunatic was off her nut. 'With you?'

'Not like that, cretin. We'd be a good team. Do that shop act all over Rome.' She went all coy. 'I've extra space. My daughter's away studying. We'd be a great team, Enrico.'

This was getting out of hand. Anyway, I had to phone Marcello to get myself off the hook. I unlatched her arm but I couldn't help smiling.

'You're a scream,' I told her. 'Get lost, Granny.'

She weighed me up. 'You're too dumb to be a good thief.'

'*I'm* not a thief,' I corrected with asperity. 'That's you, remember?'

'Better than you'll ever be,' she said, rather sad. 'I'm in the open market eight every morning if you need me.'

I felt myself warm to the stupid old creature. In her own way she was courageous and vital, and for a senile geriatric she had startling eyes. I shook myself. When you get feelings like that it's time to cut out, so I did.

Smiling to myself I thought, *me*? Need *her*? That was rich. 'Good luck, Anna.'

'Keep it. You'll need it, Enrico,' she called after me. '*Arrivederci*.'

I was still smiling when I looked back from the intersection. She was trotting beside a small group of tourists, chattering eagerly and obviously in her element. I could hardly keep from laughing outright.

With considerable relief I got through to an anxious Marcello from a payphone near the Julius Caesar Theatre.

'Is everything all right, Lovejoy?'

'Look, Marcello. The job's off. It can't be done.'

Marcello sounded astonished. Gawd knows what kind of a build-up Arcellano had given me. He exclaimed, 'But there's no question of backing out, Lovejoy—'

'Oh yes there is.' I was getting narked. The whole thing had gone wrong from the start. It was all based on misconception. And, for Christ's sake, I fumed to myself, one antique's not the whole world. 'I'm backing out right now. So Arcellano has a bee in his bonnet about an antique. Haven't we all?'

Marcello's voice went funny. 'Arcellano?'

'Yes. Tell him I can't do it. Nobody can.' I sailed on. 'Just pass the message on that Lovejoy resigns. Tell him to ask the SAS instead.'

'Lovejoy! *You* know Arcellano?'

I was too mad and too despondent to chat about things that were pathetically obvious. 'See you, Marcello.'

'*Lovejoy!*' He shouted so desperately loud the phone crackled. 'Lovejoy! Tomorrow morning! Six o'clock! The Colosseum! See me there—'

'Nice knowing you,' I said, and put the receiver down. Everybody else has a thousand excellent ideas about your work. Ever noticed that?

It was only when I was actually on the point of going for a quiet glass of wine that I realized my money was missing. Then I recollected how close Anna tended to walk with one, how trustingly she'd taken my arm – on the wallet side. The old bitch had dipped me, the evil old cow.

Apart from a few coins I was broke.

Chapter 8

Next morning I escaped from the hotel – into the worst day of my life.

Usually I'm a night owl. I'm up early too, which is just another way of saying I'm hardly a ball of fire once the day is actually under way. With the extra stimulus of wanting to escape without paying I was tiptoeing out by five o'clock.

The previous evening I had laughingly made several deliberate errors of direction down the corridors. This way I learned there was a separate exit, a kind of alleyway leading to a subterranean car park. Once out of the hotel it would be simple to hitch-hike to the airport. With luck I'd be in the air by late afternoon.

I left my crummy suitcase and my few frayed belongings. The spring weather was not overpowering, so I wore two shirts and carried spare socks in my pocket. My small canvas satchel thing came too. This I stuffed with other belongings – a dictionary, an antiques notebook, passport, air ticket, underpants and singlet – and glided out into the corridor.

There is always noise in hotels, but until five that morning I'd no idea how much. It's a wonder anybody kips at all. Flitting down the stairs, I nearly infarcted whenever the lift banged or hotel staff conversed on the landings. In fact at one stage, pausing in the lift alcove while my heart hammered and my breathing wouldn't start up again, I seriously contemplated nipping down to Elsie's room on the third floor, and throwing myself on her mercy, so to speak, but common sense won. A woman finding a man at a disadvantage can be very friendly company. Be destitute, and that same woman becomes utterly merciless. So I crept on and made it safely out into the street after only seven or eight more infarcts.

Left across the Via Campanella. The great somnolent Vatican stared reproachfully down at me as I marched along the quiet streets. Cheerfully I gave it two fingers, meaning Arcellano and his daft scheme.

The bus I caught from the Piazza del Risorgimento was one of the first out. Rome was waking sleepily. A few cars were already abroad, their drivers wearing the non-toxic air of the early motorist rediscovering the freedom of the roads. In an hour they knew it would be hell. Smiling, I got off the bus as soon as I saw an open nosh bar, and with my last groat had coffee. I'd escaped from the hotel, possibly from Arcellano and his rip. I felt really great.

It's funny how your mind plays tricks. I was honestly listening to two blokes conversing about last night's football match and noshing away when I noticed where I was. I was astonished. No, I mean it. Until then I honestly thought I'd chosen a bus at random, simply got the first one leaving the bus station in order to get clear away. But there, illuminated by the slanting sunlight against the blue sky, was the great silent mass of the Colosseum; the early sun slit by its cavities into beams that stencilled its darkness and only made its prodigious stony bulk loom even more. Almost across the blinking road, for heaven's sake. Can you imagine?

I swallowed nervously. Ever since I'd arrived in Rome events had ganged up on me. You must have had that same feeling, when no matter how you plan you finish up having no real choice. There was a girl serving.

'Have you the time, please?' I asked.

'Nearly six, signor.'

Six. Marcello's hour, the time he said to meet him at the Colosseum. I hadn't taken all that much notice of what he'd said – being more concerned with getting my own resignation in. Until this chance bus journey, I honestly hadn't the slightest intention of meeting Marcello. That is God's truth. And if old Anna had not pinched my money . . . See what I mean, about events? I want to get this clearly understood, because the deaths weren't my doing – well, anyhow not my responsibility. If I'd had my way I would have been back in my crummy East Anglian cottage instead of walking towards the curved stone storeys of the Colosseum.

There was hardly anyone about. An ice-cream van arriving, a police car dozing, an almost empty bus wheeling round and a couple of little kids waiting for the day's tourist action to begin. One early car half-heartedly tried to run me down. The city had hardly begun to wake.

The Colosseum's real name is the Teatro Flaviano. It stands at a big intersection of the San Gregorio and the road leading to the Forum. From the outside it has the appearance of a huge gutted edifice still in its undressed fawn-coloured stone. In its heyday it held as many as fifty thousand spectators and is beautifully planned. Believe it or not, it had enough exits and enough room for its audience – an architectural miracle. Find a modern building that has decent doorways and isn't hell to be in. Lovely.

I stood listening a moment between the pillars of the entrance. There was no sign of Marcello, just a great horde of cats insolently giving me their sneery stare. None bothered to move, and I even had to step over two as I entered between the scagged stones.

An empty ruin can be quite spooky, even in the centre of a bustling city in the bright cold sunlight of morning with the occasional car door slamming and noise of a passing bus. I called Marcello's name. It came out a bleat, for no reason because I wasn't scared or anything. I shook myself and called his name a bit louder. No luck. I trod inside, under the stretching stone.

The actual floor of the amphitheatre itself has long since gone. You come out looking up the length of the Colosseum's open space, with the huge slabbed divisions of the cells below now occupying all that is left of the vast arena. All round and climbing upwards are stone galleries for the spectators of long ago. I went to the right along one of the contoured terraces. A sprinkling of cats yawned and prowled after me.

I called softly, 'Marcello?'

A pebble dislodging somewhere practically made me leap out of my skin. There was a light echoing thud, probably some moggie nudging a piece of crumbling mortar off a stone buttress. For some reason I had the jitters, but then I'm like that, always on edge over something that isn't there. Cats are nice, yet when you are in a place like that you can't help thinking of their bigger relatives noshing Christians by the hundred, and spectators howling for blood.

Like a fool I found myself going on tiptoe round the terrace, and this with an ice-cream-seller whistling outside as he put out his awning and in clear shout of that splendid police car out by the pavement and, and . . .

The terrace ended about halfway round the great ellipse. An iron railing barred my way. To the right lay the outer wall and its splendid arched fenestrations showing the city of Rome slugging out of her kip. To the left, the central cavity of the arena. If I hadn't been in such a state I'd have found time to marvel at the construction. As it was, I barely had the inclination to glance ahead and down to where the buttressing was being restored. The new giant blocks of stone were symmetrically arranged on the sand to either side of . . . of Marcello.

He lay in the ungainliest attitude twenty feet below, one arm folded behind his back and his head turned at an impossible angle as if he were listening hard. Blood from his nostrils and mouth spattered the pale fawn dust. Pathetically, an ankle was exposed where the fall had rucked up his trouser leg. A moist stain was still gradually extending down his trousers. His bladder had voided under the impact when his body had struck. There was no question of life. An early fly was already at his lips.

I looked about, frightened out of my wits. Dithering like a nerk, I put my satchel down with some daft idea of climbing down, but finally thought better of things. Nearby a cat licked its paw with complete disdain. The vast terraces were still empty. Nobody was yet photographing Pope Pius IX's wooden crucifix across the other side. No talk, no other sounds. I whipped round nervously, but was still alone.

The Colosseum was fast becoming no place to be. People would be here soon, and that meant the police.

I looked over the edge of the terracing into the recess. My instincts were right – get the hell out. I was sweating and prickling. If Marcello had only just fallen – the sound of that thud came back to mind – his pushers were still here.

The sun was warming the vast bowl as I flitted from pillar to pillar in a feeble attempt to leave undetected. I was disgusted with myself. Some people would be sensible, brave it out. It's called being responsible. Others, like me, chicken out. I bulleted into the main thoroughfare.

The two little lads were still hunched over their game. Neither looked up. The ice-cream-seller had successfully manoeuvred his van into position a good fifty yards away and was smoking over his morning paper. I was mainly interested in the police car, though, which had gone. I had a vague idea I just glimpsed it leaving down the San Gregorio but wasn't going to press the issue.

The streets looked a bit more built-up towards St John Lateran so I strolled that way, my heart in my mouth. A couple of cars took turns trying to get me, hooting noisily as they screeched round the Colosseum. Somehow nearly losing my life crossing the road made me feel better, even when I realized I'd no longer got my satchel. I thought, oh Gawd, and half started to go back for it, but cowardice won out.

Rome was almost fully wakened now. I was still shaking, but improving. At least I had a great living city to be broke in, and a whole living day before me. Better still, I was alive in it. Marcello wasn't.

I watched Anna. Grudgingly I had to admit she was bloody good.

By ten past eight I'd picked Anna up in the market on the Andrea Doria. She first worked a crowd of tourists from a coach in the Conciliazione, the long broad avenue between the River Tiber and St Peter's. At first I was a bit slow guessing what was going on. She bumped into people and tripped up, always getting in everybody's way. Her profuse apologies were so sincere. She picked two tourists' pockets, and following her down the little intersecting street towards the Borgo San Spirito I was almost certain I saw her discard an extra handbag in the box of a passing pick-up truck, slick as you please. If you've ever seen the traffic hurtle down the narrow Borgo you'll understand my admiration. There is hardly an inch of pavement.

Poor old decrepit Anna was obviously fit as a flea despite the pronounced limp which returned when she was back in the growing crowd. In fact it was all I could do to keep up with the crummy old devil. I had seen enough to have no worries when an hour later she was spectacularly run down by a tourist coach at the corner of the Mascherino. She lay moaning and twitching with her few pieces of fruit scattered in all directions. I waited patiently while she gradually recovered and the sympathetic tourists had a whip-round for her, then followed her back towards St Peter's.

For the next couple of hours she worked the crowds brilliantly, leaving no scam unturned. It was as good a sustained lurk as anything I'd ever seen and I was glad – she was my one possible helper. For her age she was beyond belief. All in one dazzling hour-long spell she did three phoney fetches (you nick something, then 'find' and return it, absolutely brimming with honesty). She even did the fetch gig with a kid and got away with it. You can imagine the father's demented relief. She was unbelievably fast, smoother than any I'd seen for years. The old bag even managed to get *on* a coach as everybody else was getting off, to emerge carrying two cameras and a lady's handbag through the coach's emergency exit and zoom down a side street. I never did see how she got rid of them, but by the time I headed her off she was tottering and being helped by some sympathetic Americans near the Angelica. I decided the young nerk who'd started following me was no more than a stray pickpocket and could be safely discounted for the moment.

By one o'clock the pace hotted up. A pattern was becoming evident. Anna kept strictly to one area, roughly bounded by St Peter's Square, the Borgo and the river, and she only did a fixed number of scams. The dip seemed to be her thing, that and a careful selection of cons of which the spectacular 'accident', the faint and the phoney fetch were her favourites. I followed, marvelling, and stuck to her like glue.

It was about two o'clock when it happened. I was reeling bewilderedly after her hunched, limping, amorphous form when I realized the old bag was pausing. She was by Bernini's fountain in St Peter's Square, with me thankfully trying to get my breath and her sprightly as ever. She did something extraordinary. Quite openly, she deliberately placed a postcard in the water of the fountain. Just layered it with great precision so it floated. I stared as she moved off at a sedate limp towards the great Colonnade pillars among the tourists.

Fascinated, I approached the fountain. There it was, a postcard, still floating. I glanced about. People were clicking cameras, gazing at the great architecture, chatting and strolling or simply staring up at the Holy Father's narrow window in hopes he might show. Nobody noticed the old lady's odd action.

It was barely soggy. I got it and turned the picture over. Her writing was large, decisive and brisk.

Enrico,
The Ponte Sant' Angelo, about six-thirty.
Wait if I'm late. Love, Anna.

I thought blankly, Enrico? Who the hell—? Then I remembered. Enrico was me, her 'nephew'.

I put the card in my pocket and set off in the direction she had taken. Within two minutes I realized the old sod had slipped me. Furiously I searched for her high and low but finally chucked in the sponge. She had vanished.

I slumped exhausted on the Colonnade steps to wait till six-thirty. The old bag had shown an oddly consistent interest in me – particularly *me* – ever since I'd showed up. There was something odd here. I felt pushed, manoeuvred. The same feeling, in fact, I'd had since first meeting Arcellano that day in the auction. Surely Anna had nothing to do with Arcellano?

I put my head on my knees and pretended to doze. The showy idiot who had been following me since about nine o'clock was now leaning against a pillar forty feet away. He was on his umpteenth bottle of red wine and looked like a villain from bad rep theatre. He was about eighteen and had seen too many cheap movies. He terrified me so much I nodded off.

Chapter 9

'I saved your life, Enrico,' Anna said, wading into ninety square yards of pizza, a horrible sight. 'From Carlo.'

'Who the hell's Carlo?'

'Look back.'

We were walking at a slow pace away from the Angelo, the great circular castle by the Tiber. We had crossed the bridge and just turned left down the Coronari. A tangle of narrow streets was beginning, the kind I had yet to see in Rome. Anna was clearly at home here, never needing to check direction.

Behind us the youngish bloke was leaning against the wall of a barber's shop, cleaning his nails with a stiletto.

'That 1951 Bogart is yours, I take it?'

Anna cackled. 'That's Carlo. He wanted to spit you.'

'Good gracious,' I said politely.

'He's armed,' she said mischievously.

'His sort always is.'

She fell about at that. 'You're great. This way, Enrico.'

We dived to the right and started going slightly uphill. The streets were no more than alleys hereabouts. A lovely aroma pervaded my nostrils and I started to quiver. Furniture varnish. Several small antique shops, of remarkable elegance for such a crummy-looking district, were dotted in the nooks and crannies of the cobbley labyrinth. Carlo was following, three parts sloshed and weaving from side to side. You have to laugh.

'Visit the Vatican again?' she croaked as we trotted up the alley.

'Me? No. Why should I?'

She rolled in the aisles at this as well. I found myself getting narked at the old jessie. And the spectacle of her ravaged senile face smeared with grease did nothing for me, except make me heave.

'That's no answer.' She laughed so much I had to bang her shoulders to get her breathing again. As soon as her colour came back she assaulted her pizza again. It was horrible. All she needed was some knitting and a guillotine. 'And you've been following me all day.'

The old gamp had me there. 'Actually, I'm strapped.'

'Broke, eh? Get dipped?'

I waited coldly for her paroxysm of hilarity to end. She had to hold on to the doorway of a small antiques shop to recover.

'Yes. By you, you old bitch. I want it back.'

'*Me?* What a terrible accusation!'

Her eyes were gleaming behind her specs. I turned for half a look.

Carlo was closing slowly, every inch real menace. Doubtless Anna had given him some signal because he held his knife hand at that loose angle which did not alter as he moved, a real giveaway.

Other than us the alley was empty. There was a small boozer further along and a couple of antique furniture shops and some place crammed with ecclesiastical vestments. I could see a preoccupied browser or two in one of the antique shops. Somewhere nearby an electrical sander hummed. Maybe this was the right time and place.

I said, 'Hand it over, Anna. My money.'

'You try to riddle me? On my own doorstep? *Brutto!*'

I fetched her one then, only lightly because of her age, but enough to shut her mouth while I lifted her handbag from the basket. This goon Carlo was a real comic, hissing dramatically and narrowing his eyes as he came with his knife weaving sinister patterns in front of him. By then I was just too tired to bugger about. You can't blame me. I'd had a rotten two days.

I slid my left arm into the basket for a shield and gave him a double prod – the shield at his knife and my instep in his balls. My right knee caught under his chin as he oofed forwards, then it was only a matter of kicking a couple of his ribs in while he slumbered gently on the cobbles.

Anna was staring in astonishment, holding her cheek as I teased out her money. I tossed her the handbag.

'Here, love. Buy a pizza.'

'You bastard. That's my money.'

So much for Carlo, I thought. 'It's not. It's mine.'

'Have you killed him?'

'Carlo? No. He'll just not play the tuba for a week or two.'

She was just drawing breath for a scream when I grabbed her and stifled it.

'Listen, you octogenarian conner,' I gritted. I'm as hard as nails with geriatrics. 'I've lost my passport and air ticket, been dipped by you, been forced from my comfortable hotel, had a friend killed, got stranded, and get jumped by your threepenny nerk who's too cackhanded to blow his own nose. I've had enough, hear? Enough.'

I released her and took off. I'd reached the end of the alley by the time she started screaming. Like a fool, I had assumed the old devil would only be able to manage a senile mumble but she put up a wail like the QE 2. Bloody hell, I thought, and in sudden panic hurtled along a few zigzaggy alleys until I came out into the Piazza Navona, a place I recognized from the famous pictures in the little guidebook I'd owned until this morning. I subsided in a chair on the pavement outside a restaurant to get my breath.

Well, somehow I'd messed up the chances of having Anna as a potential ally, but at least I had a bit of my own money back. In any case she was a doubtful quantity, and her sidekick Carlo scored a definite minus. I hoped I was better off, but didn't feel it.

I celebrated my recovered wealth with a quick nosh and a glass or two of white wine, and felt much better. It was that which gave me courage to ring Marcello's number. My hand was shaking.

'Hello?' A man's voice, with that practised flintiness from a lifetime of encountering misery. A copper.

In the background a woman's awful keening was just audible, some bird realizing she was alone now with two kids in a hostile world. I put the receiver down quickly in case calls were being traced. I desperately needed to ask who Marcello had contacted between the last time we'd spoken and six o'clock this morning when he'd been flung to his death in the Colosseum.

I could guess, though. The one person Marcello and I had in common was Arcellano, the hoodlum with enough aggro to waste a bloke like Marcello simply as a warning to me. Well, I felt warned all right.

Settling up with the waiter, there was no longer any

doubt in my mind. Arcellano wanted the rip attempted. And by me. After what I'd seen of the Vatican I knew bloody well there was no way anybody on earth could pull it off. A million to one I'd be collared in the act, which must also be what Arcellano wanted – seeing he'd done me over, threatened murder and then finally committed that ultimate atrocity. God knows what I'd done to deserve all this.

But deep within me as I waited for my change there smouldered the small beginnings of a fire which I recognized with dismay.

If I tried the rip and got nicked, at least I'd know what the hell Arcellano really was up to. *But what if I pulled it off?* I'd not only know – I'd have Arcellano nailed. I'd have the priceless antique he wanted. Either way I could call the tune and make the bastard dance. The only way to reach Arcellano was to pull the Vatican rip.

It was the thought of nailing Arcellano that did it, made me walk on air. I couldn't think of nailing a nicer bloke.

I'd do the rip all right.

Chapter 10

To stay in Rome I needed to immerse myself safely among a mob of workers. What better work than antiques?

I found myself drifting instinctively among the narrow alleys not far from the Corso Vittorio Emanuele II, near where I'd had the dust-up with Carlo, and sniffing appreciatively at the luscious pong of mahogany being planed, mixed with the glues and varnishes which antique restorers use.

By now it was getting on for eight o'clock. Most shops were shutting along the Corso – so named by reason of the horse races held down those streets in ancient days. Lovely shops, handsome people, and antique shops every few yards. I felt good. My spirits were soaring under the influence of the grub and the wine. In my innocence I believed I'd seen the last of that ridiculous old woman. Vaguely at the back of my mind was the problem of where she'd intended leading me when I'd met her at the Ponte Sant' Angelo, but I suppressed the worry. Antiques do that – leave me senseless.

So, when I saw a small mixed gaggle of tourists trooping into a small antique shop near the Vecchio I was in among them like a flash. It looked just about right for me. The tourists seemed a pleasant, talkative crew.

They were being impressed by the elegant proprietress who was holding forth on the merits of her abundant antiques. She was gorgeous in her stylish fawn twin-set and pearl choker, and knowledgeable with it. I listened with some interest but more amusement as she delivered her spiel. With luck I'd be in here.

'Silver,' she was saying about a lovely tray. 'Even after the Bunker Hunt fiasco, genuine hallmarked silver is the greatest investment you could hope for.'

Well, yes, I thought, but be careful, folks.

'It's really beautiful,' an attractive blue-rinsed woman exclaimed.

'What period?' her husband asked. He was a benign portly gent in executive rimless specs and looked worth a groat or two.

'George the Third. A London maker called Edward Jay.' The woman noticed me. She obviously hated me on sight. Well, I'm no sartorial model. I never look well dressed, and what with the recent carry-ons I suppose she thought me a right scruff. As long as the other customers were there she could hardly sling me out.

'It weighs heavy, George,' the tourist said. 'And so *old*.'

'Over two hundred and twenty six ounces, madam.'

'Is that right!'

'And absolutely original, I assure you. Worth—'

Calmly I said, 'Half.'

The proprietress maintained her pleasant smile at my casual interruption. Two goons instantly appeared, one definitely limp of wrist and highly perfumed, the other a handsome gorilla. They came smiling hard and stood to either side of me. I felt like a nut in a cracker. The Americans turned on me, still benign but with financial antennae quivering.

'You say half, sir?'

'Half. Look.' I took the tray – a genuine, lovely job with applied reeded borders, handles and four panel supports – and tilted it at the strip-light. 'See the centre? The reflection's fine until you get to the middle.'

'A forgery?' the American woman said breathlessly.

'Not really. It's original all right. But the one thing which cuts the value of a beautiful tray like this is central engraving – coats of arms, monograms – done later.'

'There is none,' the proprietress snapped. Her smile wasn't slipping, but it had definitely tightened.

'Not now.' I squinted along the tray. A definite margin showed around the centre. 'Somebody's machined it off. It's visible from an angle, like oil on water.'

'Wouldn't it be thinner there, sir?' asked the elderly American.

I was impressed. Politeness and common sense come rare.

'Not if you electroplate it time after time in the centre with silver. Still genuine, you see. Still legal. But devalued.'

'Ahem, this early saxophone,' the dainty assistant crooned, sharp as floss, trying to distract attention.

'Basset horn,' I put in. 'It's a weird looker, detachable spout and all.

Her mouth was a pale slit of fury. 'I know it's a horn, stupid!'

'Wrong.' I was enjoying myself. 'It's not a horn at all. It's a woodwind. Basset as in hound, but horn after a bloke. Mister Horn made them in the Strand.'

The dealer was a woman after my own heart. To my astonishment she suddenly smiled and took the tray from me. 'Well done,' she pronounced smoothly, turning casually to her tourists. 'Signor Giuseppe is a member of my staff, ladies and gentlemen. Our little ruse worked, as usual.'

'Erm—' I said uneasily, wondering what the hell. I hadn't liked being Enrico for old Anna. I definitely hated the idea of being Giuseppe for this luscious bird.

She coursed over my hesitation. 'Ladies and gentlemen, we arrange this demonstration to show our customers that antiques are fraught with risks. Now, with our warning in your mind, please allow me to give you a conducted tour of our excellent stock of antiques . . .'

The two blokes closed on me. I really wanted to cut out and try somewhere else, late as it was, but oozed along with the Americans for protection.

Once or twice I was drawing breath to point out the odd fact – that the *crystallo ceramico* she mentioned as being by the great Apsley Pellat was probably by a contemporary copier (his favourite best-selling trick was a porcelain medallion of some grand personage, set in glass), and that the pair of peasant love-spoons she claimed were Welsh had probably never been further north than Basle. It was no use. Her two goons were breathing hard in what can only be called a threatening manner. Anyhow, the bird was in full flight, posing thoughtfully at every painting, casually arresting everybody's eye. And I'll be frank about it. She had me as mesmerized as the Yanks, though I suppose after smelly old Anna any bird would have looked like Miss World.

She sold a cut-card silver sauceboat (the silver decoration is fretted on a silver slice which is then applied to the silverware. It's not been done well for a good century). Knowing I was there, she wisely glossed over a piece of so-called Rafaello ware (in fact Raphael did none of these; they're simply forged nineteenth-century tin-enamel porcelain maiolicas) and instead sold a little harlequin table of about 1790.

The tourists made to leave after half an hour. Uneasily I realized her two blokes were between me and the exit.

'I'll walk part of the way—' I was saying with a sickly smile, but the bird was too quick.

'Signor Giuseppe,' she crooned. 'Would you mind waiting a moment, please? Good night, ladies and gentlemen! And thank you!'

The door closed. I kept my smile up but my hands were wet and my heart was thumping. I couldn't help thinking what a bastard of a day it had been. I wanted a job, not a float in the Tiber.

The proprietress stood, hands on her elbows. Her foot tapped. 'Well? What's the game?'

She snapped her fingers and her bigger ape gave her a cigarette. She was bending forwards to accept his light, her gaze on me, when I saw her eyes widen in astonishment. That was because I had taken her cigarette and crumbled it into an ashtray.

'No smoking where you've pewter or paintings, love.'

'*Wait!*'

The ape was coming for me when her command froze him. It was just as well because the Stangengläser 'pole' glass I was innocently holding was worth about ten times the lot of us. Their long cylindrical form isn't to my liking, but I'd have crowned him with it if I had to.

'Look, folks,' I said as reasonably as I could. 'You've a choice. I'll bring you a fortune, or you can simply go on in your old ignorant way.'

'Explain,' the bird commanded.

I drew breath. This was my pitch. 'If I hadn't been here you'd maybe have sold that tray.'

She smiled like a moving glacier. 'But thanks to you, I didn't.'

'No,' I said affably. 'Thanks to me you sold a hell of a lot more. That tray dodge can be repeated ten times a day. You need somebody here who knows the difference between an antique and a telly.'

'No, Piero!' Her voice was like a whiplash. The ape halted and smouldered silently. 'Go on.'

'A third of your stock's labelled wrong.'

'And you could do it right?'

'Without a single reference book.'

She was eyeing me up and down, I felt to let. 'It's not a bad idea . . .'

'He's repellent!' the petulant nerk hissed, stamping his foot.

I admit I wasn't looking very affluent, but I thought that was a bit much. She ignored the three of us, simply speculated away behind her hazel eyes.

'Are you in trouble with the police?'

'No, but you would have been if you'd sold that crappy piece of carpet as a genuine Khilim.' I nodded to indicate the labelled rug placed centrally on the floor. A real Khilim is too light to put on the floor. It's properly used for divans or as a wall decoration. 'Khilims have no pile. That thing's a foot thick. Who made it for you?'

There was a pause, also a foot thick. Finally she nodded as if reaching some inner agreement.

'Come back tomorrow morning,' she said. 'I'll consider you. Nine o'clock. And be presentable.'

I left, backing out nervously. Not much of a promise, but I was becoming used to very little. So long as I hung on in Rome some way, any way at all.

Chapter 11

I slept that night in the park near the great Castel Sant' Angelo. Edgy as hell, I kept imagining there was somebody standing watching me under the trees but when I crept over to see who it was I found nobody. I didn't sleep well. The castle's brooding bulk added nothing to my slumber, but at least it didn't rain. Most of the night I thought about popes.

Now, popes have a very chequered history. They haven't always been sweetness and light. If you crossed them – and sometimes even if you didn't – you finished up stabbed, poisoned, burned, garotted, buried, castrated, starved, or if you were lucky simply ignored to death. Even an innocent joke could earn a horrible joke in return.

I couldn't get out of my mind that whizz-kid Sixtus V. His sister had once been a washerwoman, and he considered himself ridiculed when some wag pointedly stuck a dirty shirt on one of Rome's many battered statues. Cunning as a fox, Sixtus pretended great hilarity and offered a reward to the anonymous wag – and cut off the joker's hand when he came to claim it. 'I never said I wouldn't,' the Pope calmly pronounced afterwards, the ultimate infallible theological argument. Well, my worried mind went, if a laugh gets you maimed for life, ripping the Vatican off won't exactly go over as a comedy act. And don't try telling me we don't live in the Dark Ages any more – poor old mankind is *always* in the Dark Ages, and that includes today. No mistake about that. If you don't believe me, walk around any city at nightfall, or just read tomorrow's morning newspaper. And I had even better evidence than that. I'd met Arcellano.

Twice during that long night I had to shuffle down into a small grove while police cars cruised past and their nasty beams probed the darkness searching for layabouts. I'm hardly ever cold but by dawn I felt perished and was certain I looked a wreck. Anybody that's ever been unwashed and unshaven and unfed knows the feeling, especially when the rest of the world looks poisonously bright and contented. Rome's favourite knack is appearing elegant. On this particular morning its elegance got right up my nose.

I was supposed to be at the antiques place by nine so I scrambled about, had a prolonged breakfast, a barber-shop shave and a wash and brush up. Naturally I walked everywhere to harbour my dwindling gelt. Even so, I was early and stood among passing pedestrians at the window of the Albanese Antiques Emporium.

Piero the ape was first to arrive and unlocked the shop's glass door with a proprietary flourish. Adriana herself arrived a minute later, coolly stepping out of a mile-long purple Rolls-Royce and doubtless stopping a few pacemakers among the peasants as she did so. She was blindingly beautiful. The only person blissfully unaffected by her sleek attractiveness was her other assistant, outrageous in a silver chiffon scarf and earrings, who came rushing in after her, complaining about the traffic on the Corso.

'Morning, *tout le monde!*' he crooned. 'Like my new hairdo?'

He introduced himself as Fabio — 'Fab as in fabulous, dearie!' — but I wasn't taken in. I'd once seen a really vicious knife artist with all Fabio's exotic mannerisms.

'Good morning, Signora Albanese,' I said politely.

'Come through.' She swept past into the rear office.

Humbly I stood while she ripped through a couple of letters and checked the phone recorder. Seven messages out of hours, I noted with interest. A thriving business. As she settled herself I wondered about that chauffeur-driven Rolls. There had been a stoutish bloke with her, riffling paperwork in his briefcase. He had barely bothered to look up as she descended. I'd never seen such a distant goodbye. Presumably Signor Albanese.

She looked up at last. 'Your story, please.'

'Oh, er, I was on a tourist trip—'

'Name and occupation?'

She appraised me, her eyes level and cold. First fag of the day lit for effect and radiating aggro. She really was something, stylish to a fault and straight in the *bella figura* tradition. Her smart pastel suit was set off by matching gold bracelets and a sickeningly priceless platinum-mounted intaglio that had seen Alexander the Great embark to conquer the world. I wanted her and her belongings so badly I was one tortured mass of cramp.

'Lovejoy. Antique dealer.'

'And you are in a mess.'

'Temporarily, signora.'

She indulged in a bleak smile to show she thought my mess very permanent indeed.

'Money problems?'

'Yes, signora. I was dipped. I have to earn my fare home.'

'So last night's performance was a tactic?'

'I admitted that, signora.'

She nodded and with balletic grace tapped ash into a rectangular porcelain ash trough. 'What's your speciality?'

'Speciality?' It was years since anybody had asked me this sort of stuff.

'In antiques,' she said as if explaining to a cretin.

'None.' And that was the truth.

She purred, about to strike. 'Then let me put it another way, Lovejoy. Which of my antiques do you prefer? Even an imbecile like you must have *some* preference.'

I could be as vindictive as her any day of the week. 'The genuine ones.'

'*All* my antiques are genuine!' She even stood up in her fury.

'Balls,' I said calmly into her face. 'Half your stuff is crap, love. I'm a divvie.'

That shut her up. She made to speak a couple of times but only finished up standing and smoking. Behind me Piero cleared his throat. I heard Fabio whisper something. Both had evidently been attracted by Adriana's outburst and come in to see the blood.

'*Ask* him!' I heard Fabio hiss.

She judged me then in a different way, blinking away from me, then glancing back several times. I knew the syndrome. Before, it was merely a question of using a scruffy bloke who seemed to possess a limited skill. Now it was a different question entirely. The problem was how much I'd want, because as far as her and her little antiques emporium were concerned I was the best windfall since penicillin. She drew a long breath and fumigated me with carcinogens.

'You two get out,' she said at last. Then to me, 'Do sit down. Cigarette?'

Everybody's a born dazzler – at something. You, me, the tramps padding among the dustbins, and that funny woman down the street. We are all the world's greatest. The only question for each of us is the world's greatest *what*.

I once knew a bloke who was the world's worst everything – well, almost everything. If he drove a car it crashed. If he wound his watch up its hands fell off. If he dialled a friend the phone electrocuted somebody at the other end. He was a menace at work. Finally, in despair, his boss wrote him off and begged him, tears in his eyes, to get the hell off and out into premature retirement. Honestly, they actually paid him to do nothing. He was a brand new kind of national debt.

Then, doodling one day in the public library – which incidentally he'd accidentally set on fire the week before – he realized the singular pleasure he was deriving from simply copying the stylized scrawl of an early manuscript which was framed on the wall. I won't tell you his name, but he is now the greatest mediaevalist calligrapher in Northern Europe, and official master copyist of manuscripts for universities the world over. Get the message? Even the worst of us is the best mankind has got – for something.

A 'divvie' is a nickname for somebody with the special knack of knowing an antique when he sees one. Some divvies are infallible only for genuine oil paintings, or sculpture, or first editions, or porcelain, or Han dynasty funereal pottery. Others like me – rarest of all

– are divvies for practically any antiques going. Don't ask me how it's done, why a divvie's breathing goes funny when he confronts that da Vinci painting, or why his whole body quivers to the clang of an inner bell when near that ancient pewter dish or Chippendale table. Like the old water diviners – from whom we derive our nickname – who go all of a do when that hazel twig detects a subterranean river, there's very little accounting for these things.

If people ask me to explain, I say it's just that the antiques' love comes through and reaches out to touch me. And, since everything modern is rubbish, that's QED as far as I'm concerned.

She was staring. 'For *everything* antique?'

'Yes. Except when it's mauled into a pathetic travesty, like your mahogany occasional table out there.'

She flared briefly. 'That's genuine Georgian!'

'Its wood is that old,' I conceded. 'But it's a hybrid made up of a pole screen's base and a remade top.'

She was badly shaken. I wondered how much she'd been taken for. 'Is that true, Lovejoy? I bought it as Cuban mahogany.'

'The bit you are looking at is veneer.' It's one of the oldest tricks in the book: get an original piece of the right date, and simply remould it. Most commonly done with tables, bureaux, cabinets and chairs. Some of these hybrids have to be seen – or bought – to be believed. I hate them, because some beautiful original has been devastated just for greed. Greed, that horrible emotion which makes hookers of us all.

'And you'll divvie for me?'

I prompted, 'For . . . ?'

'You mean payment.' Meeting an antiques man better than herself had rocked her, but money was home ground. She became brisk, her old poised and perfect self again. 'How will I verify your accuracy? Of course, I can always give you a knowledge test.'

'I might fail it.' They always ask the same things. 'Then where would you be?'

She blew a spume of smoke into the air, getting the point. Knowledge is only knowledge. I was on about the actual business of knowing, which is light years ahead. 'Have you any suggestions?'

'For proof? Yes. Stick your own price on any genuine antique, picked at random. I'll work for it.'

She bowed like the Gainsborough lady but her eyes were focused on distant gold. 'Instead of money? No other pay?'

I smiled at the caution in her tone. People are always stunned by somebody who backs his judgement to the hilt. I said, 'There is no higher price than time, love. It's all a person has.'

'You're hired.'

'Lend me enough to see the week out, please.'

Her eyes narrowed. 'I thought—'

'There's no future in starving to death, love.'

'That bad?' She drummed her fingers on her desk, shook her head. 'No. You might take off. If you are a genuine divvie, I need you here. Fabio!'

Fabio was into the office instantly, waving a notebook and agog with inquisitiveness. He'd been listening, of course.

'Yes, Adriana.' He struck an exasperated pose. 'What's the verdict? Hitch him to our star, or under a passing bus?'

'Hitch.'

'Ooooh, fantabulation!' he squealed excitedly. 'I wonder what he'll say about that ebony *thing* you keep saying is an eighteenth-century Benin ceremonial mask prototype!' He winked at me with grotesque roguishness. 'She paid a fortune for it, dearie, been on tenterhooks ever since!'

I thought, oh dear. They make them near Dakar and have fooled the best of us. My expression must have changed because his eyes ignited with delighted malice. Adriana sensed the bad news and nipped it swiftly in the bud.

'Fabio. See that Lovejoy receives *no* money, no expenses of any kind.'

Fabio fingered his amber beads and beamed. 'Is it to be *entirely* a labour of love?'

'And you can stop that. We've come to an arrangement. Lovejoy will be paid in antiques of *our* choosing – after he's divvied them for us.'

'I'll book it in as payment in kind,' Fabio whispered confidentially to me. Adriana's lips thinned even more. I could see how Fabio could get on the calmest nerves.

'His food will be provided by me,' she coursed on tonelessly.

'Must I book a table, dear?' Fabio asked innocently, eyes on the ceiling.

She iced him with a look. 'By that I mean under my supervision.'

He pencilled an ostentatious note, murmuring to himself, 'Lovejoy to feed under Adriana,' then asked briskly, 'Anything else, dear?'

She gave up and turned to me 'Have you a place to live?'

I thought swiftly. If she was this careful and I was fool enough to admit that I dossed in the park she'd probably stick me in some garret over her stables, with that businessman of hers counting the teaspoons every time I went for a pee.

'Yes, thanks,' I said. 'I'm fixed up.'

They both looked dubious at that but said nothing, and we went to work.

I'd found a nook. I was in with a chance of doing the rip. And doing Arcellano.

Chapter 12

The Vatican walls seemed more impenetrable than ever when I photographed them that afternoon. Every gateway, the enormous doors in St Peter's, the Museum entrance, every Swiss Guard in sight and the Angelica gateway, with me grinning and clicking away among droves of tourists all doing the same thing. I went about like someone demented. There wasn't a lot of time.

Adriana had objected when I asked to use the camera. All known antiques firms – except Lovejoy Antiques, Inc, that is – have cameras of various sorts, though most dealers are too bone idle to use them much. She had finally let me borrow a cheap box camera that was hanging on hoping to become an antique, a century still to go.

'Thanks, Adriana,' I said. My last money would go on a film.

'Signora Albanese to you.'

I grovelled. 'Thank you, Signora Albanese.'

'And that's enough for a *rustica*.' That meant eating on the hoof.

I asked what about food this evening. 'That requirement will be met, Lovejoy,' she intoned mercilessly.

The giant purple Rolls called for her just before two.

We shut shop with Piero sourly giving me the once over in case I'd nicked a valuable Isfahan carpet or two, and with Fabio taking an age doing his eyes in a French early Georgian period swivel mirror.

Signora Albanese refused to allow the car to drive off until she saw me enter the pizzeria at the street corner and emerge with two chunks of scalding pizza in my hands. Only then did the Rolls glide away, with her businessman still doing his executive bit. He'd hardly looked up when Adriana got in, and I'd taken particular pains to notice, because . . . I wondered *why* I'd been so sly. I hardly notice anything except antiques, except when I'm scared, and then I behave like . . . like I was doing now, moving casually but watching Fabio and Piero and the Rolls reflected in every possible shop window.

I decided I was merely going through a paranoid phase, brought on by Marcello's death and loneliness maybe mixed with apprehension at the thought of the rip. After all I'd done all the choosing, picked Adriana's place at random.

The final agonizing choice came about half past three. To buy a tiny booklet on the contents of the Vatican Museum, or to enter the place to suss it out? I decided on the latter course and spent my last on a ticket. I hurtled up the wonderful ancient staircase (a double helical spiral that curiously is a better model of nucleic acid even than that flashy Watson-Crick mock-up in Cambridge). Adriana had said to be back by five, and the emporium was a good half-hour's walk from the Vatican. There were seven photographs left in my camera, and I would need to shove the film in for developing on the way. It didn't leave long.

The precious Chippendale piece was still there,

sulkily supporting the weight of that horrible nature tableau. A museum guard was being bored stiff at the end of the gallery when I nipped behind a display case and clicked the view from the nearest window. Then the other way, with a complete disregard of lighting conditions. Then the length of the gallery. A couple of times I had to pause for small crowds of visitors – still sprinting as if they got paid mileage. But by the finish of my reel (who can ever work out when a film's ended?) I guessed I had at least six good shots of the gallery. Then I crossed to feel again those lovely vibes of the true Chippendale, drawn like iron filings to a magnet.

That table really was something to see. I mean that most sincerely, and I've loved antiques all my life.

Genuine ones, of course.

It was on the way out that I realized I was being observed. There is a small glass-covered cloister between two divisions of the Museum galleries. Walk along it and quite suddenly you leave that antechamber where they sell replicas of Michelangelo's *Pietà*, and emerge on a curved terrace. You can sit in the sunshine and look out over the Vatican grounds. They look accessible, but aren't. There's no way for the public to reach either the grounds or the lovely villa situated in them, because although the terrace looks spacious it is very, very restricted. There's no way of climbing off, either up or down. It's a swine of a design.

Look away from the greenery and the Museum buildings loom above you. I guessed the windows high above – and some distance away laterally, too, worse luck still – were those of my gallery. Near, and practically begging you to enter, was the splendid cafeteria they've recently installed. The grub even looks good enough to eat. The place is spotless and – coming as a dizzy novelty to a bloke like me, raised on a diet of enteric from Woody's Nosh Bar – the tables are laminates and tubular steel, and clean. Mind-boggling.

The people noshing there were the usual cross-section of modern tourists: denim-geared youngsters with birds and blokes indistinguishable, family clusters with infants laying the law down, intense schoolish couples scoring Items Seen in guidebooks. Nobody sinister. But that prickling was still there. My shoulders felt on fire with burning unease. I had this notion Adriana might have set Piero or Fabio on to me in case I scarpered with her mouldy old camera, stingy bitch.

It was well after four when I made the exit and set off down the wide Viale Vaticano. Funny what tricks your mind plays when you feel on edge. I had this odd idea I'd just glimpsed Maria. It turned out to be a woman at least as beautiful and very like her. I first caught sight of her near the ancient Roma section and had almost exclaimed aloud. She even seemed to stand the same, one foot tilted alluringly while posing casually on the other. But when she turned and strolled away among the mediaeval paintings I could see she was very different – smaller, not so full in the figure. She seemed quieter and much, much calmer than Maria. A gentle young soul, possibly a convent novice out on parole.

The odd thing was, I felt she was as aware of me as I was of her. At the corner I looked back but the woman was not in sight. There, I told myself in satisfaction. There, see? Letting yourself get spooked for nothing. And Maria was hundreds of miles away, bollocking a new class for getting its verbs wrong.

I made the emporium with one minute to go.

* * *

That first day was a real success. We fell into a pattern, the four of us. Piero was not much help, except as a removals man; the shop muscle. Fabio on the other hand turned out to be quite good on porcelain and ethnographical items, but useless on anything else. Because of some unmentionable disaster to do with a sale of commemorative medallions he had been demoted from doing any independent buying, and had been relegated to the accounts. Like many of his kind he had a real flare for display, and I very quickly came to trust his judgement when laying stuff out. Adriana of course was our vigilant boss. All cheques had to receive her signature. All sales were pitched round her mark (ie, price) and she had veto over every single tag. What she was trying to prove I don't know, but supposed it was merely competition with that podgy businessman of hers. Women can be very odd.

Calling the place an emporium makes it sound grander than it actually was. The main showroom was about forty feet deep and a smaller room led off to one side, which Adriana called the 'specials' room. There she put anything she considered to be of high value, or which was small enough to be easily nicked by the customers – a right load of light-fingered dippers they are, too. Don't think Adriana was being horrid. The average antique shop loses one per cent of its costed stock per fortnight from thievery by decent members of the public who stop by 'just to look'.

We did our tray trick only once that first day, but it was a bonanza when it came off and I swear Adriana almost smiled with delight. Nearly. This time it was with a painting which a German lady was admiring. I was being a casual browser, strolling and looking at furniture, and only getting drawn in when I heard Adriana doing a lyrical exposition of a sentimental mid-Victorian scene, quite a good painting with very little restoration.

'I'm sorry, signora,' I interrupted. 'But do please advise this lady about the medium.'

'The medium?' Adriana was nonplussed for a second because we had planned to use her vaunted 'solid' Cuban mahogany hybrid. 'But oil paints are the most durable—'

'Not on bitumen.'

At one time bitumen was regarded as a splendid permanent ground matrix for oil painting, and reached a high vogue during the early nineteenth century. The only trouble is that nothing cracks or disintegrates like bitumen does. So whether you buy for love or investment, check that the painting doesn't contain it. I explained this to the fascinated customer. The crowd she was with took great interest and one or two were even eager that I should accompany them back to their hotel and pronounce on some antiques they had bought earlier. The lady wrote me her name and room number.

'Come for supper,' she cooed. 'We could have a really good chat.'

Adriana's expression said over her dead body so I hastily said I might give them a ring. I went on to pick out a good painting for the customer, a little-known Spanish artist's work in egg tempera on laid parchment showing an early scene in industrial Milan. Adriana invented a solid price for it and the lady paid up on my say-so. It was a bargain but I wasn't too happy because I'd had my eye on it for my wages.

As soon as they'd gone Adriana yanked me into her office. Unluckily there was no innocent browser I could use for protection.

'What do you mean by that asinine display, Lovejoy?' she rasped, slamming the door.

'We made a sale—'

'Don't give me *that*! Do you think I'm an absolute fool?'

'That painting's solid bitumen—'

She stormed round the desk at me. 'I'm talking about you ogling that German cow out there in *my* shop! And I saw you collect her hotel number from her *and I* heard you promise you'd deliver the painting personally—'

I reeled under the salvo. 'Look. She insisted—'

'I won't have it! Do you hear? Making a brothel out of my emporium! Any one of the crowd could have taken offence! I'm employing you to provide—'

I bleated, 'You heard her invite me to supper—'

She practically took a swing at me as I cringed towards the door. 'You were practically down her cleavage—'

'Now, Adriana—'

'And don't Adriana me!' she yelled, heaving up her porcelain ashtray.

I ducked out fast to get that expensive glass door between us and streaked into the yard to help Piero load up the painting for delivery to the German lady's hotel. He gazed at me sardonically but said nothing. Fabio came out to watch us, his arms folded and an ecstatic smile on his face.

'Lovejoy.'

'Mmmmh?' I was preoccupied knocking up a plywood crate for the tempera. Always remember that tempera painting antedated oils by several centuries, and that to use egg tempera properly you need a relatively inflexible support – hence it is done on copper sheeting or board. You can do it on semi-rigid supports such as parchment paging but the technique is very special. Piero, a right

Neanderthal, was all for trying to roll the bloody thing up. I ask you.

'You really bother our dear signora,' Fabio was saying.

'It isn't my fault she hadn't priced it,' I grumbled defensively. 'I haven't stopped since I came this morning.'

'She wants you. Now.'

He didn't move out of the way to let me pass, just raised his eyebrows and winked as I hurried in. Adriana had a small card ready. She held it out without looking up from her desk. I took it gingerly.

'This is the name of a restaurant, Lovejoy. You will dine there at eight-thirty this evening. The bill will be taken care of.'

'I could eat somewhere cheaper and keep the difference—'

Her voice went low and murderous. '*Lovejoy.*'

I shut up and stuffed the card away thinking, ah well, I might be able to do a deal with the waiter.

During the rest of the time until we closed at eight there was only one notable moment – notable for me, I mean. There was a small object, solid bronze, of a kind I'd never seen before. It stood only a couple or so inches high and, apart from a small flattening of its upper and lower surfaces, was almost completely ellipsoidal. It emitted strong secret chimes, so it had lived for generations in that fond symbiosis which makes genuine antiques the most wonderful things on earth. I gaped. I don't often feel an ignoramus among antiques.

She asked me, 'Well, Lovejoy? Is it genuine?'

'It feels so. But what the hell?' I was puzzled and turned the bronze solid over and over in my hands. A simple bronze solid.

She glanced oddly at me and took it, twisting its ends and pulling. 'Two pieces,' she said. 'There?'

She set down on the display case a beautiful tiny anvil. I'd heard of these rare Continental jewellers' anvils but had never seen a collapsible one in my life. There it sat, solid bronze, even engraved with vine leaves and small florets on its side. One simple twist and it had become a functional, highly specialized instrument, a positive godsend to any aspiring Benvenuto Cellini. I stared and stared until my eyes misted over.

'Lovejoy?' her voice said from far away. 'Are you all right?'

I looked at her. Ratty as hell, but staggeringly beautiful. 'I'm indebted.' My voice was a croak.

'I beg your pardon?'

'For showing me an antique I've never seen before.'

She gave me one of those eloquent shrugs. 'Don't make too much of it, Lovejoy.'

'Impossible,' I said. 'Thank you, signora.'

She moved on. For just a moment her cheeks coloured. Maybe I'd revealed too much intensity all of a sudden. I know people don't understand, and I'd seen enough to realize that Adriana was an out-and-out pragmatist. I followed meekly.

For teaching me that antique I was in love with her for life.

That evening was memorable for two things. First, I planned the rip – suddenly knew exactly how it could be done, starting right in Adriana's emporium. Second, I dined lonelier than Shackleton on his ice floe.

I was given a small table by a casual waiter. Not the slightest chance of any deal with him either, because at the other end of the restaurant in grander circumstances dined Signor and Signora Albanese. Not a word passed between them except pass the salt and suchlike. And no friendly wave across the tables to lonely old Lovejoy.

The grub was great. I wasn't told what I could have or what wine the bill ran to. I just kept a wary eye on the waiter's expression and pointed interrogatively. He swiftly got the idea.

'*Fritto misto alla romana*,' he decided, sizing me up. It was a cracking fry-up, and I waded merrily in. We'd decided on *Zuppa inglese* for pud, because I'd remembered the name from one of Maria's test runs back home, and anyway who can resist trifle in hooch?

Every so often I checked that Adriana and her wealthy businessman weren't hoofing off leaving an unpaid bill and me to lifelong dishwashing, but they stayed. He was preoccupied. As far as I could tell she hardly ate enough to last the night.

Even when I got up to make my way out into the dark Roman night I kept my cool. Partly sloshed and replete with my lovely grub, I plodded solemnly past their table and said nothing. But what was driving me demented was the bird from the Museum, the one I thought had a look of Maria. During my meal she had sat at a table near the door, dined sparsely in quiet solitude and never once appeared to notice me.

Now, Rome's not the biggest city in the world. That's a fact. Plenty of cities are far more crowded. But it isn't so small that you bump into the same person in every nook and cranny. I already knew that Arcellano had plenty of minions. And if one of Marcello's killers was a delectable female, it was tough luck on her because tomorrow I was due to start preparing to rip off His Holiness the Pope. I was in no mood to muck about.

I'd never mugged a bird before, but I went out into the darkness prepared for business.

Chapter 13

Befuddled but determined, I waited in the gloom of the church doorway. The petite woman emerged, looking from side to side and obviously puzzled. The minute the restaurant door had swung to I dived to the left and raced across the street. The great façade of the Sant' Andrea della Valle gave only little cover and the main street was well lit but I trusted the sudden switch from a cosy interior to a place of pedestrians and cars would momentarily disconcert her. I pressed back in the doorway, trying to seem casual because a cluster of people opposite were waiting for the 64 bus.

She dithered for a second, half-heartedly made to start one way, then hesitated and finally gave up. She wasn't daft, though. She pretended to stroll one way, then suddenly turned down the Corso del Rinascimento, walking at a hell of a lick. All this was in case somebody was following, which of course I was. Some instinct made me dart across the road and into the zigzag alley which leads off the main street. I ran into the dark and emerged a few seconds later in the Navona. By lounging against the corner shop and looking as though I'd been there for days I could see into the Corso with little chance of her seeing me.

Sure enough she turned into the square within minutes, starting down it past the first of the two splendid
fountains. This was a problem, because apart from the
great central obelisk and the fountains there was no
shelter for me if she suddenly looked back, and I already
knew she was suspicious-minded. The square is race-
track-shaped. Popes and suchlike used to flood it in the
old days for water pageants, and indeed it used to be a
racetrack, but now it has a couple of good cafés and a
load of artists and drifters. Indeed, some were still drifting. She was halfway down when I finally made up my
mind and streaked off left into the parallel street to wait,
breathless now and still woozy from the grub and the
wine, by the alley corner.

I was almost level with the second fountain, Bernini's
great and spectacular Nile figure with its hand to its
eyes. As I waited, listening to her footsteps approaching
down the square, I had to smile. Bernini's friends used
to joke that the statue was hiding its gaze from the sight
of Borromini's church across the square. Gianlorenzo
Bernini was Borromini's boss, and probably the greatest
religious architect of all time. He was everybody's darling – except Borromini's, who was a sullen, withdrawn,
paranoiac genius and who hated his witty, eloquent,
talented gaffer. Borromini's supporters retorted that in
any case Borromini's beautiful church was designed
to support Bernini's obelisk should its base crack, like
that ghastly fiasco at St Peter's when Bernini's proposed
south tower cracked its wonderful Maderno base. There
was no love lost between these two geniuses, such
opposites of temperament. I always wonder if Bernini
actually cracked the base deliberately – Maderno being
Borromini's close relative and all that. Anyhow, their
hatred died only when Francesco Borromini, that great

sour and brooding genius, committed suicide during a fit of despair in 1667, leaving the field clear for Bernini. I'm actually on Borromini's side, though I'm completely unbiased—

'Lovejoy?'

I nearly leapt a mile. The woman was standing a couple of yards behind me. I cursed myself for a fool. The vicinity of such lovely statuary had distracted me. Daft to lurk so near antiques of such quality.

'Yes. Erm . . .' My heart was thumping. She'd scared me out of my wits.

'Why are you following me?'

'Erm, no, miss. Erm . . .' I was thinking, God Almighty. What if she screamed for the police? 'I thought you were following me.' It sounded lame. 'How do you know my name?'

'I have a message for you.'

I was getting a headache. It was all too complicated. I realized I was dog-tired. 'From whom?'

'An old lady. A friend of yours. She says she has a proposition.'

'I don't know any old . . . wait!' It wasn't far from here that I'd done Carlo over and recovered some of my money from the old cow. 'Anna?'

Anna had mentioned a spare room, suggested I lodge with her, in fact. And there'd been something about a daughter . . . I asked what was the proposition.

'You'll have to come.'

A passing couple sniggered across the alley in the darkness. They were assuming the worst, that we were making a proposition of a different kind under concealment of night. I shivered suddenly as the glamour of the Navona faded in the chill night wind. Abruptly I was washed in the cold realization that it was here poor

Giordano Bruno had been burned alive. Original and brave thinker, he had walked this very spot, been led on to the wood pile simply to provide a spectacle for the nerks of this world. Even when the poor bloke came to London to try to scratch a living by teaching bored young ladies, we'd been so offhand he'd been driven away. And tonight was the first night Marcello would spend in his grave, the first of eternity. And the first night of widowhood for his wife. And the first night as orphans for his two infants. I swear my teeth chattered from the cold.

There was sweat on my face and my forehead was burning. I leant back against the wall, bushed.

'Are you all right?' the bird was asking.

'Will she help me?'

I felt her smile. 'She offered once before.'

I walked with her then among the narrow streets. It was only when she pulled a door open and stepped inside that I realized we were in the alley where Carlo and I had had our disagreement.

Gingerly I followed into the passageway. The minuscule light just about reached the floor from its furry flex. Plaster was off the walls. It looked unswept.

'Er, one thing, miss.' I didn't want knifing.

'What is it?' She paused, key in a door by the stairs.

'Erm, where's Carlo these days?'

'Recovering in hospital,' she said pointedly. 'At considerable expense. Come in.'

'Erm, wish him better.'

The room was tidy but small with a couple of curtained alcoves. A dressing-table with hooped lights of the sort you see in theatre dressing rooms occupied one end. A divan, two small armchairs and a vase of flowers. A radio. A curtained window. A faded photograph of a man and a woman smiling. A table lamp.

'This is it, Lovejoy.' It wasn't a lot, but I'd have settled for anything. She motioned me to a chair.

I asked anxiously, 'I suppose Anna's gone to bed?' I somehow had the idea I'd get a better deal from the old devil than this quiet young bird.

She made no reply, just looked at me as if I'd come from Mars.

I floundered on, 'Look. The trouble is I have no money for rent. Not yet.'

'Until after you do the job?'

'That's right,' I said before I could stop myself, then I thought, oh what the hell if she knew. I was exhausted, unutterably weary. 'How much is the rent?'

'We'll decide tomorrow. You sleep there.' She indicated the divan.

I was too tired to argue. I'd hardly slept for the past two nights. And the days had been hell. She discarded her swagger jacket and started putting things away. I waited foolishly.

'Erm . . . are you upstairs, then?' Old Anna must already be snoring her stupid head off.

'No. There's another divan behind the curtain.'

I cleared my throat. Well, if she said so. 'Was this Carlo's?' I noticed a man's coat hanging behind the door. Tired as I was, I didn't want there to be any misunderstandings that might cause old Anna to come creeping in with an axe to defend her gorgeous daughter's honour.

She was getting out a couple of blankets. 'Use this cushion for a pillow. You're hardly conscious. There's a loo second door under the stairs. The hall light's always on. If you're shy you can undress under the blankets.

I got my shirt off while she wiped her face with some white cream stuff at her giant illuminated mirror. She was beautiful sitting there. 'Incidentally,' I told her, thinking I was being all incisive and knowing. 'Tell your mum Carlo's a drunk. He drank umpteen bottles of wine when he was supposed to be following. I knew he was there all the time.'

She was quite unperturbed, creaming away. 'You evidently pride yourself on your powers of observation, Lovejoy.'

'I'm not bad,' I confessed, chucking my trousers out and hauling the blankets up. I decided to take my socks off the minute I got warm.

'You're not all that good,' the luscious creature said. By turning my head on the cushion I could watch her wiping her lips with a tissue. It was so lovely I had to swallow. She looked good enough to eat.

'No?'

'No,' she said. *'I'm* Anna.'

There was a century pause, give or take a year. I cleared my throat. Anna's decrepit clothes hung by the alcove. And on that dressing-table stood boxes and tubes and sprays and paints and cylinders – enough make-up to service the Old Vic in season.

'You're who?'

'Cretino!' she said scornfully. 'Go to sleep.'

My head was splitting. This bird had just said she was old Anna. Sometimes things get too much. It's always women's fault.

My cortex groped for its one remaining synapse and switched to oblivion.

Chapter 14

A clamouring alarm clock shot me awake at ten past eight. I was relieved because I'd had a hideous dream in which Maria became the bird and old Anna became Adriana, and Carlo and Piero advanced towards me with knives while Arcellano stood by lighting cigarettes. I sweated into consciousness.

Anna had gone. Presumably she was already out on the streets conning the tourists. Quite a worker. Old Anna's black dress had gone from its hanger. The old bird was nicer than this young one. For the life of me I couldn't think of them as one person.

On her dressing-table stood a paper bag with rolls and jam. One of the curtained alcoves turned out to be a tiny kitchen with an unbelievably complicated kettle that defeated me. Outside I found a shower by the loo but no telephone, which was a setback because I badly wanted to phone Maria. It was at least worth a try.

I washed and ate. Anna had left a battery shaver in clear view, and a note on her chair. It read:

Lovejoy,
Be here at three.
Anna.

Another woman giving me orders. That was all I needed.

Fabio was in a hell of a mood when I reached the Albanese Emporium dead on nine.

'Walk round him, Lovejoy,' Piero advised me laconically. 'He's had a tiff with his boyfriend.'

'Shut up, you great buffoon!' Fabio squealed.

Adriana arrived in time to prevent bloodshed and got us all working, me on a collection of prints she had purchased a week before.

That morning my main intention was to work out the details of the rip. Instead I had two successes and one failure. All three came through Adriana. By elevenish I had picked out the spoiled prints and the forgeries and took them in to the boss. She was ploughing through a catalogue from Sotheby's Rome office – only a stone's throw from us. She pulled a face when she saw how many there were in the dud pile.

'Put them back in an auction,' I advised.

'Brick them?'

'Why throw away good prints after bad?'

To 'brick' a group of sale items offered at auction is to include something really quite good or valuable – or a forgery which appears so – in among the dross. This makes for a better price. The risk you take is that the bidders will be too thick to recognize the valuable antique and you'll finish up having thrown it away for a song. I never brick my stuff. It's an insult to a superb genuine antique to make it live among a load of tat.

I told her, 'Think how you'd feel.'

She actually did begin to smile but throttled it at birth. 'Very well. Into next week's auction.'

I said, 'Erm, thank you for the supper last evening.'

She looked down at her catalogue. 'Not at all. I'm glad you dined well.'

As I made to go I pretended to notice a small stand on her desk, a simple circular base with a neatly turned stem not quite ten inches tall. She kept appointment cards in the slot at its top. It still had its screw. 'Excuse me, please, signora. Do you still have the embroidery fans?'

'The what?' She saw I was holding the stand. I knew she didn't know what it was. Fabio had its partner on his desk.

'There is a crenellated embroidered fan-shaped piece of material which goes with this.' The penny still hadn't dropped. 'It's a rare American candle screen. Ladies used them to shield their eyes from direct glare when sewing. Seeing you have the pair . . . Look, signora,' I suggested. 'Why don't I restore these in the workshop? I could clean them up and maybe we can find the screens. They're really very valuable . . .'

That was my first success, gaining access to the workshop. My second came when Adriana, passing for the umpteenth time to check I was still hard at it, actually came in and commented, 'You seem at home here.'

I was concentrating on milking the screw out. 'I am. Why is it such a shambles?'

She gazed about and did her shrug. 'The business can't run to a craftsman.'

'Because *that's* tragic.' I indicated a small table in the corner. I'd not had time to have a look at it, but it looked a good early nineteenth-century French occasional table. Some goon had stuck its broken leg with sticking plaster. A couple of planks lay across its precious surface. 'The poor little sod,' I said. 'I'll do it for you.'

'Can you? Having them mended costs the earth.'

'I can do better. I'll make you a reproduction piece, something really splendid.'

'The true wood will be expensive.'

'I'll make it pay.' I'd nearly said worth your while. Adriana got the switch and went all prim.

'Do you have a piece in mind, Lovejoy?'

'I think so.' I had a piece in mind all right. 'A Chippendale rent table.'

She thought a second, weighing time against lire. 'All right. Go ahead. But don't botch it. It's a highly specialized—'

That word again. 'I've heard,' I said drily.

Curtly she told me to get on with my work and left me to it, not quite slamming the door.

My failure was my phone call to the Pinnacle Peak Language Academy in East Anglia. Adriana took some persuading to let me use the blower and even had Fabio, full of sly satisfaction, to sit and time my call. Even the few browsers bulldozing their way through our porcelains could hear as Jingo Hardy came on the other end.

'Maria Peck?' he bawled. 'No, Lovejoy, old fruit. She left the day you did.'

I felt sick. 'Why? Where did she go?'

'Dunno, old boy. I'll try and find out if you like.'

'Please.' I gave him the emporium's number and explained it was in Rome. He fell about.

'Got the language bug, eh?' he chortled. Only people like Jingo chortle. I'd never heard anyone chortle before. 'Er, sure. Listen Jingo. Could you find out the address of the bloke who paid my fees? It's rather imp—'

'Impossible, old thing. Maria did her own tuition-fee acceptances.'

That sickened me even more.

'Hey!' he exclaimed. 'Would you count Albanian loan-words in the Brindisi dialect for us, seeing you're there—?'

I cut off. I was in enough trouble without linguistics ballsing things up.

Back in the workshop I set about the candle screens again, but started thinking. Until now I'd been like a leaf in a gale, at everybody's whim. And my dithering had helped – all right, all right: had *caused* – Marcello to die. And made my friends hostages to Arcellano. It was time to mend my ways and set my sights on the rip. And on killing Arcellano. The kindly affable old Lovejoy image would have to go.

'Lovejoy! Will you stop that *riot*?' from Fabio in his mini-office up in the showroom. 'My *head*!'

'Sorry, Fabio.'

I'd been whistling cheerfully. First time for days.

Watching Anna take off her make-up was one of the worst experiences I'd ever had. I mean to say. I'm normally attracted by women who wear a lot of cosmetics. The more the merrier, as far as I'm concerned, even if the headshrinkers these days are always on about how it shows you're full of primitive urges and all that. In fact I wish women would wear a lot more mascara and lipstick and jewellery. But seeing Old Anna become young again was unnerving. Fascinating, but weird.

'What's the matter with you, Lovejoy? Don't nudge.'

I must have got too near. 'Only looking.'

She started to peel some crinkled plasticky stuff off her forehead with little ripping movements. It came like chewing-gum. Lovely smooth skin began to appear. I felt ill.

'Tell me about the Vatican, Anna.'

'Right. Sit and listen.' She started to tell me in an excited rush. 'Nine-tenths of Rome's tourists don't know what the Vatican actually is. That's a proven fact. Like you, dunce. It is a private city. It has a helicopter pad, railway station, twenty-four galleries and museums, radio studios, a supermarket, bank, barracks, garages for ninety-eight cars, newspaper printers, motor work-shop, a fire station, a population – everything.' Calmly she dissected an eyebrow. I hate things to do with eyes and was dreading seeing her start on those stubby eye-lashes but couldn't look away.

'You're lucky, Lovejoy, in one way. Ten years ago the Vatican also had its own gendarmerie, Noble and Palatine Guards. They were disbanded. Now there's only the Swiss Guard, but there's a hundred of them and they're good.'

'Don't people just go in to the bank or the shop? Or get the train?'

Anna laughed then, really fell about. '*Cretino!* Listen: the bank – called the "Institute for Pious Works" – is guarded inside and out. The railway station accepts no passenger trains, only goods. And as for the Anona supermarket, you have to be SCV.'

'Eh?'

'One of the 450 citizens of the *Stato della Città del Vaticano.* All except sixty are in Holy Orders – and you obviously are not, Lovejoy. There are nearly fifteen hundred Vatican employees, and nearly two thousand functionaries and diplomatic hangers-on. They can go in to shop at the Anona supermarket and the liquor store – as long as they remember to bring their ration cards and special personal passes. There was once a black market, you see!' She pulled small slivers from her mouth. Immediately her face filled out. Years dropped off her. It was miraculous. 'We Romans joke that SCV means "*Se Cristo Vedesse*"!' If Christ were to see . . .

This catalogue of security was getting me down. A

bigger shock was seeing her catch at her temple and simply sweep off her wispy hair, shaking out dark lustrous waves almost to her shoulders. I hand it to her: she was a real artist. The pads and teeth caps she placed in a coloured solution. The wig was instantly brushed and hung on a wicker stand. Her eyes caught mine mischievously.

'There are four ways in, Lovejoy. The main Museum entrance, from the street. Museum guards. Then the Cancello di Sant' Anna, St Anne's gate where we met – leading into the walled-in courtyards for the barracks, the *Osservatore Romano* offices, the whole service area. Swiss Guards, there. Then the two entrances near the front of St Peter's itself, the Portone di Bronzo for papal audiences, also Swiss Guard. And last the Arco delle Campane.'

I knew the giant bronze door. The Arch of Bells has two flamboyantly dressed Guards with halberds. Anna caught me drawing breath.

'No, Lovejoy. There are two more Swiss Guards just inside. Marksmen with guns.' She started creaming her face, a mask of slithery white. Jesus, but Max Factor has a lot to answer for. 'You look put down.' Only her eyes and mouth were showing as she turned on me. 'Look, Lovejoy. I saw you case the Vatican. I've seen it done by experts – *real* experts, not a bum like you, wet behind the ears. And they all missed out.'

'What's it to you?'

She swung on me then, youthful eyes shining. 'It's never been done – that's what it is to me, Lovejoy! Never. Oh, an army or two have pillaged Rome now and then. But no one living man.'

Light dawned. I stared at her. 'And *you* . . . ?'

'Why do you think I've worked the Vatican geese for

121

two years?' Her blazing eyes softened into rapture and she gave me a blasphemous blessing. 'I dream of the rip, Lovejoy,' she purred, looking past me into some paradise of her own creation. 'I've schemed and waited. And now you've come, Lovejoy. A man with the same dream. We can do it. I know we can.'

'Me . . .' wishing I didn't have to say it '. . . and you?'

'Don't make me sound like a penance, *cretino*!' She began smoothing cream off with tissues. 'You need me. Together we succeed. Alone, you sleep in the Castel Sant' Angelo garden.'

So she knew about that, too. She rose abruptly and flung a leg on to the chair, peeling a stretch stocking. Varicosities were clearly painted on the inside. I'd already seen her black buttonstrap shoes and their crafted supports, real works of art. She donned a shabby dressing-gown. 'Don't overestimate me, Lovejoy. I've no private army. Fine, I make a living, though the Mafia don't lose any sleep. But I'm good. You've seen me. We're ideal.'

She went to shower while I lay back and looked at the ceiling. I now had a job which provided sufficient cover, and an ally whose only fault was that she happened to be the best con artist on the streets. And a place to stay, providing I accepted her as a partner. And a workshop where I could make the Chippendale replica, which I desperately needed for the rip.

As a lurk it wasn't so bad. Maybe it was as good as any I could hope for. And the rip was my one sure way of getting to Arcellano. I should have been quite content, but I don't like coincidences. And for the only two people in the world planning separate Vatican rips to finish up living in the same room was too much of a coincidence for me. By a mile.

Chapter 15

The next three days I worked like a dog, had a terrible row with Fabio and a worse one with Anna, and nearly killed the bloke who was following me. At least, I *think* I nearly killed him. I may have done worse, but I'm not going back to find out.

I explained the barest essentials.

'Just a single table?' she had asked incredulously.

I'd told her yes, then lied like a trooper. 'I go for systems, not singles.'

'Explain, Lovejoy,' she demanded.

A gleam in Anna's eye told me she'd developed that basic mistrust so natural to all womankind. I tried to speak with a sneer. 'Tell me this.' I strode about the room belligerently, Marlborough on campaign. 'What *is* the perfect rip, eh? Ever thought?'

'Where you get clean away.' She was fascinated, but doubtful.

I was emphatic. 'No, love. The perfect rip's the *un-detected* rip. And why?' I paused to poke a finger towards her. She was all gleaming from the shower and sat mesmerized by my act. 'Because you can do it again. And again. And—'

'– And again!' she breathed.

'Right! You have a system. See?'

'System, not singles!' She was radiant. 'Lovejoy,' she murmured, 'that's beautiful.'

We shook on it. I saw from her manner that she had taken a deep decision.

'Now we're partners, Lovejoy,' she said, primly sitting opposite me, 'who's the man following you?'

'Eh?'

'He's outside now. To and from the emporium. He watches from the *pizzeria rustica* opposite Albanese's.'

'Oh, I'll look into it,' I said airily. 'I know of him. Spotted him within the hour.'

I hadn't and was badly shook up, but I didn't dare let Anna think her new partner was a complete imbecile. She gave me a look, said nothing.

That was our deal. Me to run the rip, Anna to suss plans and teach me all she knew about the Vatican, the tourist trade, the guides and couriers and hawkers that abounded in its vicinity.

At the emporium Adriana and I did the tray dodge a couple of times. Rested and fed as I was – and blissfully back in my natural element at last – I was on top form. Not only that, but on the way there I'd spotted a genuine Jacobean hanging bread-hutch in the side window of a small antique shop called Gallinari's, did a promising deal for a song and raced the last few hundred yards to catch Fabio just reopening. Twenty minutes later I had it safe in Adriana's.

I crowed like a mad thing as I wiped the lovely thing down with a dry cloth. 'Look, folks! We're in the presence of a genuine Jacobean period refrigerator!' Untrue really, but it was the nearest they had to it. The whole thing was a cunning wooden bread-airing device, and positively mouse-proof. It was pierced every-where, cornices and straights. Lovely. 'And,' I sailed on, 'it's not a modern mock-up.' No nasty pale edges to show where the staining's worn off and exposed for the hor-rible trick it always is. They make them from old church pews. My babbling left them unaffected. There were tears in my eyes from trying to get them to understand the immensity of the find, but there's no telling some people.

'About money, Lovejoy,' Adriana said.

'Oh, no!' I shook my head vigorously. This kind of crappy talk gets me.

'No what?'

'Look. Signor Gallinari made a deal. It's his expertise against mine. Don't dare suggest giving him a higher price. That'd insult this antique.'

I don't go for this rubbish about sharing profit, or owning up before you buy. Remember the antique has feelings too. That's what *caveat emptor* means.

A few times, as I prepared the lovely thing for sale, I caught Adriana's quizzical gaze on me. She never would meet my eye, glancing away whenever I looked up. And Fabio was sulking, earning himself a rebuke from Adriana for rudeness to customers. And Piero was in on it, pursing his lips and doing his silent-screen act. All we needed was a set of eyebrows and we'd have been music-hall naturals. Their attitudes were beyond me. As if I cared.

The row with Fabio erupted just before we closed. Adriana had this ritual which required each of us to come before her, report we'd locked up, and list our completed jobs. I went last.

'There's one point,' I said pointedly to her. 'If anybody damages that Jacobean bread-hutch like they did that early American candle screen—'

'Damaged?' she asked quickly.

I held the candle screen up to show the circular fruit-wood base was scored in several places. The scratches were new.

'– I'll break their hands.' I smiled at Fabio. '*Off*. Okay, Fabio?'

His eyes were bright with venom. 'Thinking to take over here, Lovejoy?'

'Stop it!' Adriana pointed. 'Did you do that, Fabio?'

'Maybe Lovejoy was careless.'

'I see.' Adriana appraised him. 'You resent our new assistant.' That was a step up. I'd always been called a handy-man before.

He said sweetly, 'Of course I'm aware Lovejoy can do no *wrong*, Adriana—'

'Good night,' I put in, and left them to sort it out. Through it all Piero had said nothing, just watched. But I knew I'd made an enemy of Fabio, and that Piero always went about armed from the way he stood and positioned himself when stormclouds threatened. As I left I wondered if Piero was the follower Anna had spotted. There was only one way to find out.

That night on Adriana's instructions I was seated at the restaurant by twenty to nine. The staff fawned over the Albaneses the minute they arrived. I was stuck on a corner table near the kitchen entrance but by now I was so hungry I was past caring. I hadn't spotted my tail on the way, which only proved how valuable Anna might actually turn out to be.

I only had half a bottle of wine, and ate carefully but well, keeping one vigilant eye on the exits and the other on the lovely Adriana. I'll remember her all my life, if I live that long. Her clothes were different again, I noticed, which was a real feat. She'd had less than an hour. She wore pearls – a short chain of baroques, which shows taste, restraint, and something called style because each one is deformed and relatively inexpensive. And her dress was an improbable combination of bodiced looseknit and bishop sleeves. The obsessional slob opposite her might have been a trillionaire for all I know, but he was too thick even to notice her loveliness, the bum. Most of the time he dabbled with his food and referred to his paper. Adriana again ate like a sparrow, hardly a mouthful.

The bill was collected from me and taken to Signor Albanese who was too busy reading and picking his teeth even to notice it had numbers on. I left like a stray, without even a friendly serf to hold the door handle.

Dusk was settling swiftly on the streets as I sauntered out to be followed. Last night Anna, tonight one of Arcellano's creeps.

The Via Arenula leads down to the River Tiber at one end of the Tiberina, a small island. Over nosh I'd worked it all out. I took my time because I knew exactly where I was going and I didn't want the tail to get lost.

This ship-shaped island's supposed to be where Aesculapius the God of Medicine landed when introducing doctors to the civilized world. He has a lot to answer for. There's a small sloping square on the island and a lovely old church at the downward side where the old Aesculapius temple used to be. I'd already been inside to see the woodwork on its confessional. The island has a few cramped buildings, including a pizzeria and a shop.

By the time I ambled on to the central bridge it was all very quiet. Over in the city cars were flowing in relentless streams. Buses were making their last runs. Here on the dark island an occasional car bounced over the bridge, lights on now. The Fatebene-fratelli Hospital windows were shining, and a light mist was beginning to envelope the island. Three cars remained parked on the piazza's slope. Nobody walking, and the tourists all gone home.

Still slowly, stopping every so often to look idly at the water, I wandered across the top of the square and picked up one of those polythene bags that blow about streets everywhere these days. Then I waited for him to come into view. My heart was belting along in spite of my outward calm, and my blasted hands were damp and cold. He was there, being at least as casual as I was, strolling over towards me.

My cue. I drifted down to the San Bartolomeo with its Romanesque tower, glancing in the artificial light into two of the cars. One was a French thing with a gear lever like a cistern's ballcock, the other a Fiat. I ignored the vintage Talbot over by the wall. I was in enough trouble.

At first I'd had some lunatic notion of hiding behind one of the ancient columns in the church's candlelit gloom. There's a veritable avenue of them leading to the great tomb at the high altar. The trouble is he might be armed and what could I do then? He *knew* I knew he was following me, and even had the bloody gall to light a fag on the bridge. That's nerve. The worrying thing was, he looked vaguely familiar.

Finally I could stand it no longer and strolled in. The second I was inside the doors I slid along the left side of the nave towards the north transept. There were steps up at the chancel, which baffled me for a horrible second. Luckily there was the priest's door on my left, leading outside as I had guessed into that crummy little priest's garden you can see from across the river, with the world's worst statue of Christ looking utterly lost. Emerging, I felt exposed, really prominent. The lights of all Rome were visible, the Palatine and the Capitolino looming over there in the gloom and the great floodlit avenue of the Marcello Theatre sweeping down to the water. Rome was about its busy nocturnal business – and I was about mine.

Doubling back sounds easy. On the side of an ancient church, with inhabited multistoreyed dwellings stuck on the side, it's not so easy as all that. I guessed the bastard would wait outside in the Piazza. Short of swimming in the river there was no way out. I clambered over the wall to the church stonework and groped upwards. There was some guttering, but I'd never wanted Protestant Gothic so badly in my life – the easiest churches to rob by a mile, incidentally. I swung on the crumbling stuff for five interminable yards before managing to clutch hold of a luscious slab of stonework and pull myself onto the ledges. After that it was less of a problem, but you can't help blaspheming a bit at the thoughtlessness of some ancient architects.

There's an archway to the left of the square, where lovers can stroll down and inspect the travertine marble of which the island's 'ship' prow is made. Nobody there on a chilly night with a watermist helping the honest do-gooders of this world, people like me. I dropped off the arch like a thunderclap and stood shaking in case he'd heard, but no. He was still there when I peered round. Smoking, every so often looking at the San Bartolomeo to see I'd not emerged. I was out, and he still thought I was in. The distance to the two cars on the uphill side of the Piazza was only about thirty or forty yards. I waited until he'd just glanced round, then slipped silently along the wall into the shelter of the Renault.

My polythene bag was easy to twist into a string. I pushed it between the rubber join of the driver's side window. Make sure it's doubled as you do it, then push in a bit more, and drop the loop over the button lock. A simple pull, and the door's unlocked. Why they make them so easy to burgle I don't know.

I eeled in. My keys and bendable comb were good enough to unlock the steering. Another minute. Gingerly, I raised my head. He was still there, silhouetted against the reflections from the water. He turned again to glance at San Bartolomeo, looked at a watch – doubtless the sort which gives the winter equinoxes and tidal times in Kyoto – and I undid the handbrake.

There's something horrible in setting forward to kill. I honestly meant only to scare him, show Arcellano I was no pushover. Something like that. But once I got the car rolling silently down the Piazza's slope I swear something – *somebody*, maybe, for all I know – took over. Perhaps Marcello, to be fanciful about the whole business. The wheel seemed to settle in a position, hard over. It was still unlocked, but wouldn't straighten up. And I tried, honest to God.

Anyhow it was too late to think any more. The car rolled down and he was in the way. Simple as that. Only when the bumper was a few feet from him did he realize something was wrong. He whipped round, mechanically throwing away his cigarette. Then his face appeared, puzzled at all this sudden motion and the mass heaving out of the dark mist. The silence was broken by a screech as the grille ground him against the parapet, sliding along the stonework and leaving a blackish stain. I can see his open mouth as reflex slammed his face down against the bonnet with a faint clang. Once the car connected my common sense evaporated and I sat in total stupefaction as the car scraped and bumped with that poor sod getting life smeared out of him against the stone. The metal screeched again. The car shuddered to a stop. I got out shakily, looked about. Not a soul in the little square. Not a sound from the church. Then I looked at him.

I made certain my polythene 'string' was uncoiled and dropped it into the river, of course not looking at the car. Then I carefully shut the door and walked away.

Any alibi in a storm, I always say. The German lady was in her hotel when I rang from the main railway station, just back from a play. I wasn't exactly at my chattiest, but she didn't seem to mind when I said I'd like to call round.

As it turned out she was one of the best alibis I've ever had. I got back to Anna's at three in the morning. Anna was in her alcove with the curtains drawn back. She clicked the light on and told me to wipe that smile off my face. It was a nasty little scene, straight out of marriage. She played merry hell, wanting to know where I'd been. I said for a walk, and like a fool said down by the river not knowing that one of the riverside walks is a knocking-shop, and had to endure an hour's unrelenting abuse while she reminded me I was in Rome to do the Vatican rip, not to whore about the city all night, which was a bit unfair seeing what I'd gone through. Her invective was a lot worse than I've managed to make it sound. She was a world expert. What I didn't know was a worse eruption was impending.

I undressed as usual beneath my blanket, as usual. And as usual she didn't rape me during the dark hours.

Next morning she'd got a paper at breakfast and looked at me in silence while I cleared a whole bag of fresh rolls. The news was of a fantastic accident which had occurred the previous night. A man innocently standing on the Tiberina had been crushed by a car. Its handbrake had unaccountably slipped.

I'd honestly have felt sorry for him if he hadn't been one of Arcellano's goons, the one who had pressed me down in the chair when Arcellano did me over. And it honestly was an accident, almost completely one hundred per cent accidental. That's the truth. I hadn't realized the wheel would lock that way once I'd released the car and set it rolling. Hand on my heart.

What gave me heartburn was the headline. The newspaper described him as a Vatican guard. Museum detail.

Chapter 16

The football magazine was engrossing, especially as it told me the date of the Vatican rip. No drawing back now.

'I'm going to need a van, Anna. Something the size and shape of a closed ambulance.' It had to hold two tables.

'Ambulances have windows.'

'Make them opaque, then. And a good engine. If it breaks down I've had it.'

'Right.' She was quite assured. 'Can it be a copy?'

'Yes.' I looked speculatively at her. 'Who can copy an ambulance for heaven's sake?'

'Carlo.' I pulled a face. She said cryptically, 'You've been in Rome less than a week and Carlo's in hospital, a Vatican Museum guard is probably dead by now, and you've lost a friend.'

She waited but I said nothing. 'Who was he, Lovejoy?'

'A bloke I met, er, accidentally. He has – had – a wife and two kiddies.'

'Are you in love with her?'

It was an unlikely question. I was coming to the notion that Old Anna was infinitely preferable. 'Never even met her.'

'How was he lost?'

'Killed. In the Colosseum.'

Her eyes wrinkled as she thought. 'Funny I didn't hear. It wasn't even in the papers.'

We stared at each other for quite some time.

'How odd,' I said at last. And it was.

The workshop was in some sort of order now. You can't start anything worthwhile till you get a place straight. The shelving was mended and in position. I'd gone at the toolracks baldheaded. The electric hand drill was on the blink, so I'd knocked up an old-fashioned foot-treadle spindle out of a bicycle wheel from somebody's dustbin. The one-third horsepower single-phase motor on the wood-turning lathe was crudded up to extinction. I had it off and sawed into the bench to get a foot-powered band through. Adriana graciously allowed Piero, my silent watcher, to collect a derelict Singer sewing-machine from a junk dealer.

I slogged a whole day, tidying and sorting. Somebody ambitious had once bought in a few lengths of various woods including walnut, small pieces only, but at least a start. Nowadays, when an old walnut tree is worth twice the value of the house in whose garden it grows, any piece is worth a fortune. Adriana and Piero came to look at the workshop when I'd rigged up the last toolrack.

Adriana exclaimed. 'You've created so much space, Lovejoy!'

'It was there all the time, signora.'

'Isn't this marvellous, Piero?'

'Not as marvellous as all that,' I corrected. 'Think of upstairs. Your showroom should be extended. Why not a winch?'

Adriana glanced quickly at Piero. 'Upstairs?' I looked at them, suddenly more alert. You can't help wondering, can you?

'The lifting problem,' Piero snapped, which is all very well if you're willing to be snapped at. I wasn't.

'There is no lifting problem, Piero. I could build a winch for practically nothing.'

A winch was part of the rip, so to me there was no question. Piero glared, nearly as determined as me. 'You keep out of this, Lovejoy.'

'I'll have to think about it, Lovejoy.' Adriana's tone was finality itself.

I watched them return to the showroom. What the hell was upstairs?

Anyhow, I began sketching rough plans for the rent table. I'd got Anna to collect the photographs so I should have more precise dimensions to go on. The amount of wood in a rent table is relatively huge. I'd already expected that, but the final estimate made me gasp.

Especially when I multiplied it by two

Locking up that day, Piero caught me staring up at the rear of the building. The wall looked solid, and the drop was vertical.

'It looks on, Piero,' I offered, to break the awful silence. 'See – take a drop from above the top window—'

'Lovejoy,' he interrupted, quiet and dangerous, 'when we need extra storage space Signora Albanese will rent it. Okay?'

I shrugged. 'Just remember I tried to save us money, that's all.' Let him guess.

Fabio was inside the showroom entrance, smiling and listening. He said nothing, which was another odd thing because he was practically obsessional about money. Its roof was within reach of the lower upstairs window which was near the drainpipe . . .

I got my usual paper from Adriana, with a restaurant's name and address for that evening, and tried it on as usual, asking her for the money so I could eat where I liked. As usual she said no, but avoided looking at me. Usually she managed at least a withering glare at that point. Still, I didn't mind watching her nosh for an hour or so, if that was the rule.

I departed, whistling.

Until then I thought I'd seen all possible kinds of cramped antique shops. But I'd never seen one with space left begging.

The problem was getting time to study the Vatican, among other things, because it was only open for a limited period each day. What with that and the Easter rush looming, Anna and I were on a tight schedule.

One thing I had to admit: as a caser Anna was brilliant. She recognized most of the guards, where they lived, their shifts, relatives. She was good at distances, too. Never guessed worse than five per cent error in every measurement – length of corridors, heights of walls, thickness of brickwork. Marvellous. More than once I foolishly found myself telling her she was great, but nipped it in the bud. A rip's no time for friendship. Just because we were living together was no reason to become close.

I started to get up as soon as she did, and even began tidying the room up while she put on her make-up to become Old Anna. The old thing really was endearing once she reappeared, but the actual process of watching that beautiful young bird transmute inch by inch made me feel physically ill. I asked her once what had given her the idea, and got a surprise. She laughed, really laughed, for the first time.

'An old woman isn't an obvious predator,' she said, smiling her head off. 'A young one is.'

'You don't like me doing this, Lovejoy,' Old Anna croaked that day, on her way out. 'Once the rip's done I'll be able to stop. We'll have our villa.'

'Villa?' Presumably she meant Carlo.

'It's what I'm saving for.'

So she still thought we were going to make a fortune from the rip. Her place was utterly frugal, and she ate only sparingly. No clothes to speak of. Never seemed to go out. She lived on a shoestring. Well, nothing wrong with optimism.

I called her back. 'Here. Anna. One thing.' I'd practised the casual air. 'Am I still being followed?'

'No,' she said levelly, in her young voice. 'Not since that man got injured. The night you went for a walk by the river.'

'Thank heavens for that,' I said with innocent relief. 'Have a good day.'

'*Ciao*, Enrico.'

By the end of that week I was ticking off my progress. Enough wood to make two rent tables – much of it matured, bought from various idiots who had ruined antiques by making them into something of greater apparent value. Workshop fully functional. Vatican nearly sussed out enough.

'And I'll need two tables.' I'd told Anna. 'The sort you see in cafeterias, the typical modern *tavola calda* table. Tubular steel and all that.'

She promised to take me round a couple of supply firms at the weekend to see which I liked. She counted on her fingers. 'You need a white plastic collar, two silk ropes, a disposable razor, a pencil torch. A new tie. An ambulance. Squares of cloth. That it?'

'Oh. And a pharmacopoeia.'

'*A what?*'

'A book of common drugs. But a proper one – not a granny's home guide.'

She looked doubtful. 'That might take a day or so, Lovejoy.'

'I want an out-of-date one, 1930s or 1940s.'

'Are you kidding me?'

'I never have yet, love. If you can't get one, I'll join the library.'

That stung. It was a slur on her expertise as a thief. Her lips thinned. 'I've never missed yet, Lovejoy.'

I waited till she reached the door, then said, 'And a hand grenade.'

'Okay.' She didn't even pause. The door closed with a slam. Like I said, a real pro.

Chapter 17

I waited until Anna's breathing had evened out. She had quickly become used to my reading till all hours, though at first she played hell about the light. Now she just let me read.

The trouble was we were becoming acutely conscious of each other. At least, I was of her, and a few times I saw her regarding me with an odd look. We'd become very reserved in a curious sort of way. I was worn out being polite. Still, we both understood the reason we were together: the rip, the whole rip and nothing but the rip. That's what I told myself.

I let myself out in my bare feet. She had given me a key the second day. The only risk was the couple of groups who lived upstairs, one small family right at the top and an elderly couple who worked as caretakers to the furniture place next door. It felt clear. In the alley I donned my socks and shoes and set off down the glittering, dark alleys.

A few minutes later I was on the workshop roof. It was easy enough. People forgot about roofs and floors when protecting places. Torch in my left pocket so I could cling with my right hand, and I began to climb, only partly paralysed with fear.

Some kind of gauze, a little separated, covered the window. When I think of it now it was lucky they were so preoccupied in that great oval bed. Bonny and plushily expensive, but modern crap, of course. Like the expensive Axminster carpet and the velvet drapery. And the splendid wall mirrors. And the oak panelling. It was a tasteful and elegantly appointed bedroom, and it was being put to proper use. Gold light shone from a Garian porcelain bedside lamp. Piero lay beside Adriana, hands behind his head as he talked at the ceiling. She lay on her side facing me, eyes closed. They seemed to be having words. Clinging there, my impressions were indelible: a glass with a small demilune of drink, a woman's satin robe over a chairback. The mirrors. The tight set of Adriana's mouth. Her lovely skin shining golden.

I realized with a sudden shock her eyes had opened and fixed on the window. She did not move. I froze, breaking into a sweat. My face was only a foot from the glass. I drew it slowly back and sank gently down below the level of the sill, hoping she hadn't seen me.

A few shaky minutes later I was tiptoeing into my pad. Anna gave me the fright of my life.

'Welcome home, Lovejoy,' her voice said, not a bit sleepy. 'You found her little love nest?' I could swear she was smiling. The little bitch had known about it all the time. She could have saved me all that bother.

'Well, yes.'

As I lay down, knackered after my pointless exertions, she put her geriatric voice on, for devilment. 'Signor Peci's been the pretty signora's stud for some time now. She likes them strong and handsome, Enrico. In case you're interested.'

'Don't call me Enrico.'

She cackled and I heard her turn over. I lay there

sickened. Why I should feel like that I don't know, but at least now Piero's resistance to my winch was finally explained. No wonder he'd gone pale around the gills. I'd suggested turning his private knocking-shop into a store room for reproduction 'antiques'. There'd be no question of the decision Adriana would make – after giving my scheme a token consideration, for the sake of appearances.

'Poor Lovejoy.' I heard her mattress creak as she huddled down to sleep. 'You've a worse surprise to come.'

'What do you mean?' I tried again, getting mad. 'Anna. *What* surprise?'

She wouldn't say any more. I lay there wondering why it was suddenly so important to me and finally decided it was because Adriana's emporium was the one place with everything I needed for the rip. Satisfied with my logic, I eventually rolled over to sleep.

'*Cretino*,' Anna murmured.

Chapter 18

The Holy Father blessed sixty thousand of us on that Palm Sunday. He spoke vehemently of the cross of faith and our responsibility. Not all life could be at our own behest or lived at the whim of desire, it seemed.

How right he was.

I applauded with the rest when he waved a cream-coloured frond in farewell. It was great to be part of a happy crowd. Anna thought so too, for she was busily working the dip in the thick tourist clusters round the fountains.

During the early part of the day, when the Holy Father was celebrating Mass on St Peter's steps, I reached my final decision. The well-guarded Arch of Bells was out. Its pace of life was too casual, far too intimate. Also the giant Portone di Bronzo was out. I'd glimpsed inside when somebody was admitted for an audience. The habit those vigilant Swiss Guards had of standing on the steps ready to move either way was most disconcerting.

St Anne's gate was not too bad, for all it had distressed me when I first clapped eyes on it. I decided that was our exit line. Anna had been incredulous.

'You decide the way *out* first, Lovejoy? When you haven't even got *in*?'

'In is no problem.'

She was furious. 'Might your one and only partner know why?'

I grinned at her. 'They'll invite me in, love.' I got my own back by refusing to say any more.

During the mass exodus from the Square later I missed Anna, though I observed some disturbance over near the Vatican City post office. A policeman stopped me near the Cancello di Sant' Anna, giving me a momentary infarct.

'That your auntie over there in the police car?'

'Eh?'

'That old lady. She's been pickpocketing.'

Everybody was looking. 'Er, yes. Good heavens!' I pushed through the crowd towards the car. A tired policeman in the front seat was smoking a cigarette. Anna was hunched shamefacedly in the back, putting on an act of dizziness.

'This old bag—' the cop began.

'Auntie!' I cried in relief. 'Where've you been?'

'—causes us more trouble than the rest of Rome.'

'I've been looking everywhere for you!'

'Now, signor.' The copper with me tapped my shoulder. 'Now. We tire of her. Understand? You take her in hand, or else . . .'

'I will! I promise!'

'If you looked after her properly she wouldn't need to steal.'

'You are right, signor,' I said, all humble. With my hand on my breast and my heart seething with murderous intentions towards Anna I smiled apologetically.

'We warn you,' the boss cop said, wearily exhaling smoke into my face like he was doing me favours. 'You are responsible in future. Okay?'

They took my name and address and let us off with a warning. I even had to sign for the silly old bitch. I grabbed Anna and backed off into the crowd, bowing and scraping to the cops as I went. All the way I said nothing, dragging Anna home in a blaze of white-hot fury, and once there it happened without any conscious decision. I didn't even give her time to have a shower. I gave her a damned good shaking, and called her all the names under the sun for risking the rip and getting us booked like that.

She took it in silence, struggling a bit at first and sobbing a little.

'I'm sorry, Lovejoy,' she snuffled after I'd nearly calmed down.

'So you ought to be,' I snapped. 'You're now a registered felon on the cops' frigging books.'

'I'll make it up—'

'There's no time.' As I said it my heart was in my boots. I felt ill at the thought.

'I'll ditch old Anna, build another character—'

'The fucking rip's next week, you silly cow!'

'Next week?' Stricken, she raised a tear-streaked face. 'We must put it off—'

'Rips can't be postponed. They're cancelled, or done. Silly bitch.'

'But, Lovejoy—'

Then I nicked her handbag – why change a profitable habit? – and slammed out into the alley. The trouble with allies is they try to help, and nothing is more trouble than that. Within an hour I'd got plastered on white plonk, and that evening was thankful it was Sunday. I could barely totter to the restaurant whose name Adriana had written down.

* * *

144

I worked so hard planing and chiselling that I could see wood wherever I looked.

I'd better explain. A rent table is not your usual rectangle or flapped circle, nothing like that. Think of a mushroom, a top on a pedestal. It was used for what its name says, collecting rent from the peasantry. The serfs' coins went on to a decorated centre, which sinks like Sweeney Todd's chair and drops the gelt into the pedestal below. Some are oval. Arcellano's was angled, with drawers all round. It stands to reason that *every* drawer can't be rectangular, or they would have no space to enter. Slices of cake are wedge-shaped for the same reason. So some of the drawers have to be phoney for the exterior to look right.

I was using wood cannibalized from cheap furniture about thirty years old, plus a few panels quite a bit older. Incidentally, when you are forging furniture don't turn your nose up at chipboard. It's a hell of a weight but it's cheap, it veneers like a dream, and it won't warp in central heating. Very few whole-thickness woods have all those merits.

As my plan called for two rent tables I was wood from floor to ceiling. A lucky find was a supply of beeswax and turpentine at the furniture makers' next door to Anna's place, and a reasonable range of wood varnishes from the main Corso. The adhesives you can get nowadays are great, but a few have one terrible drawback – a characteristic stink – so those have to be avoided. I'd also need a controlled temperature of 68° Fahrenheit or so to do all this glueing and varnishing, and as I'm very keen on knowing what the relative humidity is playing at around furniture, another battle with Adriana was obviously called for. The trouble was Piero would say the opposite to whatever I proposed. Him having the monarch's ear, so to speak.

During an afternoon break Anna conducted me to a couple of furniture warehouses. The tables I finally decided I liked were crummy and modern enough to break your heart.

Anna noticed quick as a flash and burbled, 'Why, Enrico! They're exactly like the ones in—'

I trod neatly on her foot and ordered three, for delivery next afternoon. 'They're just the thing I need in the workshop, Auntie,' I explained loudly.

On the way home Anna demanded, 'Has the beautiful signora said you could buy them on her account?'

'Not yet.'

'But you expect she will agree?'

'Yes,' I lied, looking Anna straight in the eye.

'They're expensive, Lovejoy.'

'They're for the rip,' I said coldly. 'What's expense between friends?'

She saw sense. 'Why did you tell the man to deliver the tables at four o'clock? The emporium's closed—'

'Anna, love,' I told her wearily. 'Shut it.' She was driving me mad. 'And you forgot your voice, you silly bitch.' Old Anna had twice spoken with the mellifluous voice of a young woman. I'd had to kick her into the right gear.

She gave me a mouthful. 'It's working with a selfish brute like you!' But I could tell she was shaken.

It was in this happy mood of fellowship we parted, Anna furiously plunging into the nearest crowd of tourists and me slamming off to the workshop for another few hours' beavering.

Mondays are always busy with customers. Several times I was interrupted by Fabio to try the tray dodge, which began to get on my nerves. It seemed every few minutes. Still, whoever pays the piper. Whether it was the row with Anna or the knowledge of Piero's special, erm, position with regard to Adriana I honestly don't know. But by closing time I was thoroughly cheesed off. When Adriana called me in to hand me my restaurant chit I refused to accept it.

'No, thank you, signora.'

Piero was bolting the back yard. Fabio was checking the window grilles.

'Where will you eat, Lovejoy?' Her frigging trump card.

'I'll manage.'

She flamed. 'Like you did the other night, I suppose. With that fat tourist?'

So she knew of that. Good old Fabio. Or Piero. Or yet another of Arcellano's goons? Christ.

'She wasn't fat.'

'And you naturally know for absolute certain *how* fat!'

I'd never seen her so pale and angry. It was one of those days. Everything was in a bloody mess at the emporium and I didn't even know if Anna and I were still speaking.

'Signora,' I said, because I was fuming too, 'all my childhood I had food tickets on the charity. I'll have no more. Please decide what you think I've earned. Give me any cheap antique you think will come near it. I'll manage the way I always have. Antiques is my game. Greed appears to be no different in Rome than anywhere else.'

I left her to make the choice and went out to help with the locking up, though one of the others always checked them after me again anyway.

We did our reporting session as usual, me last. I told

Jonathan Gash

her I'd ordered *two* modern cafeteria-type tables that afternoon and told the suppliers to bill the emporium.

Fabio started up instantly. 'Of all the nerve.'

'They were needed for glue tables in the workshop.'

'Will there be any further expenses, Lovejoy? I mean, this is your last requirement?'

'No. An old box iron, but I can make one of these.'

'Very well. But in future ask first. Is that understood?'

I drew breath to explain that there was very little future left, but Fabio broke in with an exasperated 'Oh!' so I turned to go, writing the whole bloody thing off, when Adriana said, 'Lovejoy. Here, please.'

Please? She was holding out a sealed envelope between her fingers, avoiding my eye by the trick of paying attention to Fabio's complaints. I hesitated, but took it and went to shut the workshop windows.

I opened the envelope. A posh monogrammed card was inside. It read,

Signora Adriana Albanese requests the pleasure of
Signor Lovejoy's company this evening at supper
in the Gold Season Restaurant, Rome.
Eight-thirty for nine o'clock.

I had the sense to put it in my jacket pocket before I turned round. Piero was waiting there in the doorway.

'All done, Lovejoy?' he said without inflection. It could have meant anything.

I said, 'Nearly.' And left.

I felt a real scruff in the Gold Season. The carpet absorbed me up to my ankles. The walls were discreetly illuminated along their entire lengths, gold light warming the restaurant as far as the crystal fountain in the centre.

Needless to say, an incoming tramp flashing a card and being given an ostentatiously hysterical welcome by the senior captain caused no little stir. You can't help feeling a right duckegg sometimes. Even people in the alcoves looked up to see the fuss.

I was given a dry sherry as if I'd asked for it. The offered smokes I declined. I was nervous as hell, though I'd washed. The invitation presumably meant I was to dine with the Albaneses, rather than in some quiet corner. But what did one talk about with a bloke like Signor Albanese? And I'm a clumsy sod. I was sure to drop everything or knock his wineglass all over his precious papers. Every portent indicated a really swinging time. I sat miserably listening to the gentle background music and trying to work out things to say.

There are times when even portents get things wrong. This was one of them. A second sherry had just arrived to make me hungrier still. I could hardly remember the pizza I had had at two o'clock. I'd just decided that the invitation had been some kind of elaborate joke when a cough alerted me, one of those directional look-out-we're-here coughs waiters use. I looked up, and there was Adriana, being ushered towards my table.

I stumbled to my feet, nudging the bloody table so the glasses tinkled dangerously. Calm hands steadied it and trained voices murmured apologies for the habitual clumsiness of serfs, as if it had been them and not me.

'Good evening, signora,' I mumbled.

'Good evening, Lovejoy.'

They say Queen Victoria is the only person in history never to check that a chair was available before sitting down. (One always was, of course.) Well, Adriana did it too, sinking elegantly in the sure conviction that enough kulaks were around to spring forwards with a chair. She was blinding. Her dress was a simple sheath thing in green with a scooped collar. The emerald on her breast seemed out of place at first until she raised her arms to the table and the gold bracelets picked up the emerald's gold setting. Her emerald earrings shed a million lights. I'd never seen anything so exquisite before. The waiters hurtled about to bring her sherry.

I had to tell her. 'Look, signora. I'm letting you down, being here.'

She said coolly, 'I invited you, Lovejoy.'

'I know. But you're . . . perfect. Just look at me.'

'Appearances are unimportant, no?'

'That is untrue, signora. As your husband will agree.'

'Signor Albanese will not be able to join us this evening. He's unavoidably detained.'

Until then I'd assumed he was merely telling the chauffeur where to park that purple Rolls. 'Oh. I'm sorry.' Unsuccessfully I tried to suppress my overwhelming relief.

'You're very kind.' While she accepted the sherry I wondered if I detected a certain dryness in her tone but decided I couldn't have. 'Lovejoy. I saw Signor Gallinari over the weekend.'

The bloke who'd sold us the lovely Jacobean piece. 'You didn't tell him I'm on your staff?'

'Yes. He remembered you.'

I pulled a face. 'Pity. He has two luscious early Wedgwoods, both underpriced.' We couldn't pull the same lift twice. Gallinari wasn't that dim. A lift is persuading somebody to sell an antique ridiculously cheap. Dealers are always on guard against other dealers.

Her brown eyes flicked up at me, seeming big as saucers. 'He called you *that young man who loves things*.' Lustrous. That's the word. 'You rather surprised him, Lovejoy.'

'How?'

'When I said you . . . assist me, he expressed astonishment that you had not asked for a special deal.'

'I don't do milkers.' A milker is a trade trick. You claim you've had to pay more than the real purchase price. Had I done a milker, Gallinari would have given me two invoices, a genuine and a phoney one. The loser would have been Adriana. 'Is that what Piero and Fabio expected, too?'

'Of course. And I.'

'Look.' I cleared my throat. Even a perfect woman can be dim. 'Antiques are valuable to me even if they aren't mine. They're not just hard currency. They are love. Some people – kids in slums, men and women slaving in intolerable conditions, dying as they worked – solidified love, welded it into things they made. When you think of it, it's magical. There's nothing more valuable than that.'

'There's feeling.' She was watching me again.

'No there's not.' That sort of yap riles me. 'Feeling isn't love.'

She waved away a hovering waiter. 'What are they, then?'

'Feelings are feelings. Nothing else.'

She was nonplussed. Women hate the cold light of truth. I saw a milliard doubts flicker across her face, to and fro like dappling sun on a stream. She said slowly, staring past me, 'I'm not used to this kind of discussion. You'll have to explain . . .'

'Look,' I said apologetically. 'Erm, sorry about this, but could we possibly, erm . . . ?'

'Oh, certainly!'

She ordered, and mercifully the grub started coming. I just lasted out. Apart from the prawn cocktail being so natty it was practically microscopic, the grub was lovely. I fell on it, desperately trying to maintain a light chitchat till each next lot appeared. The signora kept it coming, thank God. By the time the second lot of dessert rolled up I had slowed to a steady noshing rhythm and only then noticed that conversation had ceased at the adjacent tables. A good number of diners were watching us – well, me. Adriana had hardly eaten a thing. I reddened and glanced up at her but she only smiled.

'I would like your opinion,' she said smoothly, 'on those profiteroles. They are supposed to have quite a name for them here . . .'

'Oh, er,' I stammered, wondering if I ought to pretend I was full from politeness. Adriana overrode my embarrassment by interrogating the captain on the cream and insisting on inspecting it herself. Not knowing what the hell profiteroles were I was a bit lost and waited till all our fates were decided. They turned out to be little chocolate things that tended to vanish when you bit.

You have to admire a woman like her. Instead of being mortified by this shabby moron whaling his way through platefuls, she blossomed and funnily enough raised her voice, almost showing off. She seemed to take a curious delight in supervising what was going on. I suspected afterwards she was just covering up so I wouldn't feel bad on her account, though at the time I was just a bit surprised because I'd never seen her so animated. If I hadn't known I was a proven liability I'd almost have believed she was enjoying being with me. Like I say, women are odd. Over coffee I tried to apologize in case I'd put her off her grub. I'd just been so hungry.

She smiled. 'Not in the least.'

'You never have much.' As I said it I realized the

mistake. It meant I'd ogled her every mouthful whenever she dined. 'Sorry.'

'Don't apologize. I never really enjoy mealtimes.'

A message to cut and run? 'Erm, I think I'd better be getting along . . .'

'I've ordered coffee,' she commanded. 'I'd like you to try our famous liqueur. *Sambuca* isn't to everyone's palate, but I'm told . . .'

She insisted we finish the wine and asked where I was living.

I said, 'Over in a small street near the Castel Sant' Angelo,' but I was trying to work it out. If Piero had followed me to that hotel when I'd visited that lady tourist, and reported back to Adriana, why didn't she know where I lived?

'Is it satisfactory?'

'It's free.' Another mistake, possibly implying resentment at being fastened on her financial chain. Her colour heightened. I could have kicked myself. 'I meant it's okay.'

She gathered her handbag then, in a glitter of emerald and gold. Dinner was over. Minions panted up, quivering. She said, 'I'm afraid I shall have to ask you to drive.'

'Me? That big thing?'

'No. Something much smaller. The Rolls is . . . in use. Can you manage . . . ?'

She meant was I tipsy.

An army of waiters leapt to drag our chairs away. We processed out of the restaurant, Adriana sweeping ahead and me following.

The car was the same longish low job. Adriana passed me the keys. All fingers and thumbs, I made a pig's ear of opening the doors, and once in I took a fortnight finding the controls. Adriana said nothing, just laid her head back on the headrest and closed her eyes until we got going. Then she opened her eyes and from then on simply directed, telling me only left or right and saying nothing else.

It came on to rain after some twenty minutes. We were on a major carriageway. Quite a lot of traffic was about though it thinned as we turned off on to a smaller road. I had no idea where we were. She never said where we were heading, though when the city ended and the countryside seemed to rise, and the road with it, I began to wonder. Possibly they had two houses, and her husband had some business out of the city.

Our drive through the rain took maybe an hour or just a little less. We pulled in to the gateway of a villa. It was lit by an outside ornamental lantern so presumably somebody was home and waiting up for her. Lights of a couple of other villas were visible not too far off. I couldn't see for rain and dark, but gained an impression of palms and paths leading off a patio into a garden.

I waited, thinking, now what do we do? It was a hell of a way back, and by now so late I doubted if a taxi would make the journey out this far.

'You'll have to come in,' she said. 'No sense in sitting here.'

We ran up the few marble steps into the shelter of the porch. Dashing in the rain always makes me smile. I noticed she used keys instead of ringing. I stood feeling full of doubts while she clicked the door open and went in shaking her hair like they do. She had hall lights on before she realized I was still dithering in the porch. Her shoulders drooped as if with exasperation.

'Lovejoy.' She didn't even turn round.

'Yes, signora?'

'You now come *in*.'

'Erm, thank you.' I stepped inside. She still hadn't turned.

'And *now* you close the door behind you.'

'Right.' I did as she said, feeling a twerp. 'Look, signora,' I said doubtfully. 'About my, erm, getting back . . .'

She turned then. I couldn't tell whether she was laughing or crying. 'Lovejoy,' she said. 'I don't believe you're real.'

She said the same thing again during the night. It must have been about three o'clock in the morning. I was across in the bathroom. She came from the bedroom and stood wobbling sleepily in the doorway.

'Lovejoy. What are you doing?'

'Washing my socks.' I'd done my singlet and underpants and was hanging them on the heated rails.

'You are *what*?'

'I've only one lot.' It was all right for her. I'd never seen her in the same clothes twice. A set of heated drying pipes was not to be sneezed at. 'Finished.'

She came against me, apparently snuffling with laughter. I was glad, because I was stark naked. So was she for that matter, but nude women don't look stupid like we do. A woman like her could make a man forget Maria.

'I told Fabio to get you fitted out.'

'He must have forgotten.'

'I'll make sure he remembers.'

'Mind, signora,' I warned. 'My hands are wet.'

It was then she said it again. 'Lovejoy,' she breathed against my neck, her hands about me. 'I don't believe you're real.'

Her saying that was getting on my nerves. 'What are you on about?'

'I mean you call me Adriana now. Come back to bed.'

She meant *cretino*.

Chapter 19

Next morning was a right scramble. It shouldn't have been, but for some reason Adriana was anxious to make a proper breakfast for us, warbling in the kitchen with me gaping at the loveliest of views over a valley. I had her point the places out on the map and was delighted to learn we were near the Tivoli Fountains at the Villa D'Este. She said we would go one day.

She drove quite expertly and probably twice as well as me. Women are mostly better drivers than us. I've noticed that. I was thankful, because there was a snarl-up on the main road into the city. We had delayed getting off the bed as well, which didn't help. She dropped me with money for a taxi.

Anna had not left for the day's work. We had a brief skirmish, but that was practically par for the course nowadays. She was at her make-up when I came in and she rounded on me. Of course I had no reason to feel guilty but women always put you in the wrong.

'I suppose you've been with that posh whore? The grand signora.'

'No,' I lied. 'If you must know I've been looking around.'

'The rip?' she breathed, unbending.

'Yes.'

'I'm glad, Lovejoy.' She gave a half-smile. 'One of us messing it up's bad enough.'

She was apologizing for that business with the police. I felt a heel but quickly suppressed it. There were too many people not on my side for me to go over and join them.

'I want you to do something. Can you get hold of a camera? They took theirs back.' And asked all sorts of awkward questions when I couldn't produce any photographs.

'I'll get one.'

I warned, 'Legitimate, no stealing. Make sure you get a film that fits. Have somebody do it for you if you're uncertain. Then photograph the Colosseum.'

'*All* of it?'

'No. Go in to the right. The terrace ends about half-way round, where the ancient Romans had a sort of elevator. There are great blocks of stone—'

'I know the place. Where the masons work?'

'Photograph the stones, the recess, everything.' I didn't say that was where Marcello died. 'From every angle you can think of. It's vital, so do it properly.'

'I'll do it, Lovejoy.' She looked at me through the mirror, doing her mouth. 'And thanks.'

'What for?' I'd just given her a monumental load of work to do, one my life would depend on.

'Just thanks.' I let it go. I don't understand birds sometimes.

She came to close the door after me. 'Lovejoy. I've had news. Carlo comes out of hospital tomorrow.'

'About time,' I said as levelly as I could. It had had to come. 'Tell him I want the ambulance on standby in three days. Morning, Anna.'

'Morning, Lovejoy.'

I started making the winch that morning.

Maybe my timing was a bit unfortunate, knowing what I now knew of Piero and Adriana, but I was on a tight schedule. You can't keep Vaticans waiting. So while I was drying out some glued pieces after weighting them down I went into the yard to measure up for the beam, a plain girder with a pulley.

'What are you doing, Lovejoy? Who said you could start on that?'

Good old Piero had come to check on me. He did this about twice an hour usually. Never said much, just gave a long glance, then went back in. This time he was inquisitive and suspicious.

'Well, nobody, but—'

'You were told your winch idea's off. Listen.' He came closer, casual as anything. I glimpsed Fabio's delighted face at the rear window. 'Your job here is to *take* orders. Understand?'

'I know that. But it's daft to waste—'

'Piero.'

Adriana was standing at the top of the showroom's back steps. An entirely new outfit. Lemon was today's colour, a graceful suit and chiffon scarf. No gold, just enough silver to bend the bullion market. Her hair was lustrous. She looked straight out of Imperial Rome, a real blinder.

'Eh?' I realized she had asked a question, what was going on? 'Oh. I thought I'd start measuring up—'

'For a winch for the top floor,' Piero said. He never took his eyes off me. If Adriana hadn't arrived we'd have been having harsher words than this.

I shrugged. 'If we can't use it for upstairs, it'll do for

the showroom. A kid could use it to lift the heaviest furniture right into the ground-floor showroom. For God's sake,' I said, making out I was getting tired of it. 'Even the ancient Romans had lifting devices. Go to the Colosseum. The mason there lifted those great blocks all day long with one finger, and we hump wardrobes and cabinets up and down those stupid steps, into the loading yard. Daft.'

'Then he can make it for the showroom,' Adriana told the middle distance. 'Will it be safe?'

'Perfectly.' I smiled at her but not at Piero.

And I thought, like hell it will.

Fabio spent a contented morning after that, pouring oil on troubled fires. He took great pleasure in calling me into the showroom, innocently asking my advice on this or that antique. Twice I told him the stuff he was asking about was gunge, modern fakery, and each time he simpered with pleasure. It was only when I saw Piero's thunderous expression that I realized what game Fabio was playing. They were 'antiques' Piero had bought in. Hey ho.

Adriana spent her time being exquisitely beautiful in the office and taking customers around. We were quite busy. I was brought up to play the tray dodge again, once with Piero and once – at some considerable distance – with Adriana.

The influx always fell off about half past twelve, and it was then I really got going. Instead of working feverishly in ten-minute dashes I could tear into my Chippendale with a single mind. Of course they didn't look like tables, and if things went smoothly they wouldn't for quite some time. Piero came into the workshop about one o'clock. I was pedalling like a maniac at the spindle lathe, running a polisher into action, when I felt him there. I let the spindle creak to a halt, thinking that this was it. I gave him a disarming grin, friendly old Lovejoy.

'You rang?'

'Those bits the rent table for Adriana?'

'Yes. Want to see?'

'Not really.' He was quite casual again, in full control. I think it was then I understood what a dangerous opponent he could be. Give me somebody berserk, every time. 'There seems a lot of pieces for just one table.'

'I'm making the occasional duplicate piece,' I explained casually. 'It's called templating. Then if the signora finds it sells quickly, I can easily make another. Saves working it all out every time.'

'What I mean is, Lovejoy, you're not making separates, are you? One for the signora, one for yourself? Because I wouldn't like that, Lovejoy.' He spoke like a boss.

'No,' I said, thinking I was getting quite good at lying. I'd lied my head off all morning and it felt marvellous. 'I promise you, Piero. Everything here belongs to the signora.'

'You know, Lovejoy,' he said thoughtfully, inspecting me. 'There's something wrong with you, isn't there?'

I didn't like this. Piero the ape I could handle. Piero the thinker was an unknown quantity. 'Wrong?'

'You bend too easy. Yet I get the impression you're just not bendable. And all this honesty.'

I shrugged uncomfortably. I don't like being looked into. 'Everybody's different.'

And your gig here. Working on spec, when you're a natural at the antiques game.'

'Scratching bread, same as the rest.'

'Maybe, Lovejoy.' He was still quite calm as he left, but he said it again. 'Maybe.'

* * *

When we started to break at two o'clock I received a type-written message. In an envelope with just my name on the front: *Lovejoy*. It read:

Lovejoy,
Please phone the number below, two-thirty.

It was a Rome number.

I asked Fabio, 'Who delivered this?'

'It was with the rest of the post.'

'No postmark?'

'Just as I passed it to you, Lovejoy.' He grinned wickedly. 'Some handsome admirer you haven't told us about?'

I was on tenterhooks wondering, so I made sure I broke off on time. On the way out Adriana spoke to me as I was dismissed – turning approximately in my direction but speaking a mile over my head.

'Lovejoy. Your lunch arrangements are altered.'

I'd forgotten my nosh money. 'They are?'

'Yes. I've phoned an account in, at the pizzeria across the street and the trattoria next to it.'

'Er, thank you, signora.'

'For one,' she said absently. I felt the barb: no hungry partners share your dinners, Lovejoy.

'Of course, signora.'

I made my farewells and hurried to the trattoria where they let me use their phone. My hands were shaking as I dialled. A bored bird announced a hotel's name quite openly.

'Look,' I said with some puzzlement. 'My name's Lovejoy. I was asked to phone this number at two-thirty.'

'It's not that yet.' She was bored and belligerent. 'I'll put you through but don't blame me.'

It was Arcellano all right. I felt my flesh creep as soon as I heard the poisonous bastard. He asked, 'How's my old friend?'

'I haven't a bean,' I complained. 'I'm having to work on tick.'

He gave his cat-cough chuckle but I'll bet without a proper smile. 'Exactly as I like it, Lovejoy. Here's my instruction. As soon as you've completed our transaction, you will ring this phone number, in Bonn. The very instant. You'll be told where to deliver the item. Do you understand?'

'Yes.'

'And Lovejoy. No more accidents with cars.'

'What do you mean?' I was all innocent.

The phone went dead. I wrote down the number he'd given me and had a sombre meal.

I left the trattoria thinking resentfully that half of the people in Rome now seemed to be my bosses. I had Anna bellyaching that everything I did was wrong. I had Adriana telling me where and when I could eat, and now who to sleep with. There was Piero fighting me every inch of the way. Fabio was stirring it. And Arcellano, probably having me watched now even as I walked through the Piazza Navona towards Anna's.

It was then that I got the other half. A familiar motor was waiting as I emerged on the south side of the Navona. Familiar because you don't get many of them that ghastly purple colour. The chauffeur stood out as I crossed over.

'Signor.'

Like a fool, I was smiling as I got in, but the thing was empty. I sat, puzzled. Adriana had said nothing about sending her car for me.

We rolled like a mobile cathedral into the river road. I listened carefully. There was not a cheep out of the clock.

'Where are we going?' I asked the driver, peering out at the car roofs. I'd never been this high without a ladder. 'Look. I have to be back at work—'

'One moment, signor.'

That was all I got from him. The interior of the car was carpeted and there were more cupboards around than I had in my cottage. It was lovely. With my B-movie memory I tried the door handle at a traffic light. It wasn't locked, so I wasn't going to be gassed. Only Adriana, probably, wanting to talk.

We were only a few minutes reaching the block of apartments. Not too tall a building, and very discreet. The ground floor was occupied by a suite of offices, some kind of property development company by the looks of things. I'm thick sometimes. I was still smiling in anticipation when I realized the place was Signor Albanese's, not Adriana's.

A suave young bloke showed me in. Signor Albanese was reading documents behind a rosewood desk. I trudged the mile between the door and the chair. He had more sense than keep me waiting by pretending preoccupation, and looked up immediately with a smile that told me once again it was not my day.

'There you are,' he said, smiling at the secretary to bring a sherry. 'You are much younger than I'd imagined, Lovejoy. I put you in the mid-forties.'

'Some of us never make it.'

He smiled and invited me into the chair.

'You can leave us, Ernesto.'

'I'm afraid I don't have much time,' I said.

'I know. You must be back at the emporium fairly

soon.' He nodded as though that side of things was of the slightest importance.

I sussed him. He was a calm, immaculate sort. You immediately received the impression that nothing could possibly take this man by surprise. It was a troublesome world, clearly, but controllable. His thinning hair was flattened, his suit brand new. Behind all that cleanliness and order he was tough, and in charge.

'About your presence in Rome, Lovejoy.' He raised a podgy palm to arrest my run of falsehoods. 'No fabrications, please. Save those for others. You are, I believe, a divvie?'

'Yes.'

'An impressive attribute.' A pause. 'For one so poor.'

'My stuff was stolen. I got dipped.'

'So you say.'

'It's the truth. I'm earning my wages in antiques. Signora Albanese decided the deal, not me.'

'I heard. But that still leaves a gap in your story, no?'

'Not that I'm aware of.'

'Perhaps I should explain, then. You come here, ostensibly as a tourist. You are relieved of your wallet. So you gravitate to a job in an antique shop, simply to earn your fare home.'

'That's it.'

He continued smoothly, 'I am reliably informed that your country's authorities have an enviable record in establishing administrative systems the world over. I am further informed that they can cope with a stranded tourist.'

'I never thought of it.'

He leant forwards, shaking his head.

'Lovejoy. I swear to you, I do not intend to destroy you, or any plans you might have. And whatever you say will go no further. But I must know. Do you understand?'

I was getting sick of people uttering threats at me and then demanding if I understood. They'd all been at it today and it was getting on my wick.

'No, I don't understand.'

'You were merely one of the crowd,' he said gently. 'At first, that is. Until now. When you and Adriana . . .' He paused to make certain it sank in. 'Naturally my wish for Adriana is that she enjoys a stable relationship. I condone it. And, until now, that which has existed between Adriana and Piero Peci has been eminently suitable. I am naturally very concerned when Adriana shows signs of changing her arrangements.'

I was. lost. It was all too liberated for me to take in at one go. 'You mean I'm sacked? Or I'm not to see Adriana?'

'Not at all. Some relationship, of the kind Piero has previously provided, is essential. All I want to know is what your game is.'

I drew breath. He didn't mind Adriana having another bloke, even if it was in the plural, and all he wanted was for me to be frank about my presence in Rome? I began to get a headache.

It's . . .' I hung my head, as if in shame. What the hell could I tell him? Tinker always says you should get your lies in first. Second and you're sunk. I started to talk, praying something would come. 'It's . . . somebody I've met.'

'Adriana?'

'No.' That road might be even more dangerous. 'I admit I have some motive for staying . . .' *Anna!* Anna! I burbled, 'I . . . I want to stay for a while, at least until I've worked things out. She . . . she isn't free. She has obligations. I'm not at liberty . . .'

'Somebody else? Not Adriana?' There was a dry rasp. I looked up. The blighter was laughing, heaving up and down in his chair. 'So. It isn't really Adriana at all? By acquiescing to Adriana you were merely demonstrating unfailing obedience to your employer?'

'Well, if you put it like that . . .'

He took off his specs and wiped his eyes. I didn't think it was all that funny but he was rolling in the aisles.

'I'm sorry, Lovejoy,' he said, wiping his eyes with his glasses lifted on to his forehead. 'Very remiss of me. But if you only understood the context . . .'

'Is that all?' I rose, trying for a bit of dignity. It can be useful in the right place.

'My abject apologies, signor,' he said, still falling about. He came with me to the door. 'But Adriana playing second fiddle to some other woman is delicious.'

I went frosty. 'Can I go now?'

'The car will be at the entrance for you. Don't be too offended, Lovejoy. Let's say it's our little secret, shall we?'

'Look, signor.' I had to get one thing straight. 'What if the signora says I'm to dine with her again, and . . . ?'

'Be her guest, Lovejoy.' He smiled and patted my arm. 'After all, everybody's different. And you are merely . . . what's the expression? . . . scratching bread, same as the rest. Isn't that so?'

'Yes,' I said, wondering where I'd heard those words spoken recently.

It was returning in the Rolls, wondering about the rum world we live in, when I remembered where I'd heard those words before recently. And who spoke them.

It was me, to Piero. Word for word. My headache got worse. Well, whatever they were all up to, Piero, Adriana, the signor, and Fabio, the rip had to go ahead.

I made the driver drop me near the emporium, seeing

it was getting on for four o'clock. The three cafeteria tables were delivered on time, to my satisfaction. I'd told Adriana two, and instead had ordered three. I was very, very pleased, because two from three leaves one. Smiling at last, I covered them with a sheet of plastic and walked home to see Anna.

Chapter 20

In the heat of the day the Colosseum induces a curiously offensive languor, inducing scores of cats to live there. God knows where the Italians get all their moggies, but it's by the gross. I'd never seen so many. Anna came with me, still in her old gear and occasionally conning a few lire from stray tourists. And she was in a bitter mood. 'You tell me what magnificent photos I took,' she complained, 'then waste our rest time wandering about these old stones.' And her photographs really were great, every nook from every angle. Real skill. I like talent like that. But you really need to get the feel of the place you might die in, I always say, and you can't get that from photographs.

There was hardly anybody in, just us and a straggle of Scandinavians. Anna kept asking me why we were looking at the same recess over and over again. Finally she got on my nerves and I told her to shut it. That did it. Nothing's quieter than a bird in sulk.

The recess was the stonemason's place. Presumably the animals for Rome's great circuses had been fed into the great arena through this kind of entrance. What I liked about it was that it stood just below a great mason's hoist, complete with block and tackle, and with an almost-completed block of stone in the centre of the sandy flooring. Obviously, from the tools and the stone chips scattered around, the workers were still at it. Before long they would be ready to haul the missing stone into place.

But what I really liked most was that the recess was at least forty-odd feet deep, and had smooth walls impossible to climb.

'Why are you smiling, Enrico?'

'Don't call me Enrico.' I asked her, 'What would happen if somebody were to get himself trapped in that recess?'

'He'd have to stay till people lifted him out. But nobody could get trapped down there.'

'Why not?'

'Don't you see?' Scornfully she pointed across to the opposite wall below us. 'He could just walk out, couldn't he? That great stone's missing. *Cretino!*'

I shaded my eyes at the great beam overhead. 'But if that unfinished stone were to fall into that hole . . . ?'

'*Then* he'd be trapped!' She took my arm. I was still gaping skywards. 'Enrico? I don't like you when you're like this.'

'You don't like me anyway,' I reminded her acidly. I'd slept in the same room for what felt like a lifetime, and we were as chaste as Abelard and Heloise – different reasons, of course.

'It'd be an open-air prison.' I realized I was smiling at thoughts of Arcellano.

'Enrico.' Her eyes looked at me, enormous with a deep beauty. 'What has this place to do with the rip?'

'Don't call me Enrico.' I was feeling a lot more confident as we left. The arena was after all just one great maze made up of those stone blocks. If anything went wrong I'd be off like a scared rabbit, being the fastest coward ever recorded. And in my time I've been chased by experts. Yes, I was pleased – fool that I was. Nothing could go wrong. So I thought.

During the rest of our spare time I either pored over the photographs, went over Anna's Vatican Museum measurements, or intently read the pharmacopoeia. In this last Anna had excelled herself, having an epileptiform seizure in the huge bookshop on the corner of the Leone IV and nicking the pharmacopoeia while people ran about for water. She kept asking what I wanted it for but I shoved her away and said it was rude to read over other people's shoulders.

'I've indigestion,' I told her snappishly.

'You eat like a horse when that cow of a signora feeds with you at those expensive restaurants!'

'She hardly eats anything,' I corrected.

'Only people! In her grand villa!'

Which told me a lot. For one, Anna obviously didn't trust me. For another, she had some means of knowing where we dined each evening, and about my visit to Adriana's villa.

Now we'd done the Colosseum I needed a little money and a chance to finish in the workshop. Then it would only be a question of checking the van. But first we had to welcome the great man himself.

Carlo came home like a wounded hero, groaning in a taxi, overacting and being brave but in pain. Sickening. It was all the same to me, but you couldn't help being really peeved at the fuss Anna made over him, snatching everybody else's cushions to make sure he was comfortable. For once she'd bought in a load of provisions and made him a tantalizing mound of unrecognizable food. He managed to force it all down, the greedy pig, while I sweated my guts out over the photographs and sketches. I've never seen anybody look so sorry for himself, the pillock.

No use asking Anna for a loan after the argument we'd just had, though I wouldn't need much. I'd have to work on Adriana, which was a nuisance because being a bird she'd be as mistrustful as Anna. But there was another problem, just as serious and far more urgent. What did Lovejoy do now hubby was home? So far there hadn't been a single bad vibe – not more than usual, anyway – but it had to be faced.

'Look,' I began when Carlo mournfully started on his second bottle of wine. (Naturally, I'd been offered none.) 'Do you think Carlo's up to it?' As is the way with invalids present I spoke over Carlo's head to Anna.

'Of course he is.'

Carlo straightened up briskly. 'You questioning my ability, Lovejoy? You can't do without me.' Well, I'd been told that by indispensable allies, and they'd been just as wrong as Carlo.

Nastily I demanded, 'Has he ever done anything before?'

'Tell him, Carlo.'

He got up to stride the room, obviously full of beans. Clearly a good recovery. 'I've ripped off every film crew which has ever come to Rome.'

'Great,' I said drily. That meant pinching a plug or a bulb and selling it back to the cameramen. 'Anything with cars?'

'I can drive faster—'

'No,' I told Anna flatly. 'You tell him he's to drive like a fifty-year-old, not Fangio. Get that into his thick skull or it's off.'

Anna smiled, but I could tell she was annoyed. 'It's

not off, Lovejoy. You know it. I know it. Carlo will do anything you say.'

'He'd better.' I moved towards the door.

'Hey,' Carlo called, now mirror boxing and admiring himself. 'You've not said what the plan is.'

'If we get it right, Carlo, you'll never know.'

'You going back to work, Lovejoy?' from Anna.

'Yes.' I hesitated to give Anna time to follow me into the gloomy passageway. 'Erm, what's the arrangement for tonight, Anna?'

'Arrangement?' she was honestly puzzled.

'Well, now your bloke's back . . .'

She pealed laughter and clapped hands. 'You mean . . . *Carlo*?'

'Yes,' I said irritably. 'What's the joke?' Women like Anna nark me.

'He's my brother.' She fell about some more. 'He sleeps on the folding camp bed.'

'Oh, right.' I felt even more of a nerk and backed out into the alley. 'See you tonight, then.'

'*Ciao*,' she called, slamming the door on me. '*Cretino!*' I heard her laughter as I walked the uneven alley towards the Castel.

That same day I had luck, which was important. By nightfall I had become practically independent in Adriana's business. A trustee instead of a convict.

The antiques game's the queerest on earth. Some days – weeks, months, even years – you come across nothing worth a second glance. Then they roll in, and everywhere you look there is some genuine wonderment, preening its lovely feathers and shrieking to be bought.

We hit a purple patch. Adriana had reluctantly agreed

to visiting a small antiques bazaar about a mile away. I'd felt vibes almost like never before while passing on a bus. The dazzling spiritual glow from beyond Piazza Argentina all but blinded me. I was almost certain I'd glimpsed a monk's chest – neither a chest nor for a monk – being unloaded in a small street. The funny thing was I could have sworn I'd seen its photograph in one of Adriana's catalogues where a great deal of miscellaneous items, arranged as job lots, had been listed. (This in itself is a serious mistake and argues a cataloguer too idle or inexperienced.) I persuaded Adriana to come and see if they had picked up any of these items as well as the monk's chest. It turned out like Christmas.

It was a small quickie business run by three lads and their birds, you know the kind of place, everything for speed. They had bought indiscriminately, and hadn't even unpacked the smaller stuff. So eager to display their larger pieces, they let me go through and buy four small cardboard boxes of stuff practically without doing much more than unwrap a couple of top items in each. I made out I was in a great hurry, wanting stuff to trade for period reproductions in Turin the very next morning. It was a steal. Of course it cost Adriana more than the same pieces would have done had she attended the auction itself, but that was okay.

Adriana waited round the corner in Piero's car with him while I did the deal. She'd collected enough money for me to buy outright, and I came haring across the Piazza Argentina practically crowing with delight. I was so chuffed I nearly downed a fat bloke ambling across the road. The youngsters had been hugely pleased – we always say the first profit is the best, and best means fastest – but I'll bet they weren't as pleased as me. I swear I'd felt the clamouring of the eighteenth-century malachite green decorative jewellery inside among all those newspapers, and nobody could help feeling that ringing emanation from the Chien Lung agate-tiled silver box. The only William IV lead funereal marker I've ever bought was among them – and you know what's happened to the price of those. Ten years ago these flat lead pieces were thrown out with the beer bottles. Practically everything was worthwhile, and some pieces – like the little box of early model French soldiers – would pay for the rest.

She took the receipt while I hugged the stuff to me on the way back to the emporium. Unbelievably, there was a travelling dealer waiting with Fabio. He was a pleasant but tatty little Milanese bloke and had with him a collection of miniature early furniture, probably used for display in some furniture maker's in the 1830s. We call these geezers 'sweepers' in the trade because they do 'sweeps' through the country trying to gather up anything and everything which could be regarded as antique. They're the blokes who come knocking at your door on dark nights. (Take my tip: *always* send them packing. No bigger crowd of rogues exists on earth, and I should know. I was one for years.) The BBC and Sotheby's do 'sweeps' too – respectable ones, and at least as honourably, I'm sure.

I urged Adriana to buy the stuff. When the sweeper had gone we all looked at each other. It was only half past six, and I'd made the emporium a fortune.

'We overpaid the sweeper,' Piero said sourly, the miserable sod.

I wasn't having that. 'We'll make twice the cost on his stuff.'

'Of course, we still have to sell them,' Fabio said waspishly, another ray of sunshine. 'And as for buying those little balls—'

I'd bought two balls of compressed feathers wedged inside a small fraying leather case the size of a shaving stick.

'We paid the price of two beers,' I said gently. 'We'll sell them for the price of a car. They're early golf balls. Rare as hen's teeth. I'll bet you—'

'You haven't a bean to bet with, Lovejoy,' Fabio countered waspishly, sweeping back to his accounts.

I felt myself go red but Adriana said quickly, 'You were very astute, Lovejoy. Thank you.'

'Not at all, signora.' I hadn't meant to sound bitter but it came out different from what I'd intended. The workshop was clearly the place for me, though I was itching to go through the rest of the job lots to see what other brilliant stuff we'd got.

Time was getting short, though Adriana's rent table was coming along fast. It would soon be finished and good as new. Better still, good as old. One difficulty was not having the sketches of the Vatican Museum's period piece with me, but I'm not that daft. If Piero or Fabio found drawings like that they'd smell a rat. So I worked in the old way, from notches cut in sticks. Every morning at Anna's I tied the sticks to my calf inside my trouser leg. Once I was at the workshop an extra stick or two went unnoticed.

Another difficulty was assembly. The reproduction rent table I was making for Adriana to put on display had to be ready fairly soon or they'd be wondering what the hell I was doing down here, especially after they'd all commented, each in his pleasant little way, on my working speed. So I did a zillion test assemblies of every drawer and every joint, and never put it all together. The outer surfaces of her table I copied precisely using light plywood but giving them the same kinds of finish.

These were the pieces I'd told Piero were my patterns for copying.

Like hell they were.

Somehow I made room for the two cafeteria tables, scattering bits of wood about on them to show how useful they were being. The third one I left out in the yard, allegedly ready to be returned.

A further stroke of luck came about thirty minutes before we closed for the night. Signor Gallinari phoned us to say he was ready for swapping – we were doing a trade of chairs to make up complete period dining sets. Piero and Fabio went off in the van grumbling and sulky. I immediately put the metal saw across the tubular steel tips of the cafeteria table's legs. I put the four tips in my pocket, wrapped in a hankie so as not to clink, and stepped off to look. Nobody could tell. I was whistling happily and splitting some thin dowelling when Adriana came in.

'Here, Lovejoy.' she held out an envelope.

'Thank you, signora.' It was thicker than usual.

'Open it, please.'

There was money inside, besides the invitation card. I drew breath. I needed money badly, but not that bad.

'No, thank you, signora.' I kept the card and held out the notes.

'Why not?'

'We've agreed what the rules are, signora.'

She avoided my eyes. It gives you the choice, Lovejoy. Where to dine, what to do in the evenings.'

I tried to make light of the whole thing. 'With all this gelt I might streak off.'

'No, Lovejoy.' She sounded listless. 'Not you. You do what you want. You're here for your own reasons.'

So she'd realized too. 'But signora—'

'No more, Lovejoy. Please.' All the day's successes were forgotten. 'No more hypocrisy. I don't ask why you stay. From now on you won't be forced into anything. I'll see you are paid money each day.'

Her eyes were wet. I was lost. 'What about Fabio? He'll realize . . .'

'I'll find some way. Take it out of the petty cash. He won't know.'

That seemed odd, almost as if she was apprehensive about Fabio. She was the boss, after all, and Fabio was only a hireling, like me.

'Am I to be at the restaurant?'

'Only if you wish.'

I hesitated while Adriana dabbed at her eyes. Women get me mad because you never know where you are. 'Did Signor Albanese say anything? He had me taken to his office.' She looked merely resigned as I told her about it, word for word. 'I made up some cock-and-bull story about having fallen for another bird and wanting to stay here to work it out.'

'What woman?' she asked immediately.

I had a hard time convincing her there was no such woman, that she was a figment invented on the spur of the moment. 'The signor thought it hilarious.'

'I see,' she said, finally convinced. It was more than I did.

'The only thing is, he seemed to know that, erm, you and I, erm, at your villa . . .'

The others came back at that moment, so we got no further.

When we locked up later Piero was unusually affable while Adriana was still there, and walked with me as far as the corner. I wondered if this was it. There were plenty of people about, but he was such a bloody size.

'Lovejoy.' He'd made certain the purple Rolls had floated off. 'Time for you to go away, no?' He tried a wintry smile. It wasn't a patch on Arcellano's, but he was quite patient, and that disturbed me because calm fighters always do. They've seen it all before.

'Why now, especially?'

'Before, I didn't mind you too much. You were . . . incidental.' He meant insignificant, the pillock. 'But now, Adriana begins to take you seriously. You're a good antiques man, the best I've seen.' He shrugged. 'A divvie's special. Okay – so you're good for her business. But I won't be displaced by a bum that's planning some crazy rip, and using her for camouflage.'

I gave a hollow laugh. 'Rip? You're off your head. It's my hobby.'

'You joke.' He nodded gravely, eyeing me. 'Though everything you do is serious, Lovejoy. Deadly serious. You're a driven man. So I'll make a deal. go tomorrow.'

'Where to?'

'Anywhere, Lovejoy. Name the place and you'll receive money, a passport and ticket.'

'And what's my part of the deal?'

'I save you from gaol, Lovejoy.' He picked his teeth, wrinkling his eyes against the fading sun. 'I've got your fingerprints, your photograph. Fabio will provide evidence of pilfering. The Rome police are serious about antiques, Lovejoy. Whatever the rip they'll have you. You've got till tomorrow. *Ciao.*'

I watched him go, working it out. Now I had to leave, to stay, to do the rip, not to do the rip, chat up Adriana, leave her alone . . .

And that evening we dined together in the Gold Season, just the three of us: me and Adriana, and her husband. I felt between the devil and the deep blue sea because I was now sure I was being followed. The fat bloke I'd nearly knocked down in the Piazza Argentina was shown to a corner table five minutes after we arrived. A different digit, but definitely Arcellano's finger.

That wasn't all. After a couple of hours' nosh and one-sided chat – Signor Albanese was in fine form, with Adriana unresponsive and me demented – we rose and departed, and this time a Jaguar waited for Adriana. Beside it was the purple Rolls, with a familiar figure standing peevishly by, handbag on the swing.

Adriana resolved all doubts by passing me her keys quite openly. 'Drive, please, Lovejoy.'

'Erm—'

Signor Albanese gave me effusive thanks for my company and said he would not rest until we dined so pleasantly once again.

'Come *on* Emilio!' Fabio shouted petulantly. 'I've waited hours!'

'I'm hurrying!' Albanese called.

I stood while Adriana slid into the Jaguar. Emilio Albanese waved to us once and joined Fabio at the Rolls. I watched it glide away before getting in beside Adriana. I drew breath to say something and then thought better of it. Adriana was looking away. Evidently that was the other surprise Anna had promised me, the night I learned about Piero and Adriana. Piero and Adriana because of Signor Albanese and Fabio? And now Lovejoy and Adriana because of . . . ? I gave it up.

'To the villa, darling,' Adriana said. She sounded a hundred years old.

Chapter 21

It had been an uptight morning, with Fabio and Piero giving smouldering glances at the clock to warn me I should be gone by nightfall. I trotted home to Anna's eating pizza on the hoof.

I could tell Carlo was already there from the blaring transistor echoing pop music down the alley. Sure enough he was dancing sinuously before the mirror, admiring himself while Anna was removing her make-up. Ominously, he looked sloshed. Three empty wine bottles projected from the waste basket.

'Get your knickers on, troops,' I said from the door. 'And turn that bloody thing off.'

'Miserable man.' Carlo glared sullenly at me while Anna flicked the tranny, and slumped on his camp bed, obviously ready for a hard afternoon's kip.

I said, 'It starts, lad,' and toed him beneath the canvas. 'Up.'

'What does?' Carlo propped up on an elbow.

I leaned down, smiling. 'The rip, comrade. Now.'

'This instant?' from Anna, suddenly pale, her lovely face rimmed by those theatrical bulbs.

'Finish your make-up, Granny,' I said heartlessly. 'Carlo's going to show me the ambulance van.'

It's ready,' he was saying, insolently starting to lie down again, when I tipped him out and heeled his knife hand. The knife fell clear. 'He thinks I'm a kid,' he complained, staggering up.

'Kid, no. Stupid and drunk, yes.' I yanked him into the corridor. 'Anna. You be here at four.'

The van was in the smallest garage in the world half a mile from St John Lateran. We got the Metro, Carlo paying – obviously in blood – and leering at women. That journey was a record: he only combed his hair a couple of dozen times. Pests don't come more pestilential than Carlo. He was doing his spy theatrical all the way out of the Metro and crossing the road. We got more attention than Garibaldi's entry. I still don't believe it – he gave eight significant raps on the garage door, looking cloak-and-dagger as he hissed a secret code word through the gaping slats, even though the door was half off. Bloody fool. Wearily I pushed it open and stepped through while Carlo was still at it. He swaggered after me undismayed, narrowly failing to light a cigarette. That was because I took his matches and fags off him and dropped them underfoot. He was standing next to a petrol pump and a drum of waste oil.

'Patrizio.' Carlo leaned against the garage wall, flicking a coin. The nerk was unbelievable.

A tubby cheerful bloke in trousers and singlet emerged from the engine of a derelict one-tonner. He was glad to see me and smeared me with oil in an effusive greeting.

'Patrizio, this is the boss,' Carlo rasped, his eyes hooded. He missed his coin which plopped into an oil puddle.

'Ah, Signor! You like her, eh?'

'Like who?' I looked about.

'You want the van tomorrow, no?' Patrizio slammed

a hand on the ancient relic – it nearly fell apart – and grinned enthusiastically. 'Big rip, eh?'

I swallowed carefully. There wasn't another vehicle in the place. '*That?*'

'Sure!' Carlo thrust out his lower lip. 'Me and Patrizio done a deal. She'll do a hundred, boss.' Carlo screwed the words out the corner of his mouth in a crude American accent.

Stricken, I walked around the van. Patrizio came, exclaiming and extolling with enthusiam. It had obviously done service in the Western Desert, World War II graffiti and all. Now, the old banger was having a hard time standing upright. 'Fine, eh?'

'No, Patrizio. Carlo must have misunderstood.'

Patrizio's thought winged instantly to money. 'Cheap, Lovejoy.'

I sighed. He knew my name. Carlo had probably given him my address as well.

'Carlo,' I said. 'Keep watch outside.'

'Sure, boss.' The duckegg hunched his jacket collar up and sidled out, tripping over an immense air hose as he did so. He slammed the door so a plank fell out, and stood outside pretending to chew gum.

'Now,' I said carefully, giving Patrizio one of my special looks. 'I need a professional driver, and a pro van.'

Patrizio was no fool. He glanced at the garage door and shrugged. 'Apologies, signor. I thought—'

'—I'd be a fool, too?' I smiled, quite liking him. 'Be frank and there's no harm done.'

'Tomorrow, no?'

'Tomorrow, yes.'

He nodded, gauging me. 'You need my boy Valerio.'

'What's he like?'

Another mile-high shrug. 'I'm his father, signor.'

'You'll need uniforms, Patrizio. Possible?'

'Certain. But if it's tomorrow the van'll have to be . . . obtained, not fabricated.'

'Do it. One thing.' I shrugged, at least an inch. The best I've ever been able to manage. 'It'll have to be a flat fee.'

Patrizio looked at me as if into the teeth of a gale. 'Never heard of a straight-price rip, Lovejoy.'

'You have now.'

'And Carlo? Anna will be furious if he's left out.'

'I'll deal with Anna.'

He grinned and slapped my hand. 'Good luck, Lovejoy. You get your van. Where and when?'

I'd met a pro at last. Smiling with relief, I told him.

Back home Anna was incredulous. 'Carlo dropped? He can't be!'

'You want him so badly?'

She nodded. She was wearing a young print dress and was all ready for me when I returned a few minutes after four. I'd sent Carlo to count the traffic at the traffic lights on the Leone IV, telling him it was our getaway route, the berk.

'Please, Lovejoy. I know what he is, a child still. But he is all I have.' She was ashamed.

I recognized the symptoms from my own career, and relented. 'I've got him a part, love.'

Her face lit, like sunrise. 'You have?' She flung her arms round me wildly. 'Oh, thank you, Lovejoy! Thank you!'

'A vital one,' I said into her hair. 'I'll see he's useful.'

I was thinking, by the time she realized exactly *how* vital, I'd be a thousand miles away from Rome and in the clear. Like I say, sometimes I'm just too thick for words, but you can't be right all the time.

*   *   *

On the way to the emporium for my late stint I popped into the church on the Borgo San Spirito. It's one of the churches still burning honest-to-God candles instead of those gruesome candle-shaped electric sticks they have in Rome nowadays which for a hundred lire give you a few minutes of electron-powered devotional flicker.

Feeling vaguely embarrassed by the novelty I lit five candles, stuck them in the holders and knelt down. I won't tell you everything I said, but I promised God I'd take Arcellano alive. Then, mumbo-jumbo done with, I emerged blinking at the sun – and saw Anna across the road and waved. To my relief, she was smiling and nodding, so I knew the clever girl had got it, that dark old-fashioned brownish bottle from the chemist's shop by the Via del Mascherino. All systems go.

That evening Adriana and I stayed at the emporium. It was the oddest sensation, climbing the forbidden stairs and seeing Adriana move about the bedroom as if we'd been together there all our lives. Adriana tried to act casual but I saw her hand tremble as she hung up her stole and I realized that bringing me here was a big thing for her. Another worry.

She insisted on making us both coffee and bringing it over to me. She'd taken my jacket and sat me on the couch, promising to show me around once I'd become accustomed to the idea of being alone with a rapacious woman. I smiled to show I too was solemnly concentrating on lightness of heart.

'New locks,' I observed.

'The stair door? Yes. There are so many thefts nowadays, darling.' She swept her hair from her face. 'I thought it was wiser.'

Which meant that Piero's key was now obsolete.

'Adriana. Will you get in trouble?'

She concentrated on not spilling the cream. 'With Emilio? Hardly. You saw, Lovejoy. Him and that creature Fabio. It's beyond a woman's control.'

'Piero, then? He's the sort to play hell.'

She only had one lamp lit, that lovely minareted Garian case which dappled gold about the room. Her face was silhouetted in a deep bronze fire. She was sitting beside my chair, looking away. I'd never seen anything so wondrous in all my life as that miracle of line and form. Sorrow enveloped me. What a mess it all was, the whole fucking rip.

She said rather sadly, 'He can be got rid of.' The words were so matter-of-fact I hardly took them in at the time, especially as she continued talking with her head on my knee and her breast against me. 'Are you married, Lovejoy?'

That took my by surprise. 'Rescued.'

Her eyes deflected, all casual. 'A dragon?'

I thought a bit. 'A pretty laser.'

'So sometimes you too plan badly.' She continued, 'How could I have known about you, Lovejoy? You weren't here.' I suppressed exasperation at the bitterness in her voice. I hadn't known about her, either. Nor that Marcello would be murdered. 'A woman needs a man.' She turned quickly to loan me a half-smile, an on-account sort of expression. 'Not as badly as a man needs a woman. You've taught me that, Lovejoy. With you it's one hundred per cent yourself. The rest is incidental.' She indicated the apartment vaguely. 'This. The money, the firm. With Piero it was a percentage. And the others were the same.'

I returned her defiant look, trying to smile. It was a hell of an effort. She was so lovely.

'People make allowances for men.' Bravely she explained, 'A woman taking a lover is a hedonistic bitch. A rich gentleman is merely a roué, a gay old dog. And it's women do the damage – at least, in Rome it is. They're on to you like wolves.'

'What now?' I asked after a pause.

'Now?' She raised her lovely head and smiled. 'You've come at last, Lovejoy.' She smiled gently and reached back to ruffle my neck. 'I don't care what you've done in the past, darling. I take you as you are. And you'll please forgive the measures I've taken while enduring the long, terrible waiting.'

Until then I'd been absolutely determined to go back to Anna's divan. Honestly, I really had. The trouble is, women can be very assertive. I'd be well-balanced and even-tempered all of the time if it weren't for them. So I stayed. I swear it wasn't anything in the way of a deal between Adriana and me. Honestly it wasn't. Adriana in her mind had simply given Piero the push, that was all there was to it. I knew divorce from Emilio was out of the question for Adriana. I sighed inwardly. I'd have to give Anna the excuse that I was working on the rip. Anyway, this couldn't last.

What a mess it all seemed. I'd have stopped to work it all out, but now there was no time left anywhere. The rip was upon us. Here. Now.

Chapter 22

Teaching Carlo the rip was like talking to a frigging wall.

'Repeat it,' I said wearily for the umpteenth time.

'Lissern you guys,' Carlo ground out, flicking ash into his own coffee by mistake. 'This is the plan, see?' He did a Cagney hunch-up and chewed gum. 'We cruise into the saloon—'

'We walk casually into the cafeteria,' I corrected.

'—Get a shot of bourbon—'

'Wine and cream cake.'

'—And wait for the Big Wheel's signal—'

'And read a newspaper until I say.'

'All rightee!' he said grimly, grinding out his cheroot – *cheroot*, for God's sake. I ask you. 'Get your holster on, boss, and let's *go*!'

'Not till two o'clock this afternoon. And leave your knife here.' So help me, he'd got a knife long as a sword especially for the occasion.

'Right, boss. High noon.'

He burned his thumb trying a one-handed strike for another cheroot. The goon was actually wearing a white tie with a black shirt and a black suit with shoulders a mile wide. In the cold light of early morning he was utterly unreal. I could have throttled him.

'You've warned Valerio and Patrizio, Anna?'

Anna patiently passed him some butter for his burn and lit his cheroot at the gas-ring. 'Yes, Lovejoy.'

'You got me the phone number?'

'Here.' She'd printed it carefully on the face of a postage stamp, a good touch. I smiled approval at her. 'They'll be waiting from one o'clock. If the rip aborts they'll go on stand-by until seven.'

'You've done well, Anna.' I shoved Carlo's elbows off the table and checked once again.

'Bottle.' The brown bottle Anna had stolen from the chemist's stood among the Colosseum photographs I had neatly arranged in rows. 'Photographs. Measurements written out. Suit. Shirt and tie. Case. New shoes. Towel. Gloves. Hygienic sealing tape.' We went over the entire contents, krypton lamp, coat hook, tubes of adhesive, the lot. My own toolbag felt heavy as lead. 'Thanks, love.'

The measurements were for the winch. We'd tried the dark sober suit an hour before and it fitted me pretty well. I hadn't worn a suit since my missus left home. It felt decidedly odd. Anna had lifted it from that elegant gentlemen's outfitters on the Viale Giulio Cesare. The new shoes pinched a bit, but on the whole she had stolen with uncanny accuracy. I thought uneasily, maybe she watches me as closely as I watch her. I waited while she packed everything neatly into the black rectangular briefcase.

'Now – breakfast.'

Anna brought out a cloth and began to lay the table. A dozen mental reruns later I scented the fragrant aroma of frying bacon. I looked across questioningly but she did not meet my eye as she cracked some eggs on the side of the pan. Breakfast was usually a roll in a paper bag, and mostly Carlo got to it first. I was looking at the floor when she served it up with a mound of bread and butter.

'What's all this?' Carlo demanded, for once shaken out of his acting career.

'You'll both need a big breakfast inside you!' Anna rasped. 'The rip starts today – or hadn't you heard? *Cretino!*'

She slammed an immense meal in front of each of us, and even made tea specially. Hearing somebody else called that instead of me made it a breakfast to remember. Carlo went out in a sulk, so I had his as well.

Piero spotted my little case the instant I stepped in the emporium that morning and grinned all over his face. I tried to look defeated.

'Going anywhere, Lovejoy?'

'I have to visit somebody. I only came in to clear up loose ends, Piero. I don't want any trouble.'

'Okay.' Nonchalantly he threw me the keys to the workshop. 'Finish what you can, then piss off for good.'

I've never really been able to whine, not really convincingly, but I did my best. 'Look, Piero. About that passport . . .'

'You'll have it tonight.'

Thank Christ. I pulled a face. 'Er, the signora hasn't paid me . . .'

He sneered, his lip curling. No, honestly. It really did curl. I'd never seen a lip curl with scorn before in my whole life. I stared admiringly and only remembered in the nick of time that I was supposed to be a hopeless scrounger. 'You'll get your fare,' Piero promised scathingly. 'And enough to get drunk on the way home. Now work.'

'Please don't say anything to the signora—'

He grinned again. 'I can handle her.' I could have hit him.

By the time Fabio swept in I was working like a mad thing, quietly and efficiently testing the strength of my plywood mock-up. The base of a rent table's essentially a modified cylinder, with tangential walls showing lovely wood patterns. Now, a table top's always easiest to falsify, so don't trust it when you're buying antiques. Also, remember that a table is a flat surface or it's nothing, which means its top is always the first to suffer should drinks be spilled or serving maids have catastrophes with smoothing irons. Luckily, I was in the enviable position of forging a table whose major surface would be covered by a Presidential cage of synthetic sprawling birds.

But the pedestal base would be in clear view the entire length of that gallery. It had to look genuine, solid and *old*.

Tip: polyurethane varnishes *are* superb and polyurethane hardglazes *look* superb, but only true beeswaxes *feel* absolutely correct. Antique dealers dress a falsely veneered surface by varnish, then by beeswax, which is given a microscopic craquelure by rapid drying. This is done effectively only in two ways: in front of a fan or by a chemical desiccant such as sodium hydroxide in a sealed container. I'd applied both, placing the workshop's fan heater on 'cold' during the day and stuffing the folding veneered plywood into a plastic bag with the crystals overnight. There's always plenty of these crystals in an antique shop – even honest dealers (should there be any left) use it for putting that golden gleam on oak. Like I say, it's getting so you can't trust anybody these days.

With my heart in my mouth on that day I checked Piero was fully occupied, and extracted the veneered plywood. It was beautiful, its gleaming surface now dulled by drying. Microscopic examination would reveal minute cracks in the waxed surface, such as are normally associated with ageing. The corners and inter-sections were more obviously peeling than the rest, but I helped this artefact along with a little crushed carbon from a piece of drawing charcoal (use Winsor and Newton if you can get it) blown on to a piece of chamois leather and rubbed gently along the edges.

I still had the thin top sections and hinged edges to slot under the cafeteria table, but when Adriana sent to tell me I was to stop for coffee the collapsible pedestal was folded out of the way under the work bench. I was well into machining the metal support rods which would give it strength. Two hours to go.

I was on time. My heart was banging.

Dead at one o'clock Patrizio came for the cafeteria table in his wheezy World War II van. He arrived with the characteristic boredom of the vannie, smoking laconically and humping the steel and formica job on his shoulder without a word. Piero came to see I wasn't flogging a Regency piece.

'Get a receipt, Lovejoy,' he orderd.

'You,' I shot back, getting on with my job.

Patrizio gave Piero a don't-interrupt-me look and drove off leaving Piero looking foolish, to my delight. That was my last smile for a long, long time.

We closed at quarter to two, me strolling unbelievably casual into St Peter's Square exactly at two.

Valerio was a chip off Patrizio's block all right. He was a square thickset young bloke. I'd told his dad no drinks, no smokes. Valerio was obediently sitting picking his teeth and reading the *Osservatore Romano* on the end of the lines of chairs set out between the fountains.

'You want a seat?' He made to rise. Daft, really. There were four hundred empty places.

'No,' I said, mouth dry and voice no more than a croak. 'I have an urgent appointment.'

He eyed me curiously. I eyed him. It was the first time we'd met. Anna had suggested this ludicrous interchange because security forces everywhere had these directional microphones. He nodded imperceptibly. My words meant the rip was on.

'Then go well,' Valerio said.

'Ta.' I walked past him on legs suddenly made of uncontrollable rubber and headed for the loo to the left of St Peter's façade. The Vatican post office was doing a roaring trade. Old Anna was being bothersome among a crowd of amused Americans near the great basilica steps. From the corner of my eye I glimpsed her sudden querulous departure. Judging by the burst of laughter she had made some crack. Her job now was to find Carlo and hurtle him in to the loos after me.

The two usual women attendants were sitting at a little white table by the door. They ignored me. As long as I remembered to throw a hundred-lire coin into their plate as I left I'd remain an invisible passing tourist. Once in a cubicle I frantically started stripping off my clothes, hands shaking. I was sweating like a pig. My shirt and jacket were drenched, the sleeves clinging to me from damp. I cursed and wrestled in the confined space, a couple of times blundering against the door so noisily I forced myself to slow down. Hurry slowly. Good advice for anyone, as long as they're not frightened out of their skulls.

I dressed in my new sober gear. Make sure the handkerchief's showing from your top pocket, Lovejoy, Anna had said. It's a man's equivalent of white gloves in a woman, she'd said, trying to smile brightly, and I'd promised. Shoes cleaned, and in a plastic bag so as not to soil the clothes. Money – what there was – shifted into the new navy suit. Shirt. Sober tie, monogrammed imaginatively but with careful ambiguity. Cuff-links. Surprisingly, as I flopped on the lavatory pan to lace my shoes, a note on a stolen card. It read, 'Good luck, darling *cretino*,' and was signed with three cross-kisses. The card was for a silver wedding. I had to smile, even the shaky state I was in. Obviously she'd had difficulty finding a card with an appropriate good-luck-nicking-the-Pontiff's-antique motto.

I stood with the customary stiffness of a man in a strange new suit, and checked over the discards. Items into the briefcase, one by one. A moment's stillness. A quick listen. Deep breaths for control. Hundred-lire coin in my right jacket pocket for the women attendants, a tug on the handle to flush the loo – I'd tried to squeeze out a drop but every sphincter I possessed was on the gripe – and out, walking with purpose.

One old man leaving, tapping his stick. Two German youths combing hair and talking loudly, about to depart. And Carlo, nodding and winking and chewing gum and rolling a cowboy's cigarette one-handed, doing it all wrong. Sweating worse than ever, I ignored him and went to wash my hands.

From the handbasins the women attendants were talking just out of sight. I ran the water, peering through the mirror towards the entrance. The German lads left, still talking. The old geezer was gone. All the cubicle doors were open. Nobody.

I pulled a third-bottle out of my pocket and swiftly unscrewed the cap. 'Carlo.'

'Yeah, boss?' He slid over, gum-chewing and

shoulder-hunching. His hand was thrust deep into his jacket pocket. He now sported a white trilby pulled down over one eye just to prove to the world's armies of Swiss Guards that he really was a genuine hundred-percent gangster on the prod. With virtually uncontrollable hands I poured him a capful of the dark rum. No good doing things by halves. His eyes widened delightedly. No acting this time, I noticed wryly.

I whispered, 'Cheers, Carlo,' and tilted the bottle, my tongue in its neck to stop any leaking into my mouth. 'But you said—'

'Shhh! Old custom,' I told him, gasping to good effect as if stunned by the booze.

'To the death, Captain!' He swigged it back, the poor sod. His eyes bled tears and he gasped, 'A superb shot o' old red-eye!'

'Er, yes.' I screwed the cap on and slipped the bottle into the case. Still nobody. 'You have fifteen minutes, Carlo.'

'Sure, boss. Ready? Willco!'

The poor goon slunk out, hunching and glancing, his collar up. The two women rolled eyes to each other showing exasperation at the young. Carlo looked a right carnival, but he no longer mattered much – as long as he made the Museum cafeteria at speed.

Coin casually in the dish, and I was out into the warmth of St Peter's great square, a picture of the professional gentleman scanning the sights of Rome. There is no real short cut to the Vatican Museum doorway, so it meant making a brisk diagonal under the Colonnade, down the Angelica, round the Risorgimento and along. I was panicking in case there was a queue.

Seven minutes to reach the slope where I could see three coaches reversing into the slip by the Museum doorway. I lost all decorum as I hurried up the street to reach the entrance before the scores of Dutchmen poured out, and only slowing down once I was certain I would be ahead of them.

An elderly lady sold me some violets from the low wall near the entrance. I paid, leaving my briefcase to be swiftly covered by her shawl. Anna squeezed my hand as she gave me the change. While buying my ticket I realized she had short-changed me by five hundred lire, but that was only her joke. Anyway, I was almost smiling as I made my way up that spectacular staircase. Three violets were our signal that Carlo had made it ahead of me by three minutes. A rose would have been the signal to abort, that Carlo had failed to show.

Anna had said you couldn't reach the cafeteria from the Museum entrance in less than four minutes. I had argued and argued but she'd remained adamant, and now I was glad she'd been so stubborn. The small corridors between the decorated chapels were crammed with schoolchildren. Teachers herded classes to and fro. I blundered among them in a lather, trying to keep up a steady count in my mind so I could keep on schedule, but finding to my horror I was starting over and over again at one, two, three . . .

Worse, the bloody cafeteria was bulging though its self-service line was moving forwards fairly quickly. I looked anxiously for Carlo. He was near the front, almost at the till by now and sandwiched between two strapping blondes. Apart from Carlo, I was the only person there not in jeans and tee shirt. If I'd known I wouldn't have worried about looking exactly right. My spirits hardly rose, but at least they crept cautiously out of hiding an inch or two.

We shuffled forwards. I collared a couple of wrapped

sandwiches and moved with the rest, sliding my tray along the chromed rails. Carlo carried his tray to a newly-cleared table by the picture windows which overlooked the garden terrace. He sat and immediately started wolfing his cream cakes.

'Move along, please.'

'Er, sorry.' The worrying thing was Carlo had three glasses of wine, not one. The two blondes were watching him with conspicuous amusement from a table across the aisle. Yoghurt-and-soup queens. Mercifully he was too busy stuffing his face to respond to them. I shuffled on, nervously paid up and tried to get a seat facing Carlo but a sprinting Aussie beat me to it, so I started on my sandwiches with my ears exquisitely tuned, listening for sudden activity at Carlo's table behind me two aisles away. Old Anna came through the cafeteria, on the cadge. She plumped opposite me, doing her exhaustion bit and openly nicking one of my sandwiches. I chuckled affably to show my good-humoured acceptance of the old dear, especially when I felt my heavy briefcase slide on to my feet. Idly I checked that everybody was too preoccupied to notice, and edged it beneath my chair. Anna gave me a roguish wink and departed, chewing gummily on my sandwich. By now I trusted her enough to know my briefcase would be emblazoned by a Department of Health sticker. But that Carlo . . .

Ten minutes later I was beginning to wonder if I'd poisoned him all wrong. There was no sound other than the usual cafeteria din. He must have had a stomach like a dustbin liner because at least a third of the rum which I'd given him was a mixture of jalap and colocynth, the most drastic purgatives known to the old nineteenth-century doctors – and they were experts in drastic purgatives, if nothing else.

It happened just as I was about to chuck it in and abort the whole thing. A chair crashed over behind me. Somebody exclaimed in alarm. Casually, I glanced round in time to see Carlo streak through the doorway into the loo across the other side of the cafeteria.

The eddies created by Carlo's passage had not stilled when I moved purposefully among the tables and into the men's loo. Ominous noises came from one of the cubicles. A worried man was hastening out.

'I think somebody's ill in there,' he said. 'You think I should go for help?'

'I'm a doctor,' I said calmly in the best American accent my Italian could stand. 'Wait until I see . . .'

'Oooh. Lovejoy—' Carlo's voice moaned from the cubicle as I glanced in. I could have murdered the fool, giving out my name, except I was worried that maybe I had. He sounded in a terrible state.

'That must be his name,' I pronounced glibly to the man. 'Signor. I want you to stand just inside this entrance. Let nobody in. I don't like the look of him.'

'Yes, *Dottore*.'

'Don't you worry, Signor Lovejoy,' I called loudly to Carlo in the poisonously brisk voice. 'I'll have you safely in hospital in no time at all.'

I strode purposefully out into the cafeteria and headed round the queue of people at the paypoint. I had the full attention of the customers. A lady emerged from behind the line of servers. She wore the harrowed look of a superior longing for obscurity.

'Good day, Signora . . . Manageress? I'm Doctor Valentine.'

Her eyes widened. 'Is anything wrong? She'd glimpsed the sticker on my briefcase.

'Have you an office, please?'

'There's nothing wrong, is there?' she pleaded over her shoulder, leading the way behind the terrace of stainless steel and bright cookers.

'Nothing that cannot be efficiently handled, signora.' I kept my Americanese variation of Italian going. 'A man's been taken ill after eating your cream cakes—'

'They are perfectly fresh—'

'Of course. I know that.' I smiled bleakly to keep some threat in the words. She trotted ahead into a neat pastel-blue office. Her name was on the door stamped in white on brown plastic. Signora Faranada was a pretty thing, understandably distrait but the most attractive manageress I'd yet seen in the whole Vatican. If I hadn't been terrified out of my wits I'd have chatted her up. She pulled the door to. 'Signora,' I said, instantly becoming terse. 'He is very sick. It looks like Petulengro's.'

'Petulengro's? A *disease*?'

I reached for the telephone, laconic and casual the way doctors always are when putting the boot into suffering innocents. 'You've heard of Legionnaires'? Similar thing.'

'Legionnaires' Disease?' she moaned. 'Oh my *God*! But—'

'Nothing that can't be handled quietly and efficiently,' I reassured with my wintry smile. 'You're lucky. I was just calling on you – courtesy visit. I'm from Communicable Diseases, Atlanta, USA. Currently with World Health, on loan to the Rome Ministry. Here.' I passed her the receiver as if disgusted with the slowness. 'Get me an outside line.'

She frantically spun the dial.

'The Vatican has its own children's clinic and physicians. Am I right?'

'Yes, Doctor.'

Impatiently I dialled the number as if I knew it by heart, reading it off Anna's postage stamp I had stuck to my left wrist. 'But no resident epidemiologist expert in communicable diseases, right?' I barked the question, the old lawyer's tricks of two knowns followed by an unknown, all to be answered with the same word.

She hesitated. 'I don't think so, Doctor—'

I turned away impatiently. Valerio came on the other end. A sweat of relief started to trickle down my collar. 'Doctor Valentine. Get me the epidemic section – fast.'

'Epidemic!' moaned Signora Faranda.

'Hello?' I made a conciliatory gesture to the lady as I spoke commandingly into the phone. 'Hello, Aldo? Great! There's a rather problematic issue here – Vatican Museum. Cafeteria. Looks like a case of Petulengro's . . . No. Only one, a man. I've got him under control in the toilets . . . Of *course* I applied emergency treatment, brought him round . . . No. The place looks really superbly clean . . .'

'We scour and disinfect every half-day,' Signora Faranada bleated, tugging my sleeve.

'Sure, Aldo.' I laughed reassuringly, the expert all casual in the presence of somebody else's catastrophe. 'No, I agree. We can't take chances . . . Look, Aldo. Can I leave it to you to . . . ? Fine . . . No, no sirens. Quietly does it . . . The least noise the better. No sense in being alarmist . . .' I smiled and nodded at Signora Faranda. 'So you'll send an ambulance . . . ? Good . . . No. I'm sure the manageress can handle that . . . Agreed?'

I slammed down the phone.

'I'll get back to take charge,' I told the lady. 'I've arranged hospital transport.' I stilled her protests with a raised hand. 'Infectious diseases are always sent to a special unit because they are, erm, infectious.' I smiled a cut-rate Arcellano smile. 'You know how patients just love to sue places these days, I don't doubt.'

'Sue?' she gasped, the poor thing.

'It won't come to that,' I said smoothly. 'I promise.'

'What must I do?'

'Do you have a rear entrance to the cafeteria, where the ambulance can pull up?' She nodded anxiously and reached towards the top filing drawer. 'The gate will need notifying,' I said, ticking off the items. 'Aldo – that's Doctor Cattin of the Public Health Division – said St Anne's Gate. Is that acceptable?'

'Yes, yes. I'll telephone—' She clutched feverishly for the phone.

'And the table. It may be contaminated. For taking specimens, and disinfection.'

'I'll see it's brought round—'

I snapped, 'Tell everyone it's in need of repair, wobbling or something. Use your discretion.'

'Yes, yes. Discretion,' she gasped, dialling frantically.

'Get your duty security man. I'll need that terrace quietly sealed from the public. It overlooks the drive-in, correct?'

'Yes! Yes! I'll get him right away—'

'Do you have a store room?'

She was gasping. 'Yes. By the loading bay.'

'Good. And I'll seal the lavatory cubicle until it's proven clear. Don't worry.' I rounded on her like I'd seen on the movies. 'Do as I say and people'll hardly notice. You have a beautiful clean restaurant here. We don't want to attract attention—'

'Thank you, Doctor!'

She was in a worse state than I was when I left and strode commandingly through the cafeteria. I cautioned

Carlo's relieved custodian to silence and thanked him for waiting. Carlo looked so bad I grew really frightened but there was nothing I could do.

The duty security officer was a stout Turin chap with the intriguing name of Russomanno. He was delighted at the whole thing and determined to be pompous, thank God, and proudly showed me the tiny loading bay. Signora Faranada wanted instructions so I told her to parcel up Carlo's table and the utensils he had used in sealed plastic. She dashed off up the steps.

I glanced about. There were occasional faces peering from the Vatican Museum windows overlooking the tiny roadway and the loading bay, but with an ambulance backed in all sight of the loading steps leading into the rear of the cafeteria would be blocked off. From the other side walkers on the upper terrace could see over.

'I wanted that terrace cleared,' I said tersely.

'It's entrance will be closed immediately, *Dottore.*'

An ambulance was trundling slowly down the narrow thoroughfare. Time the security man went. 'You'll have the numbers of diners checked, of course?'

'Of course, Doctor.' He looked quite blank.

I smiled, nodding. 'Forgive me. I forgot I was dealing with a professional. Rest assured my team will be discreet and swift.'

The stout man puffed up the steps as Valerio reversed the ambulance – a full-blown, genuine ambulance – smoothly up to the loading bay. Patrizio sported a moustache, to my alarm. Did ambulance men wear them? Both he and Valerio wore some kind of dark blue uniform. Valerio's peaked cap bore an impressive but anonymous badge.

We had one nasty moment when I couldn't yank the

door of the store room open, but Patrizio's hand gently pushed me aside and turned the handle.

'The table, Lovejoy.'

My work of art – still apparently nothing more than ordinary steel-and-formica cafeteria furniture, though with a thicker top than usual – was wedged between the two stretcher slots. I stood on the steps ready to use delaying tactics should the manageress come fluttering down to do some ground-level panicking. Valerio and Patrizio carried my table into the store. I mopped my forehead.

'Let's go. Bring the stretcher.'

Eight minutes later Carlo was inside the ambulance with Captain Russomanno standing proudly on the running board. Poor Carlo was ashen and almost comatose. Anna would go for me if I'd really killed him. With him went the table at which he had been sitting, his plates and drinking glasses.

I trudged upstairs, nodding confidentially towards the worried Signora Faranada to show everything was in hand. 'I'll seal off that one toilet cubicle,' I said in an undertone. 'It might be contaminated. The rest of the loo can be used with safety. Then I'll slip out. I'll return tomorrow. Just tell your staff to continue as normal.'

'Very well. Doctor, I am so grateful—'

I smiled nobly, wishing there was more time for this sort of thing. She was lovely.

'Only my job, signora,' I said, smiling. 'If only I met such charming people every day . . .'

The cafeteria was full as ever. I melted among the crowd and made my way over to the loos. Inside my grand case I had tape labelled 'Hygiene. Sealed by Order' to seal the cubicle.

And in the sealed cubicle would be me, sitting silently waiting for the closing hour. The ambulance by now would be rolling into the Via Porta Angelica.

For the rest of my team the rip was practically over. For me it had only just begun.

Chapter 23

I sat in the loo, that powerful creative location, thinking and listening.

Sealing the outside of the cubicle door with that impressively worded sticky tape had been a simple matter. I had written 'Out of Order' on a piece of cafeteria notepaper and stuck it to the door then climbed inelegantly over and dropped inside. There was enough of a hubbub in the cafeteria to convince me the manageress would assume I'd slipped out as I'd promised. Now, short of some nosey-parker peering in, I was safe.

People came and went in gusts of noise from the cafeteria. I heard all the languages under the sun. I learned a dozen new jokes, but only one was even vaguely amusing and anyway I always forget the endings. There was a two-inch gap under the cubicle door, so at the faintest sound of approaching customers I sat with my knees hunched and toolbag on my lap, just in case. Once I actually dozed, probably reaction to the state of abject terror in which I'd lived all day.

Somebody wiser than me – or even more scared – once said hell was other people, or something. Sitting in the foetal position there on one of His Holiness's loos was the loneliest place I'd ever been in my life. I'd have loved to go out for a minute, just for a cup of coffee, with normal happy people all around and noise and light reassuring me that everything was as it should be. But there was no chance of that. While blokes came and peed and chatted and were replaced by others I sat miserably on, convinced it was the end of the world. Hell, I couldn't even have a pee myself in case of noise.

The trouble was Arcellano. Even though I was tormented by visions of Adriana worrying herself sick about my sudden absence it was Arcellano's vicious face which kept recurring. Throughout those long moments, while I waited for the Vatican City to quieten, the evil that was Arcellano seemed to dominate my mind whichever way it turned. What maddened me was how little choice poor old Lovejoy had in all this. There just no way round the bastards of this world. If they conscript you into their army, you're a draftee for life.

Unless . . .

Sitting there in utmost privacy, I gulped audibly and shook my head. None of that. No sinister thoughts of revenge, no creeping desires to fight back as savagely as Arcellano himself, because I'm a peaceable bloke at heart. I've always believed (and I really do mean it) that *Homo sapiens* is a higher being, noble and even God-like in his innate purity and benevolence. Okay. Occasionally you do come up against evil. When that happens the natural inclination is to grab the biggest howitzer you can find and let fly, but that's all wrong. Maybe it was the gentle atmosphere which was getting to me, but there in the loo I vowed fair play for Arcellano. I nearly moved myself to tears. Maria would love me for it. Anna would lash me up a lovely unhealthy breakfast of polysaturated fats for it. And Adriana would forgive me everything for it. Noble and even God-like in my innate purity and benevolence, I dreamed on about my final confrontation with Arcellano and his pair of psychopathic killers. I would be smiling, persuasive, kind.

But as I sat on, hunched and fretting and dozing, some little gremlin in my head kept sniggering and saying, I'll be frigging kind all right. You see if I'm not.

As long as my homemade winch was strong enough.

Eventually the cafeteria noise settled to a steady muffled banging as the servers gave the counters an end-of-day scouring. It was poisonously familiar. I'd dishwashed often enough to recognize that sound anywhere. Twenty minutes later some heavy-footed bloke stopped by the loo, presumably the security, banging the doors of the other cubicles back and giving my door an experimental rap. I heard him spinning the stopcock on the ascending water main, obviously a security man of the most careful and pestilential kind. His footfalls receded and the outer door went again.

I listened to my sanctum's silence, holding my breath as I did so. Presumably I was now alone and the whole loo empty. Just in case I counted slowly to a hundred and listened again. Nothing. I did another hundred. Nothing, not a sound.

You feel better with your feet on the floor instead of dangling. I lowered them carefully, put my briefcase down and slowly stretched. A quick peer underneath the door made me feel even better – no nasty boots waiting motionless for poor unsuspecting intruders to emerge whistling. I was alone.

Nobody's had more practice than me at being scared witless. The trouble is, every time's the worst. With the caution born of a lifetime's cowardice, I gauged the time. Anna said the security shift of eight officers signed on at seven o'clock. The international football came on the television at half-eight, a live screening from West Germany which meant two untroubled spells of forty-five minutes, briefly intersected by that worrisome fifteen-minute interval. Some conscientious nuisance could trot out of the telly room for a quick listen for burglars in that gap. I couldn't repress a surge of irritation at weak-kneed footballers actually needing a rest between halves. Soft sods. When I was a kid we simply switched ends and carried on. You get no help when you need it.

I'd planned a couple of hours' calm reflection at this point, but being calm doesn't work for some blokes and I'm one of them. I just can't see the point of serenity. My inner peace lasted three minutes. After that I sat and sweated.

Anna had assured me that the Vatican Secret Police were mythical. There's no such body. Security guards, yes. Secret cloak-and-dagger artists, no. I'd believed her. Alone in the gathering gloom, I wasn't so convinced.

In fact I was shaking as I peered into the deserted cafeteria. Empty places are really weird. Not bad in themselves, but you're used to seeing them filled with people, aren't you.

The cafeteria was spotless, shining and neat. And silent. Long curtains were drawn across the long curved picture windows. Through them a weak light diffused, presumably the floodlights which played along the Stradone di Giardini, the low road which runs straight as a die between the four-hundred-metre stretch of the Museum and the Vatican gardens. The central security possessed eighty closed-circuit TV monitors arranged in banks five screens high before a control console. They needed light. I *had* to trust Anna's map of the security electronics.

Slowly I stepped out into the cafeteria, feeling curiously exposed though I made no noise, almost as if I were performing on a stage with some vast silent audience watching my every move. Absurd.

The downstairs store room was locked, which meant an irritating ten-second delay while I pressed my plastic comb through the crack. A quick lick to stick my suction-pad coat-hook on the door, a series of rapid push-and-pull motions, and the lock snicked back. The delay was minuscule but worrying. That it was locked meant some bloody guard was doing his stuff, and that was bad news. I wanted them all cheering and booing in that staff telly room between the Museo Paolino and the Sala Rotunda.

No windows in the store room, thank God. I locked the door, took the thin towel from my toolbag, rolled it into a sausage and wedged it along the door's base to prevent light leaks. My krypton bulb beamed round the room. Two spare batteries weighing a ton were the heaviest items in my toolbag, nearly, but I couldn't risk working blind for a single second. They'd be worth the effort before the night was out. A rectangular black cloth to hold the tools, a swift unpacking, jacket on the floor and I was off.

My cafeteria table on which I'd laboured so much was the same as all the rest, except that its top was thicker, and an X-shaped strut reinforced the tubular steel legs. A security man might pass it over at a glance as an average modern nosh bar table. To me it meant ripping the Vatican.

I inverted the table and levered off the gruesome shiny edging strips. The main section I wanted was held on the underside by eight mirror brackets with their flat-headed screws. For one frightening second I thought

I'd forgotten my favourite screwdriver, but I'm always like that when I've a job on. It was there all the time, beside the hand drill. The wooden section was only a series of oblique triangles. To fold a polygonal surface you can only hinge it along three lines. (Experienced forgers will already know this. You beginners can work it out.) I'd done this by linen hinges, for flatness, and now I unfolded the wood. It was a lovely Andaman surface. Some call it 'Padouk' wood, a rich rosewood-like Burmese wood which has been with us since the eighteenth century. Now I took my prepared rectangular blocks and made a quick swirl of the resin adhesives. I hate these modern synthetics, but a lovely old-fashioned smelly gluepot was a wistful dream in these crummy circumstances. I laid the inverted polygonal disc on the floor and glued the little blocks across the linen hinges, which had now served their purpose. In thirty minutes the disc would be rigid, and would become the 'Chippendale' rent table's top.

Meanwhile I unplugged the tips of the four hollow legs and from two drew out the slender steel rods carefully packed inside. The tissue paper could stay in, to save telltale mess. From the other two legs I shook out a dozen pieces of quartered wooden dowelling. The glued blocks had holes to take the rods which slipped in easily, to my relief, though I'd rehearsed this a million times. The polygonal rent-table top was now reinforced.

The cafeteria table's steel legs themselves and my added cross-strut came apart once the screws and clasps were undone, which only shows what modern rubbish stuff is nowadays. I had long ago dissected away the thin formica layer back in Adriana's workshop. Now I simply pulled it off and leaned it against the wall behind some stacked chairs.

That gave me the cafeteria table's rectangular chip-board top. One of my most difficult pieces of work had been cutting the rectangle into four so that it could become an elongated cube. The tubular steel legs would hold it rigid enough to carry practically any weight. They already had screwholes, made three days ago with a noisy electric drill. I'd veneered the exterior, of course, but the travelling had done it no good and I wasted time worrying about the shine. Anyway, the top central spot would be covered by that monstrous case of stuffed doves. The pedestal's lock keyhole was phoney but looked good.

The real rent table upstairs had a base plinth as deep as the drawers – always a good sign in an antique of this kind, because the plinths got deeper as fashions changed. the narrower the plinth, the earlier your antique. This place of honour was reserved for the last bit of chipboard which I screwed along the base. It was only stained African white wood and the colour was too dark compared with the thing upstairs, but it was the best I could do.

The metal X-shaped strut I placed across the centre of the polygon. By now the adhesive was setting well. I turned the huge wooden polygon the right way up and screwed it to the strut through the six holes I'd sten-cilled there. Solid and lovely.

Sweating badly in that confined airless room, I found my jacket and carefully removed the six tiny circles of Andaman veneer from the top pocket. I'd pencilled a number on the underside of each to show which screw-hole it came from. A touch of synthetic glue, and the shiny screws were covered precisely by the matching veneer.

I was having to hurry now. The false drawer fronts

were the weak spots. If people fingered underneath the edge of my table, nosey sods, they would realize the game instantly, because there'd be only a sharp edge instead of a lovely smooth underface. I'd have to risk that. Once the rip was over they could laugh their heads off at my folding copy – because a million miles off I'd be laughing too.

The drawer fronts had come fitted easily between the undersurface of the cafeteria table's top and the folded polygonal section, being only veneered three-ply. My pieces of quartered dowelling rods came in handy now to hold the drawer façades completely rigid. It had to be glue, though my heart ached for a small brass hammer and a supply of fixing pins. I hate doing a job by halves.

So, in total silence, I completed the table margin with rotten modern adhesives and stood the polygonal top on its façade of drawers to set firm.

Looking at it, I was quite proud. It looked really great, even in the harsh beam of a krypton torch. Once the gleaming top was plonked on the pedestal it would be indistinguishable from the real thing, unless you looked underneath or pulled it to bits. The only good thing you could say about it was that it was twice as sound as the jerry-built modern crap they sell nowadays.

I must have taken about an hour. I was on schedule. Time.

Chapter 24

The Vatican places great faith – charmingly quaint, really – in the reliability of mankind. As I say, it takes all sorts. There are the pilot lights at each of the corridor inter-sections, set high by each of the main doorways. They indicate the security time clocks where the patrolling guards clock in. No hidden infra-red sensitor beams, unless you include the sets indiscreetly built into the walls near the Viale Vaticano entrance and between the Cappella Sistina and St Peter's itself. You mustn't know about them because they're secret. And the secret cam-eras which connect with the screen-outs in the security room which I mentioned can be seen quite clearly from the galleries They're not quite archaic, but striving hard for obsolescence. They're about as secret as Mount Palomar. Anna had mapped out the camera blind spots, and I had them by heart. Anna had reported that there were more magic rays to trap unwary burglars at St Anne's Gate. Big deal. That's the trouble with museums. They're crazy about entrances.

Nervous as a cat, I locked the store-room door with a horrible loud click and walked in silence up the stairs to Signora Faranada's office. There were two risks: a wandering guard, and some unexpectedly simple alarm system like a bell on a door.

The office door came apart at a waggle of my comb. The top filing-cabinet drawer was locked, but they all have that fatal flaw of a spring-loaded catch, and old Joe Bramah showed civilization the way round that in the 1880s, so I hardly paused. The box inside was unlocked, and held the set of master keys the manageress had used earlier in the day. I was worried about the light from my pencil-torch and did all I could to shield it. The trouble was, I was going into places where windows would be a constant risk. The Vatican has more windows than a mill.

Outside the signora's office a narrow corridor ran about ten yards to end at a door. The fourth key worked. With my hand clutching the rest of the bunch to avoid jingling, I turned the lock. My stupid heart was banging loud enough to wake the dead as I pulled the door open and waited a second for the alarms and sirens to sound off. Dead silence. A brief dizziness swirled in me. God knows how long I'd held my breath. Unsteadily I clung to the door a moment to recover and had to close my eyes for about a fortnight until the nausea passed.

I stepped out nervously. I knew where I was. To understand the layout of the Vatican Museum you have to think of a huge letter H, except that now with the new wing it has a double crosspiece with the great library between the two struts. From Anna's drawings I was somewhere underneath the Paoline Room and the Biblioteca. One floor up and across, and I would be in my favourite gallery beside my least favourite museum showpiece. To the right and along.

Stairs are the ultimate risk. You can peer down a corridor, count doors, watch for shadows at the far end. But staircases are a swine because you can't see who's having a crafty smoke in cupboardy alcoves beneath.

I reached the top stair on hands and knees. I squirmed flat and squinted at right angles down the long gallery. The ranged series of long rectangular windows, the slanting shadows from the outside lights in the grounds, all there in frozen gloom. And no glow of a cigarette.

Opposite the faint white blobs of the odious stuffed doves the shadows thickened. That would be the blue-and-gold double cupboards, full of stored early Christian figurines. Happily, ancient cupboards with natty antique locks. They sound and look impregnable, but believe it or not they were my one stroke of luck.

I eeled out into the main chamber a yard or two. Not much light from the Stradone. Mercifully no curtains at the long gallery's windows, not since that time ten Popes ago when His Holiness had done his nut and the drapery was retired in disgrace, which served them right for mixing maroon and blue. Nothing moved. Better still, it *felt* right. Silence everywhere and that precious feeling of loneness. The football was probably midway through the second half by now, maybe twenty minutes before the security round. Yet . . . there was something wrong. Nothing to stop me, but definitely a wrong vibe somewhere. Still, no time now for imagination.

I got up and practically sprinted back the way I had come, flitting along the camera blind lines, snicking past Signora Faranada's office and through the cafeteria. I reached the storeroom excited and a little breathless, but it felt good. Really great. Except . . . again there was something vaguely wrong, but I couldn't put my finger on it. The rip was on. Scramble, Lovejoy, and worry about vibes when celebrating afterwards.

Inside my bag were two slender coils of silk rope. It costs a fortune – at least, it would have if Anna hadn't nicked it. Both were exactly the right length. The longer one stretched double, over and under my great polygonal table top so it lay on my shoulders like a set of clumsy wings. A top loop to put round my forehead, Indian style, leaving my hands free, and my pedestal easily carried by the smaller length of rope slung over my shoulder. Clumsy, but with care not to bump I could do it. My toolbag I looped on my wrist.

Creeping along in the semi-dark hunched under my table-top like a tortoise, pausing for breath at corners and manoeuvring my pieces slowly round them, I switched between panic and exasperation. Shuffling along the gallery towards those pale blurs, I was pouring sweat and burning at the unfairness of it all.

It took about ten minutes and seemed a month. Close to, the stupid white birds' glass case was a good landmark. Wheezing with the strain, I lowered the pedestal and then slipped the table top off my back. The relief made my head swim and I had to shift, and fast. My bag of tools.

Looking along the gallery to check, I slid across to the cupboards which stand on the Stradone side of the chamber. There are six double ones, each about six feet wide, though other galleries have as many as twelve. Two minutes to pick the lock and I creaked one cupboard door open.

'Jesus,' I muttered. My pencil torch revealed scores of small terracotta figurines staring back at me. Lovely and nearly priceless, but in the circumstances a real bloody nuisance. Feverishly I began lifting them haphazardly from the middle shelf and stowing them on the other shelves. God knows how long it had taken the curators to arrange them. I thrust them anywhere, scooping their labels up and rammed them towards the back of the lowest shelf. That feeling of sickly confidence had evaporated in my sweat. Now this whole dig felt bad and that depressing sense of wrongness enveloped me, but I'd no idea why. I began to feel I was being watched from somewhere further down the long silent chamber, which was impossible. I knew that. But I was starting to shake. Maybe it was all those unnerving terracotta eyes.

My sense of time deserted me. I don't know how long it took to clear the middle shelf, six long feet of valuable early Christian figurines. I'd been quite prepared to saw out any middle divider to give me room to lie down, but the cupboards are without vertical divisions, as sensible cupboards ought to be. I hate those modern coffin shapes they call cupboards nowadays.

By the time I'd cleared the shelf I was close to babbling with fear, feeling invisible avenging angels closing ominously about me. Without looking about, I slid across to that glass-cased monstrosity and lifted it clumsily to the floor. There was a nasty moment when my foot entangled itself in my carrying ropes. I rammed the two lengths into my toolbag out of the way and carried my pedestal over to the cleared shelf. End on and pushed to the shelf's extremity, it still gave me room to lie down – as long as my feet were stuffed down the hollow pedestal's interior.

I made myself stare down the gallery. No sign of movement. My confidence began to creep back when something intruded into my consciousness. In the distance I could hear motor-horns in regular cacophony. For one horrible second they suggested police sirens. My mouth went dry from fright till I recognized it. *Dah-dahdadadadadadada-dah-dah*. The universal rhythm of the soccer fan's applause. I turned to jelly. This was it. The televised match from West Germany must be over, and jubilant fans were parading Rome on their way to a celebratory beer-up. Lucky I'd heard the racket, but how long had it been going on? Was *that* what felt so wrong? No chance of calm now. My worksheet to protect Arcellano's rent table, then three wobbly goes to lift my phoney antique table top on top. My measurements were too generous if anything. I'd allowed three extra inches, which turned out plenty. A little sliding adjustment of my phoney top, and I could replace that glass case of doves. In a sweat of relief I stepped back. Done. Only an expert would realise that the precious table had widened slightly. There was no other visible difference. I was supremely confident of my veneer. I'd sold worse to experts.

Lying down on a shelf is harder than it sounds. Why I'd chosen the middle shelf when the lowest one was so much more logical I don't know. I was mad with myself. Probably some daft idea of peering through the lock to see the security guards pass. Even that was lunatic, because I'd have needed an eye in my bellybutton. Stupid, stupid. I was in a hell of a state by the time I'd slotted myself along the shelf, breathless and tired. The toolbag fitted in the crook of my knees. I lifted the pedestal up and shoved my feet down inside it. A blue cotton thread from my pocket, wetted and threaded through the keyhole, enabled me to pull the door gently to.

And there I was, safely shelved among the precious early Christian figurines. The important thing now was not to nod off and start snoring. I'd never felt so knackered in my life, but it was going perfectly.

Which raised the important question of why it felt so frigging *wrong*.

The security guards came an hour later.

I'd dozed fitfully, jerking awake and imagining a

million noises. The cupboard was unbearably stuffy. I'd allowed for a mere fifteen minutes on the shelf. The temptation recurred to open the door briefly for air but I never change a winning team. And by all possible estimates I was undoubtedly winning. I'd made my replica. I'd smuggled it into the Vatican. I'd fiddled myself in. I'd left no traces. Not a fingerprint, not a mark. All I needed now was for the security guards to hurtle past, leaving me five precious uninterrupted minutes to somehow lower the true antique down to the Stradone. Heavy as it was, from there I would simply carry it across to the loading bay steps and conceal it in the storeroom among the cafeteria tables. I hadn't quite worked this bit out, trusting to Patrizio to pull a switch with the ambulance again, but you can't think of everything. And the security blokes knew their cafeteria table was due to be returned once it was proved contamination free.

There were two of them, talking in undertones about the big match. Two-one, apparently. A last-minute decider after untold agonies, the opposition as unsportsmanlike as ever. The usual crap.

Luckily they were disagreeing about the team choice, a famous Milan striker having been dropped – unaccountable stupidity or the wisdom of ages, depending on your viewpoint. They passed, muttering arguments. I was worried because their shoes hardly made a sound on the luscious antique flooring, which proves how basically unpleasant these security people actually are. There's no cause for suspicion that bad.

I listened them out of earshot. Anna maintained they went one way first, then retraced the route at the next circuit. We'd argued time and time again over this. I kept telling her it was too good to be true. She called me a cretin. Twice I'd done the entire circuit myself, among tourists. Pausing a full minute at the position of each time-clock and walking at security guard pace, the whole route took forty-six minutes dead. I waited at least that long in the confined space, horizontal and running sweat. Inevitably their meal would come between circuits.

It took longer to climb out of the cupboard than it had getting in. My legs were stiff as hell. Grunting at the effort I had to re-educate my muscles before I could even put my foot down. I practically whined with pain as pins-and-needles tingled up my legs. The feeling had never got that high before.

I lifted my pedestal out, having the wit to recover my blue cotton thread and leaving the cupboard door unlocked in case I suddenly needed to hide. No sign of lurking guards. I was about to start across the gallery to assemble my phoney 'antique' when I froze. I knew what was wrong. In fact, *I'd known all along*. Only my abject terror had prevented me from appreciating the unpleasant truth.

I slipped across the gallery and reached underneath to touch the wood of the precious piece of Chippendale. Not a single chime of ecstasy. I tried again. And again. Arcellano's genuine antique table now wasn't.

Being a divvie's not as easy as it sounds. It's hard work. Okay, so you *know* without understanding how it is you know. You're absolutely certain that Grandad's old clock is a genuine Jerome, and not a modern copy. You know you are one hundred per cent right, that the rough old timepiece is actually made by that great Yank whose shelf-clocks popularized brass (instead of wooden) movements and whose clocks are now worth a fortune. (Tip: look for Jeromes in East Anglia. It's where genuine examples are commonest found. God knows why.) But all this inner certainty only helps as long as you *let* it. You can stay an ignoramus, if you're determined. It takes hard work to learn who's making today's best Jerome forgeries, and how many genuine pieces Jerome himself exported from Bristol, Connecticut, to England between 1821 and 1860, and memorize information on his contemporary rivals. You can be an ignorant divvie, and I should know. In that terrible moment nobody was more of an ignoramus than me. I'd been fooled.

I'd been sent to nick a bloody dud.

I felt my face drain of blood. I stood there like a fool, holding my useless bag of tools and licking my lips, looking about for a trillion Vatican Guards to spring out of the shadows and nail me. A frame. A set-up. Hunted. I was hunted. In an instant I was transformed from a clever supercool burglar about to pull off the greatest rip of all time to a nerk who'd been had.

In a sudden panic I began slipping down the gallery towards the marble staircase. And just as abruptly paused. A good steady listen into the dark silence. Nothing. A quick kneel to press an ear to the flooring. Nothing. I sat back on my heels, thinking quickly.

Whether the Museum's 'antique' was valuable or not, I hadn't been rumbled. At least, not yet – and not by the guards. There might still be a score of police waiting outside to nab me, but the fact remained I was still in the Vatican without a single clamouring alarm bell. A memory came – of a day, among crowds of sprinting tourist groups, I'd stood in this very gallery before that 'antique' and been stunned by the clamour and radiance emitted by the loveliest pristine *genuine* Chippendale I'd ever seen in my life.

Which meant someone else had already done what I'd intended, nicked the genuine item and substituted a dud. In the antiques game we call it 'doing a lady', after the card game of dummying queens. For maybe another minute I remained there, trying to flog my poor old tired cortex into action.

How long had I got? Say an hour for their break, plus five minutes for starting the reverse circuit. Sixty-five minutes. Take away twenty minutes for shifting the phoney table. Say forty, forty-five at the outside. I managed a swallow. I'd need luck, and every ounce of skill I possessed. I flitted silently back towards those gruesome doves, undoing the toolbag as I went, with cold murder in my heart.

Chapter 25

I woke with a muffled squeal of terror, instantly stifled by the even greater fright which swamped me as I realized where I was. I'd fallen off the lavatory, knocking my head against the wall. The clatter of trays and the sound of vacuum-cleaners close by was almost deafening. How long had they been on the go, for heaven's sake? A trace of blood from my chin worried me for a second. Then I remembered. I was in the Vatican Museum cafeteria's loo, for the moment safely ensconced in a cubicle, sealed. I'd pulled off the rip, but the Museum's Chippendale was a fraud.

Blearily I remembered I had shaved in the early hours according to plan by means of the disposable mini-razor. Blisters wept painfully on my right palm where I'd gouged and slaved to dismember Arcellano's supposedly precious antique Chippendale in the long gallery. Sitting on the loo I smiled at the memory, weak with relief. I'd never been so vicious with any piece of furniture before, modern or otherwise. With a complete disregard for the ridiculous copy that his supposed Chippendale was, I'd unscrewed what could be unscrewed and sawed what couldn't, using a fine-gauge metal saw for stealth. Three times – actually at the pedestal joins – I'd levered off the supporting brackets using my work-cloth to dampen the creaking as the modern toothplates lifted away, and then gathered the sawdust under the pedestal. My entire concern had been speed. Arcellano's 'antique' was a piece of crap, and I treated it accordingly. I'd gone to all this trouble to nick it, so I swore it would get duly nicked. But as for respecting it any longer . . . As far as I'm concerned, a bad forgery's the ultimate insult.

Leaving my own – much superior – mock-up proudly looking every inch a thoroughbred, I did two journeys with the disarticulated pieces of Arcellano's table. The top surface was heavy as hell, almost uncontrollable, waggling from side to side on my bowed back, and once I accidentally clouted it on the bannister with a loud echoing thump that made me freeze, despairing that I'd finally blown it. Nobody came and, in a state of collapse, I finally tottered into Signora Faranada's corridor almost unbelievingly. It took me almost half an hour to recover enough to get the pieces down into the storeroom.

For the rest of the night, way into the early hours, I slogged quietly in that airless room inhaling its stale cloying aroma and steadily whittling Arcellano's phoney but solid pieces into sections. I settled after a lot of sluggish thought to use two of the modern cafeteria tables, and simply sawed the 'Chippendale' into sections for screwing underneath one of the cafeteria jobs. That left the drawers and pedestal and a few angled pieces from the surface. These I arranged like bits of a child's jigsaw beneath a second table. I used the spare sheet of formica, which I'd earlier left in the room against the wall, to hold the pieces against the underside in a kind of concealed sandwich. The only odd thing was that the two tables both had formica surfaces top and bottom. I covered both with my one plastic sheet and reeled back to the safe haven of the loo.

I listened to the cafeteria kitchen preparing for the ten o'clock rush, gathering my resources for the last act. At ten past ten, as Signora Faranada's staff coped with the influx, I would make my way out of the cafeteria under cover of the queue. The two sedentary guards permanently stationed at the staircase leading to the Gallery of the Candelabras would be questioned at ten-fifteen by Dr Valentine in his grotesque American-accented Italian. He would be professional as ever – clean collar, new tie, smart briefcase – but would have missed his way while taking the cafeteria manageress a good report. Could the guard please phone ahead to announce his arrival . . . ?

Signora Faranada would of course be delighted. In the flush of victory, she'd be only too happy to arrange that Captain Russomanno issue a transit permit for her own table to be returned from the health laboratories. I could ask to use her phone to summon Valerio from my 'department'. Anything to get shut of me and the suggestion of contamination, to wind up the whole problem. And I would promise the fullest report to the tiny Vatican emergency clinic.

Wearily muttering my plans to myself for the last time, I smiled. I would promise her a special certificate, a clean bill of health, if not more. She had a lovely mouth.

At eleven-thirty that morning I walked wearily out of the Vatican Museum into the Viale Vaticano. It was straight ahead, across the road, down the street shops towards the market. My face felt white. My nape prickled and my hands were tingling. I could hardly move my legs for shaking.

There was a public phone in a store entrance on the Via Candia. I dialled, but not the number Arcellano had given me. I kept missing the hole from nerves. I cupped the mouthpiece and asked the Vatican City switchboard – nuns run it – for the boss priest in Security. They kept trying to give me a captain and I kept refusing, telling the switchboard it was a matter of life and death. I've always wanted to say that, but not in these circumstances. It took three feeds of the coin box. I had to trust somebody, for God's sake.

'Very well. I'll put you through.'

As the clicks went I wondered what the hell you call them. Monsignor? Sir?

'Hello?' a distinguished voice intoned gravely.

'Er, hello, ah, Reverend; I want to speak to the, er, bishop in charge of the Vatican City security.'

'Cardinal Arcellano speaking.'

I closed my eyes and put my forehead against the cool wall for a moment before asking him could he please repeat that.

Five minutes later, my mind numb from the shock, I made it across the Via Candia, turned right among the barrow stalls displaying shoes and leather goods. Immediately on the left is the best bar in Rome. I reeled in, went through to the back and sat.

The girl brought me a glass of white wine and a *cappuccino*.

'And one for that old lady,' I told her, nodding towards the far corner.

'*Grazie*, Signor,' old Anna wheezed.

'*Prego*, Signora,' I said back. It was our signal we'd pulled the rip.

I'd never seen tears in Anna's eyes before. Women always surprise me. But then so does everyone else.

That afternoon I did two things, bushed as I was. Anna and I became lovers, and I phoned Adriana. I realized at the time one thing was stupid and the other profoundly wise. To this day I don't know which was which.

Chapter 26

Piero came on the line. There was no time left for mucking about, so I owned it was Lovejoy wanting to speak to Adriana.

'Where are you? If you're still in Rome—'

'Sod off, lackey,' I said, bone weary. 'Get her.'

'Lovejoy?' Adriana sounded breathless, not as furious as I'd expected.

'It's me, love. Listen. I've been held up.'

'Darling. Are you all right? Do you need—?'

'Nothing. I'll contact you tomorrow. I have to see you.'

'Darling. Just tell me where and I'll come . . .'

There was more of this. In a daze I broke off and floated home to Anna's. Adriana was lovely in that spectacular Roman way I was coming to worship. And when she rose up so fragrantly to meet me swathed in the opulent creamy linen of her bedroom—

'You fucking swine!' Anna went at me, spitting and scratching.

'Eh?' I ducked among the furniture. 'What are you on about—?'

'You poisoned Carlo! *Cretino!* Assassin!'

Poisoned? I moaned. Don't say I'd got the dose wrong, not after all this. She raged after me. 'He's in hospital again!'

'Put that knife down, you old lunatic!'

I had to belt her before she would stop. She sobbed uncontrollably on the couch. I was so utterly tired, but credible lies were called for. My strong suit.

'It wasn't me, love,' I said. 'He'd had a whole pint of Scotch and threw up. I merely turned it to my advantage.'

'Is that true, Lovejoy?' she sniffed. With her aged make-up running uncontrollably she looked horrible.

'Honest,' I lied. 'Cross my heart and hope to – er, honest.'

'Poor Carlo.'

Well, quite. I argued persuasively, 'You know what he's like, Anna. By tomorrow he'll believe he pulled off the whole rip single-handed.'

'That's true.' She dabbed her face, making things twice as bad. 'Only . . . Lovejoy. If you didn't dose Carlo with that stuff, what was it for?'

'Last-minute varnish,' I lied. There was no answer to that. 'It's my secret,' I said as coldly as possible, to freeze her off. 'We're allies, Anna, but if I let on to you exactly how . . .'

The dear bird jumped to a woman's favourite conclusion in the pause and breathed, 'You are afraid that would be the end of our partnership?'

'Not really *afraid*,' I said nobly. In fact my greatest craving was to get shut of this maddening old crone and her goonish brother.

'I see,' she said, looking at me in a new way.

I cleared my throat after a year's uncomfortable silence. 'I'd, er, better have a lie down,' I said eventually. 'I've more night work ahead.'

She rose then and crossed to the dressing-table. 'Shower while I make up your bed.'

When I came tottering blearily back her alcove

curtains were pulled aside. My couch wasn't made up at all. Uncaring, I reeled towards it, clutching my towel round my middle.

'Here, Lovejoy.' I felt her guiding touch on my arm and collapsed on her bed. She looked down at me, her make-up gone and only her lovely young face hovering. 'You'll sleep better here than on that old couch. Are you very tired?'

'Done in.' My vision blacked. 'What are you doing?' My towel had gone and a smooth lissom body was moving alongside my exhausted hairy neck.

'You need keeping warm, Lovejoy.'

Actually I didn't, but when your hostess offers you tea it's rude to refuse. And as it turned out I wasn't as tired as all that.

'That you, Arcellano?'

'Where the hell have you been, Lovejoy?'

It was my old friend all right. 'Pulling the rip.'

That shut him up, for about ten seconds. 'You what?'

'You heard.'

Another pause, then much quieter: 'Lovejoy. Are you serious or drunk?'

'Serious.'

'But it's impossible.'

'*Was.*' We both listened to heavy breathing.

'So you'll deliver—' *But he was uncertain!*

I cut in. 'No, Arcellano. No nice long trips to Bonn. I deliver here, in Rome.'

'You're off your head.'

'In the Colosseum. Exactly at sunrise. No sooner, no later.'

'Lovejoy.' His sibilant voice made my skin crawl.

'Lovejoy. If you're planning to work a fixer, I'll have you crisped. You do understand?'

'Perfectly,' I told him. 'And if I find you skulking in ambush when I arrive at the Colosseum, Arcellano, I'll take to the hills.' I put a whine of anxiety into my voice. 'I want no trouble.'

'Very well, Lovejoy,' that voice purred. 'I'll be there.'

'Alone, Arcellano. Agreed?'

'Agreed.'

I walked the half mile to Patrizio's garage. I had remembered to bring the keys to Adriana's workshop so Valerio and I could nick the winch and bring it over in his van. I walked quickly. It was already dark, and I still had work to do.

Chapter 27

As the first sun ray touched the high rim a cool breeze wafted through the Colosseum's gaunt stone honeycomb. Fawns and dark browns started stuffing the blackness out of sight among the pits and arches. A pale midnight blue appeared above the jagged edge of the great interior. All around me the huge crescents were thrown into relief.

I sat there like a nerk, daintily at breakfast on top of one of the great masonry teeth which protruded from the floor of the vast arena. Even the most suspicious-minded crook could see I was alone, unaided and completely vulnerable.

I had been there an hour, perched on my stone block. Anna's white tablecloth fluttered indolently in the stirring air. My elbows on the coffee table and the coffee almost gone. What dregs were left in the cup were now stone cold. I was only saving them for effect.

Getting the table up had almost proved too much for me and Valerio. Patrizio and Anna had sussed out the entire Colosseum at four a.m., reporting all clear in whispers. Apart from one sleeping old drunk and the inevitable prowling cats, the place was empty. I made Patrizio and Anna promise to leave once I was in position. Anna was all for staying and taking on the universe with me. I refused to explain, saying it was all part of the rip. I felt utterly alone.

The sky lightened. Rectangles of pastel blue began to appear, stencilled out of the enormous brown stone rim above me. I shivered, half wanting the sun to reach down into the enormous bowl and warm me but too frightened to wish really hard. When it rose, Arcellano would come. Some murderers come alone. Others come with a band of assassins. I knew which sort Arcellano was.

A distant bus revved up and chugged out into the streets. First sound of the day. A few moments later a car came close, changed gear, droned away to silence. Nearby a cat stretched, scaring me to death by suddenly being there. I calmed myself as best I could by rehearsing my movements. Arcellano would send his goons to go over the Colosseum inch by inch. I'm not that dim. With a little luck – and the speed which my terror would lend me – I'd be off out of the whole frigging mess with the speed of light. I looked down and along the sandy ground across to my left. There, half the arena's width away, was the spot where Marcello's broken body had lain My eyes lifted, as casually as if I were idly waiting, to where my pulley and beam overhung the stonemason's area. The massive stone block which hung suspended there did not even stir in the cool shifting air. I swallowed. It represented safety, but the bloody thing looked miles away. I'd have to run that far, dodging among the vast blocks.

I was becoming worried. Time was getting on. I let my gaze move inch by inch round the scagged interior. No sign. No movement. Only one of the cats coughing gently in the gloom directly ahead. The place was dappling swiftly. And the sky blueing, and gold touching the stonework. Soon, visitors would be waking to start the day and there was no way I could cajole Arcellano into a rerun of this meeting . . .

That cat coughed again. And I remembered the sound. Too late.

Against the weakening shadows a pale shape was emerging. About as tall as a man, a big man, with a fawn overcoat draped elegantly over his shoulders. And he was laughing. The laugh was short and dry, unvoiced barks like a coughing cat. I glanced involuntarily towards the long sandy run towards my recess. The pale shape saw my glance and began to drift that way. I thought, Oh Gawd.

I took a sip of coffee dregs to wet my throat and called, 'Is that you, Arcellano?' The cup rattled in it saucer.

'Charming tableau, Lovejoy.'

'Coffee, or have you had breakfast?' It was the best I could do. Everything I possessed had got the wobbles.

'You're allowed one cigarette, Lovejoy. Before execution.'

'Don't be daft, Arcellano. You owe me. I pulled the rip.'

'Wrong, Lovejoy. My men checked. The Chippendale's still there.'

I lifted the edge of the tablecloth to show the pedestal and the rent table's unmistakable edge. 'It's here, friend. Your antique from the Vatican. The one now in the Museum gallery is a forgery. I made it.'

He thought about that before speaking. 'Then why no alarms yesterday?'

'Because I made a *good* forgery. Go and check. I'll wait here.'

That cat cough laugh really sounded then, maybe a

whole minute. He wiped his eyes, but all the time he was drifting to my left along the terracing. I had to look upwards at a slight angle to see him.

'You bastard, Lovejoy,' he called down. 'How?'

I explained the outline. All the time he was drifting, drifting in the direction I had glanced earlier. The swine suspected that was where I'd try to make my escape. He paused, leaning on the iron tourist rail. I could see him clearly now. With every second the day was rushing into brightness.

'You clever bastard,' He honestly sounded full of admiration. 'The old fiddle switch to rip the Vatican. I might have known. A bluff on a bluff.'

'It was nothing,' I said, all modest.

'They said you were really something, Lovejoy.' He was chuckling. 'Robbery without alarms. The only way it can be done. Congratulations.'

I thought, Here goes 'Thank you,' I said with careful loudness. 'Captain.'

I moved my trembling legs ready to leap off the stool and run.

He paused, tilted his head. 'Captain? What are you talking about, Lovejoy?' He waited. I tried not to glance again at the million miles of sand which stretched between the recess and me.

'You're a senior officer of the Vatican Security guard, Arcellano.'

'You're insane.'

'You thought up this rip to test the Vatican's security. On the quiet.' I let that sink in. 'So you had a grotty copy made of the Chippendale original. This is that copy.'

'So where's the real piece?'

'You have it stashed away.'

'And why should I go to all that trouble?'

I smiled, the thing I least felt like doing. 'If I succeeded in pulling the rip, you naturally assumed there'd be a gap left in the gallery's exhibits. Then you could put the real Chippendale back. Nobody would then know there'd been a rip at all.'

'And if you failed?'

'Then I'd be nabbed,' I said evenly. 'By you. Your men would have me in clink.'

'Doubtless telling tales, no?'

'Yes, but an improbable tale people would laugh at. You gave yourself away, Captain.'

'Really?' The bastard was too calm by far. I could feel his two goons smiling in the morning shadows behind me and tried not to look round, to concentrate on this murdering bastard who had now resumed his oh-so-casual stroll round the terrace towards my only escape route. 'Really, Lovejoy? How?'

'A clever geezer like you would naturally want to protect his interests, in case things went wrong,' I said. 'Captain Blood put an end to the straight-lift caper, nicking the Crown Jewels from the Tower of London in 1671. Substituting the dud showed your hand.'

'But why should I bother, Lovejoy?'

'Because you had the greatest prize of all in mind – a method, Captain. If I succeeded, you'd know how it could be done.'

He was smiling, the fucking swine, thinking he'd won. 'And you've given it to me, Lovejoy. A method which can be repeated times out of number.' He grinned. 'I'm indebted. Now I can drain the whole Vatican, item by item. I thank you. Sincerely.'

'But you murdered Marcello, Captain.'

'Well.' He spread his hands. 'He started asking around about Cardinal Arcellano.'

'That was my fault,' I cut in. 'I knew no other name for you except that. I should have realized as soon as Marcello sounded suddenly so different, full of urgency.'

'Silly of me to use the honoured Cardinal's name at that little auction. It seemed just a joke at the time.'

'It misfired, Captain. You had to kill Marcello because of it. Am I correct?'

'Near enough. But it's over, Lovejoy. Once that table's out of sight all your evidence has gone, right?'

'You've forgotten one thing, Captain.'

He snapped his fingers. The stockier of his gorillas stepped out of the terrace shadows. A second appeared far over to my left. My exit run was now overlooked by them both. Arcellano made some light quip to the goon, the pleasant way his sort do before knocking somebody off. He turned back to me, a picture of mayhem in classy suiting. His voice was suddenly flint hard. 'If you mean payment, Lovejoy, you'll get paid – well paid '

I said shakily, sweat stinging my eyes and my voice quavering, 'I don't mean that. You're under arrest, Captain.'

It should have come out crisp as a western gunfighter's threat. It came out a feeble warble.

His famous non-smile was back. 'I'm . . . *what*?'

'You heard, piss-head '

A car droned by. It didn't stop. Yet this was the moment Russomanno and his Keystone Kops should have come bursting in with lovely protecting howitzers. There was silence. A cat yawned extravagantly. Arcellano was glancing about swiftly. His two goons had reached inside their jackets. With innate skill they backed against the supporting pillars, fading from the daylight into shadow.

'*Get him!*'

I flung myself sideways, dropping to the ground, and was off, keening with fright. I ran like a stag down the narrow avenue of tall stones, hunched and babbling imprecations, begging for my life. Instinctively I weaved, ducking in and out among the colossal rectangles and scuffing the sand. If only I'd trained. Something plucked the air by my head, clipping stone chips from the masonry. My face stung. A bang, echoing. I heard Arcellano screaming instructions. I could hear footsteps along the terrace.

Frantic now, I cringed behind an upright slab as a piece of stone exploded at eye level ahead of me. Three cracks sounded. More stone chips. I moaned in terror. The bastards were everywhere. It was all wrong.

Arcellano should have come down to this level so I could imprison him by my ingenious falling block in that recess up ahead, for the police to arrest at leisure. I ducked into view, saw Arcellano on the terrace, hurled myself back into cover. Two more gunshots, one from behind and to the side. My leg went funny. Bleating with terror I tottered forwards, weaving among the standing stones as fast as my sudden limp would allow. I whined, 'Please, please . . .'

'Halt! Halt!'

'Get him!'

Along the stone avenue, with shots going everywhere and people shouting. I glimpsed Arcellano directly against the metal railing. He swung over ahead of me and dropped lightly to the sand, to my level at last. But he carried a shiny slate-blue length in his hand. For a big man he moved like a dancer, soft and easy. I moaned in terror at the sight. He was only twenty yards off and floating like the hunter he was, his teeth bared in a silent hiss. I'd never been so frigging scared of anything or anybody. I limped to the right. More shouts and a small fusillade of echoing shots. Somebody screamed. It wasn't me, thank God.

'Lovejoy!' some lunatic yelled, as if I wasn't out of my skull with horror.

Gasping, I lumbered along the arena wall and across the straight avenue of standing stones. The bastard was gliding away from me, looking from side to side. I must have made a noise, maybe scraped on a stone or something, because he spun instantly and the blue thing in his hand flashed. The air near me warmed and splinters flicked blood splashes from my face. I tumbled to one side, scrabbled lopsidedly across to the far side where my chain hung. The only place I could go was my recess. My own bloody prison.

The space was the size of a large room. Masonry tools lay scattered. Chisels, hammers, mallets and set-squares, some as Valerio and I had dropped them during the dark hours. Too late to think of using those now. I made it to the coil of chain and gave it a yank to set it firm on the pulley. My throat was raw with fright. Somebody shouted again up on the terraces. I heard rather than saw Arcellano step towards the gap through which I'd come. I flicked the chain once, released it and stepped aside as the dull rumbling began.

Arcellano came into the space. The fucking gun looked enormous.

'Okay, Arcellano,' I yelled, though he was only a few feet off 'I surrender! I'll say it was me!'

'Too late, Lovejoy.' He was smiling now. 'You're resisting arrest, you see.' He raised his voice and shouted, 'The table, Maria! Just push it off that stone. It'll smash.'

'Who?' I asked dully. He'd said Maria.

The gun lifted. My belly squeezed. He glanced up

then. Maybe it was the sudden swiftness of the rectangular shadow, maybe the rumbling of the descending block. I don't know. It was all in an instant. But he glanced up and froze, appalled at the sight of the massive block plummeting towards him. He hesitated, started to step back.

'Forwards!' I screeched. 'Step forwards, man!'

He halted, then leant towards me into the space left for the great stone, his eyes on mine. It was only then that I realized I'd told him wrong. I'd said forwards when I actually meant to shout back. Either way I'd have been safe, but somehow my mind got the words wrong. It was unintentional. I swear it. Honestly, I never meant him to suffer like he did. The great stone settled into its allotted area with a faint scrape and hiss, pressing Arcellano's broad shoulders down and crushing blood into his face, and forcing the very life out of his mouth. His eyes popped in a spurt of blood that sprayed over my face. His face puced, swelled, burst out of its expression in a splatter of blood. The gun in his hand cracked once, sending splinters round the confined area. Needles drove into my neck and thigh but what the hell.

Maria. He'd shouted instructions to *Maria*. His woman, Maria. To push the table, my evidence, off the central stone and break it to smithereens. I suddenly remembered why the table was up there on the stone, and drew a great breath.

'*Maria!*'

The name echoed round the Colosseum. 'Maria!' No sound but a distant shout – man's voice – and rapid footsteps.

I screeched. 'Maria! Don't touch the table. Please! For Chrissakes, leave it—'

Her dear voice came clear as a bell over the great

arena. 'It's no good, Lovejoy.' Then those terrible words I'd give anything to forget. 'Get rid of him, darling.' Her voice had a finality I'd hoped never to hear. '*Do it!*'

She wasn't talking to me. She meant this dead thing under the stone. She obviously couldn't see – hadn't seen – the block fall on her man Arcellano. Frantic, I drew breath to scream a warning, but she was telling her man to do it. To kill me. Me, who loved her.

And I uttered no sound.

I slumped to the sand. It was all happening too fast. Dully I heard footsteps, people running. I sat against the wall of the recess, staring at that horrid mess of Arcellano's popped face squeezed bloodily from between the giant stones. His arm protruded in a great purple sausage. The other arm was nowhere to be seen. Tears streamed down my face, for what or why I don't know to this day.

The explosion came exactly four seconds after I heard the table crash to the ground. The whiplash crack of the hand grenade's plug against the stonework sounded near my head. I didn't even flinch. They always say, don't they, that the plug of a grenade seeks out the thrower. Maria did not even have time to scream before she died.

I don't know how long I was there, sitting in the sand of that accidental prison. The first thing I remember is a face grinning over the edge up there against the blue sky and saying into the scream of sirens, 'What is it? Filming?'

It was the drunk, wakened by the war. 'Yes,' I told him.

'Where are the cameras?'

'Hidden.'

I saw him fumble and bring out a tiny bronze disc. 'Want to buy a genuine ancient Roman coin?'

I squinted up against the light. The same old acid patina, two days old. 'It's phoney. You've used too much acid to get the verdigris.'

He mumbled, nodding. 'I told my mate that. He's a know-all.'

He made to withdraw. 'Hey,' I said. 'Want to buy a genuine antique?'

Somebody up there was yelling everybody to freeze because this was the police, that the place was surrounded. Sirens were going, car doors slamming. Now it was all done for them.

Typical.

Chapter 28

No airport's pretty.

They gave me my green boarding-card after an hour's wait. It's always a relief because it means you are going to get aboard and some other poor nerk's going to be left behind. The passengers I was with were a cheerful, talkative crowd. I sat to one side trying not to remember the inquest, the harsh post-mortem evidence given over the verdict on my lovely Maria and on Menotti, her murderous lover. In the official hearing I had been gently reproved by Cardinal Arcellano for calling Menotti 'Arcellano', but explained I'd known him by no other name. The Cardinal was a quiet little bloke with a mind like a computer. He'd been understanding, even compassionate, when I'd given evidence about the killer Menotti's attempt to finish me. On the way out of the hearing I'd tried to avoid saying a farewell. He got in my way and told me he'd pray for my peace of mind. I'd said thanks and passed on by. I don't know what people are on about half the time.

'Signor Lovejoy?' An air-terminal policeman stood there, all phoney boredom.

'Yes?'

'Would you come this way, please.'

'But my flight's nearly called—'

'Only a moment, signor.'

Obviously a slight passport difficulty, easily resolved. I got my bag and followed him to the manager's office, trying to exude a sense of confidence towards the other passengers. I even swaggered, for show.

There were four policemen in the office, including a captain. He had his thumbs in his belt.

'You are Lovejoy?'

'Yes. If it's this passport, I can explain . . .'

'You know this old lady?'

A photo of Anna in her pickpocketing clobber. 'Yes.'

'Your aunt, I believe?'

I thought swiftly. 'Er, not exactly. You see—'

'You lodge at this address with her?'

'Well, er . . .' The signature on the form was oddly familiar. It was my handwriting. That time Anna got nicked by the Via Porto Angelica. No wonder two of these cops looked familiar. The two in the car, who'd made me sign to get Anna off the hook.

'Yes or no, signor?' That phoney boredom again. I'd rather have hate. It's safer. 'And this is your signature?'

I swallowed, took a chance. 'Well, yes.'

'You went surety for this old lady?'

'Not really,' I burbled. 'It wasn't meant to be taken seriously—'

'You signed a police form *frivolously*?' The officer swelled ominously. 'Intending to default, slip the country, leaving your aged aunt—?'

I said desperately, 'She's only twenty-odd, for Christ's sake. It's all make-up—'

He smiled a wintry smile. 'She told us to expect all sorts of ludicrous explanations, signor.' He dropped another photograph on the desk. 'You recognize this antique shop?'

'Yes. It's . . .' I hesitated. My job there was illegal. No work permit.

'Albanese Antiques Emporium, signor?'

'Yes.' I had a headache. It worsened abruptly as he reached for the phone and dialled without looking the number up.

The police stood about with the terrible patience of their kind. I noticed two were now between me and the door.

'*Pronto*, signora! Yes, we have him . . . At the airport.' He listened attentively, full of importance. 'Yes, signora.' He turned, placing the receiver on his chest in token of confidentiality. 'Signor Lovejoy. You are in default of a contract of employment with Signora Albanese, no?'

'No!' I cried desperately. My bloody flight number was being announced. 'Listen! I never had any legal . . . er . . .'

The captain's eyebrows rose in mild surprise. 'You are saying, signor?'

'Erm . . .' Adriana had me either way.

'Having given surety for a vagrant,' the captain said affably, '*without* gainful employment?'

'No.'

'Then you've defaulted, signor.' He lit a cigar one-handed. It was clearly his trick. Carlo should have seen him.

'Let me speak to her.' Furious, I snatched the receiver from him. 'Adriana? Now you look here! This is Lovejoy—'

'Hello, darling.' She sounded quite pleasant, even chatty. 'Speaking from police custody, I believe.'

I deflated. 'Er, yes. Only temporarily. Some crazy mistake. I want you to tell them that—'

'That you have a job, darling, and are not a vagrant?'

'Yes, that's it!' I cried eagerly. My flight number was blipping on the monitor screen in the corner of the room.

'But, *darling*! There's this slight matter of those tables, the ones you wrongfully purchased on my account.'

I thought. 'Is there?'

'Yes, darling,' she cooed, sweet as a dove. The police were staring patiently at the ceiling as Adriana went blithely on, 'And I'm in such a mess here. A load of antiques being delivered tomorrow, ready for the new season. Such problems.'

I waited, but so did she. 'So?' I said weakly.

'Well, darling. You know how much more expert you are at this sort of thing . . .'

I swear there were tears in my eyes as I watched that monitor screen. I tried for a last-ditch stand against the unfairness of all womankind.

'Okay, then. But I want a good rate of pay.'

'You'll work for your keep, Lovejoy.'

I yelped. 'For *nothing*?' I eyed the police, wondering if oppressed antique dealers got a discount from the judges in Rome for murdering their tyrannical employers.

'You'll receive, shall we say, payment . . . in kind, Lovejoy.' I could tell the sadistic bitch was falling about with delight at the other end. 'The most intimate kind, of course. In fact, I shall insist on delivering it personally. Think of yourself,' she added sweetly, 'as providing an essential service.'

The captain blew smoke. He slid an employment form across the desk to me in silence.

I read it swiftly, my face red. 'Erm, Adriana.'

'Darling?'

'Listen,' I croaked hopelessly, 'I, er, have this police form to fill in.'

'Do it, dearest. I'll come for you directly.'

'Erm, there's this space. *Nature of occupation.* I can't write—'

'Hired consort?' She was rolling in the aisles, though her voice was sugar.

'What shall I put?'

There was a pause, then a smile crept back into her voice, and she said, 'I know, Lovejoy. Apprentice.'

I thought, I'll kill her, but said, 'I can't put that. They'll assume—'

'– The truth, Lovejoy?'

The phone went dead, purring anonymity. I looked at the receiver for a long minute before replacing it carefully on its rest. The tannoy announced my Alitalia flight, final call.

'Your elderly aunt is waiting for you outside, signor,' the police captain said. He too was carefully out of smiles. I glanced about, frantic.

The four cops inhaled, ready for the dust-up. Brokenly I thought of Adriana streaking out to collect me, of Anna prowling outside the door. The trouble with women is they win so bloody often.

The captain demanded, 'I take it you are staying a while, signor?'

'Yes, Captain.' Bitterly I pulled the form towards me and wrote *Apprentice* in the space provided. I said, 'I may not survive, but I'll definitely be staying.'